# Violent Summer

# H. B. Broome

# Violent
# Summer

A DOUBLE D WESTERN
DOUBLEDAY
New York  London  Toronto  Sydney  Auckland

A DOUBLE D WESTERN
PUBLISHED BY DOUBLEDAY
a division of Bantam Doubleday Dell Publishing Group, Inc.
666 Fifth Avenue, New York, New York 10103

DOUBLE D WESTERN, DOUBLEDAY,
and the portrayal of the letters DD
are the trademarks of Doubleday, a division of
Bantam Doubleday Dell Publishing Group, Inc.

Library of Congress Cataloging-in-Publication Data

Broome, H. B.
   Violent summer   /   H. B. Broome — 1st ed.
      p.   cm. — (A Double D western)
   I. Title.
PS3552.R6598V5   1990
813'.54—dc20   89-49365
CIP

ISBN 0-385-26567-0
Copyright © 1990 by Horace B. Kelton
All Rights Reserved
Printed in the United States of America
June 1990
First Edition

BG

For Jack Broome and Monte Noelke

## AUTHOR'S NOTE

The community first called "the sinful village across the river from Fort Concho," variously named Saint Angela, San Angela, and finally San Angelo, is fictitiously represented in this series of books as Santa Rita. Certain family names that are known in West Texas have been used, but it is to be emphasized that every character in this book is fictitious.

# ONE

THE MAN who'd been following him since midmorning stopped in a clump of mesquite trees on the high ground and stayed there, hiding out of sight.

The noon sun turned the day into shimmering pale gold and caused bright shafts to glint off the shallow river. While locust noises seesawed through the windless air, Tom English lengthened his left arm to permit Deuce, his dusty mount, to lower his head into the slowly moving current. The thirsty dun gelding raised his dripping muzzle, pawed the already muddy current with a hoof, then drank again. Slick black water bugs scampered about in skimming circles on the thin membrane of the river's gray-green surface, and a cluster of stick-bodied dragonflies, suspended by invisible wings, hovered nearby.

Tom's right arm, hanging slackly at his side, moved very slowly back to his saddlebag. He slipped the small rawhide loop over the flap's leather knot and then slid his hand into the bag until it fastened on the handle of his Colt. At the same time he pulled his horse's head up with his left hand. A moment later, cradling the six-gun in his lap, he backed Deuce from the water and dismounted, keeping his weapon out of sight.

The dun, reins dangling, raised his head, ears up and forward, and whinnied a fluttered greeting. Tom stood with his feet spread slightly, holding his right arm down behind his leg as he waited. He looked at the horseman leaning back in his saddle as he made his way down a small bluff to the flat ground near the Concho River. He rode a limping horse with a jagged brand barely visible through the caked lather on its hip—and pulled up not ten feet away. The rider, wearing filthy clothes, propped a rifle on the swell beside his saddle horn. He had a hooked nose and deep lines leading down to a lank mustache. He shifted ever so slightly, leveling the rifle's bore on Tom's chest and fixing hooded, rheumy eyes on him.

Neither man spoke at first. Tom waited in the oven heat, feeling a prickling sensation run up his back, hearing a sudden wire-whip swishing sound as his horse's tail lashed at flies.

"You startled me," Tom said at last.

The stranger leaned in his saddle to one side and spat a short arc of brown tobacco juice. "Good-lookin' horse you got there," he said. "Mine is wore out, so I'd like to propose a trade." He sat very still a moment before adding, "Besides that, I been huntin' for you."

With a quick movement he started to pull his rifle to his shoulder. Tom threw himself sideways, his Colt exploding as he did, and its heavy slug bludgeoned the hook-nosed man from his horse in a backward cartwheel. He landed with a heavy thud but rolled over, still holding his rifle with his right hand, and sat up, legs outspread. Dark blood, almost black, pumped from a big hole in his belly and he looked at it, bending his head down, then raising it. His eyes widened in disbelief.

"You done kilt me," the man gasped. Blood mixed with tobacco juice trickled from his mouth and a spasm twisted his face. He slowly pulled the rifle around.

From the distance came the sound of hoofbeats as the stranger's horse clattered away. Deuce had retreated some twenty yards, neck drawn back, the whites of his eyes showing, but he hadn't bolted.

"Don't," Tom warned.

The long barrel of the man's Winchester dug a little trench in the dirt as he pushed it forward.

"I said, don't try it!"

The rifle cleared the ground, and the wind shriek of a bullet went past Tom's ear a split instant before he heard the blast.

Tom's hand bucked three times, the shots going off so fast that they sounded almost like a continuous explosion. The first hit the man's stomach, the second his chest, and as he doubled, the third split the bone of his forehead.

Crouched over, stunned, echoes ringing in his ears, Tom stood with his right holding the Colt outstretched toward his blood-drenched unknown enemy.

A host of frightened sparrows whirled up into the clear June air as if hurled from the trees by the sharp crashing of the handgun.

Tom English sat in a rocker on the shaded east porch of his headquarters house at the Lazy E and waited for his friend Calvin Laudermilk to appear. He'd seen him a short time earlier, riding up on

Sully, the dappled gray Percheron he'd owned for years. Standing seventeen hands high and weighing almost a full ton, the ponderous animal still had a certain grace. Long feathery-looking hair hung down over his fetlock joints and pasterns, brushing near his pie-plate hooves. Sully supported his owner's bulk of more than three hundred pounds with ease, a fact which Calvin deeply appreciated since more than once he had mounted a normal horse only to have the animal stagger, legs spread wide, and look back with dismay at its furious rider.

Tom fidgeted nervously, toying with the glass of bourbon he held, trying to forget what had happened by the river. He'd had these empty, guilt-strewn feelings all too often now. "I hope I've learned enough to know that it won't help things to get drunk," he said to himself. In fact, he'd given up whiskey altogether more than once, but there were times, like this one, when he persuaded himself that he needed something to mask the pain.

Calvin lumbered around the side of the house and labored up the steps. With a wheezing sigh he squared his broad shoulders and balanced his great barrel of a stomach as he eased himself down into the sturdy armchair which he normally claimed. He dropped his sweat-stained hat on the floor, revealing a weathered face with a fine-boned straight nose and laugh wrinkles around his inquisitive hazel eyes. In spite of his bulk and his various chins, he still was a handsome man. His collar had been fastened all the way to his throat and he undid the top two buttons, cursing the heat with slow intensity as if this might help matters.

Then, accepting a glass of whiskey from his host, he said, "Once as a child I borrowed my daddy's ten-gauge. He normally used that gun in heavy brush in the hill country when he went after deer. Well, without asking his permission, I took that shotgun and some shells loaded with buckshot and went dove hunting. When I came home I had a poke full of birds but they weren't of much use. All that was left of them was some feathers, one claw, and a couple of beaks."

Tom drank from his glass and looked across the valley past the tree-shaded Concho toward the low purple hills on the far horizon. Calvin stared curiously at his host, noting the sun-darkened skin of his face and the surprising contrast of his ice-cold pale blue eyes.

"You may wonder why I thought of this, but when I went out to the barn to look at that feller who considered taking a shot at you, it struck me that your reaction was a little strong. You killed him four times."

Tom winced.

"Sorry. It's just that, well, I don't know that I've ever seen anyone so tore up."

Tom said defensively, "My first shot caught him low—I was jumping sideways when I let it off, thinking that he would be firing at the same time. But he was slower than I'd expected."

"So you made sure that wouldn't happen again."

Tom frowned slightly before assenting.

"You certainly don't believe in half measures," Calvin said, downing his bourbon and refilling his glass, "and that's what brought to mind those doves I shot with ten-gauge shells loaded with buckshot. Well, who is he and why did he want to kill you?"

"I haven't the slightest idea. I'd seen him trailing me during the morning. So I stopped at the river and dismounted, figuring he'd take the chance to catch me unawares. Which is what happened."

"Except you weren't unawares."

"No."

"Why'd you bring the body in? Couldn't your boys bury him where he lay?"

"We don't do things that way anymore, Calvin. Besides, I want to make a full report to the law in Santa Rita. They may be able to figure out who he was—and why he was after me."

"I don't want to sound indelicate, Tom, but it's mighty hot to keep a body around."

"Pepe and Luis plan to load it in the hack this evening and leave before daylight in the morning. They'll get to Santa Rita by early afternoon."

"Will you need to show up for a hearing or the like?"

"Wouldn't think so. The boys are taking a letter I wrote to Jedediah Jackson which explains everything that happened. They'll deliver it right after they drop off the body at Massie's."

Tom spoke of Massie's shop, which made and sold furniture, among other things. Noah Massie and his son Japheth had set up an undertaking parlor in a back room as a sideline, which tied in nicely with the family trade since for years they had been making coffins.

Calvin waited patiently while Tom added, "Jedediah should be able to get things cleared up. He's always done everything I've needed along legal lines."

"Since he's the only lawyer in town I think you made a wise choice," Calvin observed.

Tom ignored the sarcasm. "Anyway, everybody knows me—and since it was a clear case of self-defense, that's all there is to it."

Calvin obviously agreed. He changed the subject by asking, "Where's your pretty wife and your youngsters?"

"They're at the Lower Ranch," Tom said, speaking of a spread which had its main house not six miles from the town he'd been mentioning. "I'll be there tomorrow—and may decide to go see Jedediah."

They sat without speaking as the sun sank lower. After a few more drinks Tom mentioned his daughter. "I promised Rebecca that I'd avoid gunfights. But, as you know, I still practice, and keep a Colt handy most of the time. Today I had the old six-gun that Jason Field gave me when I was seventeen. I've been carrying it in my saddlebag—but, after what happened, I guess I'll strap on both Colts again."

"Things like this tend to make a man jumpy," Calvin said, nodding sagely. "Though why anyone on earth would be fool enough to go up against Tom English is beyond me." He sat for a time, patting his stomach, then asked, "How many does this make, anyway?"

"I've lost count," Tom replied tersely.

"Don't get short with me, lad," Calvin snorted. "As you know, I have a tendency to get curious about all manner of things that aren't any of my business. Well, if you don't want to sit out here and talk, you might as well be a good host and feed me. Let's go roust out the cook and see what we've got for supper."

The familiar weight of the matching .45s in their tied-down holsters comforted Tom. He sat Ross, Jr., a well-muscled bay he'd named after a favorite horse, one he'd been forced to leave on the ranch he and Hap Cunningham's boy owned up in Montana. Santiago Acosta rode beside him with a Winchester cradled across his left elbow as they passed the Mexican shacks with swept bare ground around them which marked the north edge of Santa Rita. They made their way into town and went directly to the sheriff's office to check their weapons.

Tom wrapped his reins loosely around the hitching post, then stepped up on a board sidewalk. His spur rowels clinked as his boot heels struck the planks before he stepped inside. Santiago entered right behind him.

A man he didn't know sat or, more precisely, half lay back in a chair with his feet propped on the scarred desk before him. He opened sleepy eyes and looked blankly at Tom.

"Something I can do for you?"

"Where's Jim Boy Irons?"

"He quit." The new deputy stretched his arms out wide, revealing dark wet patches of sweat as he yawned. "You lookin' for him?"

"No," Tom said slowly. He looked around the small office, taking note of the host of unused pegs on the unpainted pine wall, and remarked, "Doesn't look like people are checking their guns here anymore."

"That's right," the deputy replied. "Us havin' to run all over town grabbin' varmint guns off saddles and the like turned into a blame nuisance, more trouble than it was worth now that the town has settled down and most folks don't go heeled no more." He stared past his boots at his two visitors and added, "Although the two of you look like you're loaded for bear. If you plan to stay around here I'd recommend that you park all that iron you're carrying somewheres. They tell me you can trust a man named Dave at the Girdwood wagon yard just east of here if that's where you're puttin' up for the night. Of course, some travelers swear by the Elkhorn wagon yard right over yonder." He pointed vaguely to the west.

As Tom and Santiago turned toward the door the deputy came awake enough to ask, "What might be your name, mister?" But Tom didn't respond.

He swung back into his saddle and pulled his mount's head around. When Santiago drew even with him, Tom said, "Been awhile since you and I've been to town." He stopped talking because Ross, Jr. began to tiptoe sideways as the sudden sound of a hammer banging on a nail rang out. They rounded a corner and saw a wagonload of raw lumber being unloaded at a construction site.

"Been awhile since you came into this town and ran across someone who didn't know who you were," Santiago responded.

Max Hall, owner and president of the First National Bank in Santa Rita, showed his surprise when one of his oldest and best friends walked in. The bank had a counter with several tellers and next to it a waist-high rail divider which gave Max as much privacy as he needed. Two empty chairs rested before his desk and he rose to his feet as Tom advanced. Max, a round-faced tall man with a big frame, usually had a boyish smile on his face, but today he looked at Tom with concern in his eyes.

"I heard about the trouble," he said simply.

Tom shrugged. "I'd thought that sort of thing was behind me."

"No one can fault you, Tom. I had a talk with Jedediah and he showed me your letter. Well, what's done is done." He sighed and said,

"It's good to see you after all this time." Lapsing into his accustomed style, he commented, "We thought that you'd forgot all your old friends."

Falling into the familiar pattern, leaving his concerns unspoken, Tom said, "To tell the truth, I hadn't expected to find you here. Thought you might be down at the creek with a fishing pole—having heard stories about bankers' hours."

"Just because for a while we closed our doors at three o'clock so we could get our books caught up didn't mean that we'd taken up slothful habits. Besides, as you may be aware by that clock on the wall, it's nigh on five and we're open for business this afternoon." With a scowl he said, "With no more customers than we've had lately, our bookkeeper has no trouble at all keeping everything up to snuff."

A heavily loaded freight wagon crunched through the crusted dry ruts of the street outside. The four horses that made up the team pulling it leaned wearily into their traces and ignored a mongrel dog that yapped at their heels.

"Appears to me that all manner of business is going on around here," Tom observed. "Are you saying that you're not getting your share?"

"You know how I run this bank," Max Hall stated wryly. "However, others in this business don't pay much mind to prudence." He selected a cigar from a brass humidor on his desk, clipped the end with a penknife and, after lighting it, said, "I guess I ought to explain what I mean. Whenever I've seen you, which has been damn seldom in the last year, I've tried to tell you that something mighty strange is going on. It goes beyond the normal growing pains that any new town might expect. The simple truth is that Santa Rita has changed considerably since Julian Haynes showed up."

His voice turned bitter when he mentioned his competitor's name. Haynes, since his arrival, had bought the squat frame building that had formerly housed Johnson's Saddle and Harness Shop and also Moon's Feed Store. In a short time a host of carpenters knocked out certain partitions while adding others, remodeling the structure so that it might house the Merchants State Bank. Tom knew all about this—Max had talked of little else on his rare visits out to the ranch. Haynes had been loaning money freely, ignoring normal precautions, causing former clients of the First National to change banks regardless of past loyalties.

"With money so easy to come by, we've got a third wagon yard going in, not to mention two new livery stables. On top of that, there's a new general store to compete with the Westbrooks, when there's not enough

trade for *one* store right now. And to top things off, Haynes is going after the ranchers' business. He's announced that he'll make his own evaluation of their property and stock, and will loan them up to one third of that with nothing more than a handshake and a smile—along with their signature on a stack of papers. Naturally, he gets everything they own pledged as collateral. You know how that goes: when a man is hard up for cash he'll sign anything that's stuck before him.

"It's clear that Julian Haynes has got something up his sleeve—for he's got agents out looking for land—a lot of it. He's already bought more than a hundred thousand acres from your neighbor Henry Jameson and some of his kin, and is stocking the place easy enough since, with the drought, the bottom has fallen out of the cattle market. Most owners, as you well know, are pretty desperate to cut back on the size of their herds."

"I'm aware of that," Tom said. "But he can't carry much stock out west of my place since there's no water. I guess that's the main reason he sent some men to make me a handsome offer for enough of the Lazy E to give them access to the river."

"Smooth talkers?"

Tom smiled. "Like snake-oil salesmen."

"But you turned them down?"

"Of course." Tom looked thoughtfully at the banker. "Where does he get his money?"

"God knows," Max grumbled. "Since the flood of '82 knocked Ben Ficklen almost off the map, and Santa Rita got to be the county seat, Haynes may figure on the town amounting to something one of these days. Though with no more water than we've got, and with no railroad, I can't imagine why anyone would think so. But anyhow, the man is up to his ears in politics. You'll recall when the state formed Tom Green County we put some of our citizens up as commissioners to get the county government started. Haynes and his friend from El Paso, T. J. Hoskins, got elected to the Board of Commissioners. Along with that, Haynes has been loaning money to the other commissioners to such an extent that it's clear to me that he's got them in his pocket. The latest thing they've done, by the way, is to construct a courthouse.

"Haynes has big ideas and says that when the town's tax base is bigger he wants to bring in some German masons from Fredericksburg and build *another* courthouse, a bigger one with stone columns on the front of it."

"People like you keep me informed, Max. It's amazing how much

gossip I hear. But, while we're talking about the new courthouse, is it true that Haynes may put his own man in as judge?"

"God a'mighty, didn't I tell you about that? He's already done it—and it's none other than T. J. Hoskins."

Tom looked sharply at Max Hall. "There were rumors that something like this might happen. Jedediah Jackson came out to see us a while back and told me the little he knew about Hoskins. He sounded disturbed about the matter, as well he might be, since the idea of some outsider from El Paso going on the bench in Santa Rita—a man who's not even a lawyer—made his hackles rise."

Max nodded his head as if in agreement. "Things are happening a little too fast for me too. Of course, they went through the motions and did everything by the book—held an election for judge and for sheriff when they changed the makeup on the commissioners board."

Tom's eyes narrowed. "This is the first I've heard of a new sheriff."

"Yep. Man name of Reuben Baxter. They say he's from El Paso—same as Judge Hoskins. No use complaining, not much we can do about all that now." Max rubbed his thumb and forefinger on his mustache and said, "Aside from politics, I've got my own problems. You know, Tom, I've been in a position of being the wise old man—sitting down here in my bank, giving sound advice to folks about being frugal."

"I've heard enough of that myself."

"Then you may enjoy knowing that I've got myself in the same fix as the men I've been counseling all these years."

"Things getting a little tight?"

Max said, "That ain't the half of it, old friend. I feel like a wounded whale being trailed by sharks and barracudas. I've seen many a picture of the ocean and it always looks real smooth on the surface. But you can just imagine what goes on underneath it."

# TWO

JAPHETH MASSIE had done the best job he could in cleaning up the corpse. Rigor mortis had long since set in and it lay stiffly on a home-made metal-sheathed table built something like a large drainboard with a gutter along one side of it. He'd had to cut the man's clothes off him since the body wouldn't bend; and after scrubbing for some time at the dirt and blood, he took some candle wax and did his best to fill in the blue holes in the body's chest and stomach. The head wound, however, went beyond his talents, so he put the man's sweated-out brown hat there and pulled it over the exposed white bones. He had to force the back of its brim into a lumpy fold in order to do this. Even in the hazy light he'd been able to see clear through to the gray and red muck that had been the victim's brain.

Japheth decided that he'd had some difficult jobs in the past, but this one took the cake. At last, feeling pleased with his efforts, he straightened up and dropped his stained wet rag back in the bucket of rusty-looking water on the floor.

The visitors who had been watching Japheth at work for the last ten minutes—the banker Julian Haynes, Judge T. J. Hoskins, and Sheriff Reuben Baxter—muttered about the smell within the closed small room. In spite of an open window, the heat was oppressive.

"When will you be through?" Haynes asked.

"Won't be much longer."

Haynes turned to the sheriff, no emotion showing on his face. "You know what to do." With that he strode from the room, followed by Judge Hoskins.

Sheriff Baxter, distaste etched across his face, said to Japheth, "Just as soon as you finish, get some help and bring that body over to the Concho Street Saloon. Don't put nothin' on him, bring him just as he is."

Something over an hour later, a curious knot of men crowded into

the saloon. As they filed in they heard the sheriff's voice say, "My job is to find out if anybody recognizes this man. I'm sorry to have to ask this of you, but he's been killed by Tom English and we want to know who the hell he is."

He adjusted the overhead coal-oil lamp so that it cast a bright yellow light on the rigid form. Baxter leaned over and pulled the oily old brown hat away, revealing the dreadful head wound. The bystanders flinched.

"Jesus Christ," one man growled. All of them kept their eyes on the macabre sight, staring as if hypnotized.

The line of some eighteen curious and strangely silent gawkers, made up primarily of townspeople together with a few cowboys who'd been passing through, looked down at the whitish-gray body of the man lying flat on his back on the sawdust-strewn wood floor. His ribs and pelvic bones pushed at discolored, almost hairless flesh. His legs, bowed from a life in the saddle, spraddled apart, and one of his eyelids had pulled open.

The bartender, Chesley Upshaw, in a show of decency, went to a cabinet and returned with a torn apron which he put over the corpse's loins.

Chesley couldn't conceal his aggravation at the things that were going on. He had yielded to pressure from the new sheriff and his damn fool deputy but had drawn the line at their suggestion that he put the dead man on two tables shoved together for the purpose. He had protested, "Hell, Sheriff, my customers won't want to sit around these particular tables anymore if I do that. Would you?" But he had at last agreed to a compromise: he'd let them lay the man to be identified on the floor. It occurred to Chesley that sales at the Concho Street Saloon surely would pick up under the circumstances.

He rattled some bottles and glasses together on the top of the bar and, as if obeying a summons, men who'd been looking at the horrible sight grimaced with distaste and hurried over for a quick drink. One by one those behind them also stared down, then moved to join the others.

An old-timer who was not wearing his false teeth lisped, "I never seen nothin' like that."

Others drank hurriedly, then agreed. A cowboy drawled, "I don't know what offense that feller gave Tom English, but I sure can't believe it could have been bad enough to call for that kind of treatment."

A voice sounded from the other side of the room. "Was the poor sonuvabitch armed?"

"What differnse would that have made?" a townsman answered

sharply. "Ever'body knows English is the fastest gun they ever was. He's killed so many men that it don't mean nothin' to him. No more than drownin' cats in a burlap bag might fer you or me. In fact, it may be that if he goes too long in between killin's, he gets to *missin'* it."

"That'll be enough of that talk," Chesley Upshaw said. "All the sheriff wants to know is if any of you've ever seen this here waddy."

The men at the bar stared at their drinks and no one said a word. Each seemed lost in his own thoughts.

Chesley said, "Sheriff Baxter, if it's all the same to you, could I ask Japheth and his helper to clear that thing out of here?"

"She is a fine figure of a woman," Calvin Laudermilk said to himself as he viewed Elvira East, the spinster sister of Alvin East, the generally out-of-work journalist.

Elvira also seemed pleased with her appearance as she looked through long lashes, one of her better features, at the reflection staring back from the pier mirror in her brother's front hall. She wore a rose-colored cotton blouse which strained at her pouter-pigeon bust, and a tan linen skirt which curved over her ample hips and swept to the floor. Suddenly, as if aware of how close to the edge temptation had drawn her, she averted her gaze, turning from the sin of pride to her escort.

"I didn't think you'd actually come. I was just now telling Alvin that, if you didn't, he'd have to take me to the church social. But at that very moment we heard your buggy out front."

"But I promised."

"Well, you just never know about men like you."

"Men like me?" Calvin growled. "Miss East, there are no other men like me."

Elvira giggled.

Seated in the rented buggy, Calvin gallantly made sure of her comfort before flicking the reins and clucking at the gaunt mare which leaned forward, straining to get the wheels in motion.

"This social is going to be out back of the Baptist Church. The Women's Prayer Group has worked all week on this, and you're going to have a wonderful time. We've got paper lanterns in the trees, tables with cakes and pies and punch . . ."

Calvin interrupted. "You're sure it's all going to take place outside?"

"Well, of course it is, but why is that so important to you?"

"Haven't been inside of a church in ten years," Calvin mumbled.

"What?"

"It's a point of pride, a matter of intellectual integrity."

"I can't believe my ears," Elvira said faintly.

"Believe them, my dear."

The soft evening breeze which came with the late twilight cooled them. The mare, now with a slightly downhill pull, moved easily as their buggy jolted over the uneven road.

"Mr. Laudermilk, we have known each other for months and we haven't discussed this before now," Elvira said uneasily. "I took it for granted that you were a Methodist when I never saw you at our church."

"They're all the same, regardless of the labels they may choose to use. Their preachers, one and all, rag and fuss at you, making all sorts of personal insinuations. If even *one* of those fellows had a genuine understanding of sin, why, I might find it entertaining to listen to him. But they whine and warn us about the silliest kinds of things."

"And what should they be warning us about?" Elvira inquired with some asperity.

"Anything that takes away from the joy of life," Calvin responded positively.

"Heeyah," he hollered at the faltering mare, whapping her rump with the reins as they ascended the slight rise leading to the side of the white frame church where other buggies had been parked.

A short time later Calvin stood as if transfixed. Before him on a long table lay a marvelous sight: dozens of cakes and pies and several platters full of freshly sliced peaches garnished with plump red strawberries. Plates, cups, bowls, forks, and spoons waited in neat rows. Beside the fruit sat a large crockery pitcher full of clotted cream. A short distance away, several low fires flickered from their beds of glowing coals while oversized blackened coffeepots hung suspended from racks above them. A punch made up of cherry and apple juice sat at the end of the table in a large bowl next to a stack of thick-rimmed water glasses. A girl holding a dipper stood near the bowl, waving her free hand to keep the flies off.

The aroma from all of the freshly baked cakes caused Calvin's aristocratic nose to quiver. His great paunch trembled and from within his vitals he felt and heard a grumbling. Out of the corner of his eye he looked hurriedly at Elvira to see if she too had heard this sound, but she gave no sign that she had.

"I will have a slab of that pineapple upside-down cake for starters,"

Calvin instructed a young woman standing behind the table. "And a touch of mincemeat pie with whipped cream, if you please."

Elvira touched his sleeve tentatively. "We must wait for Reverend Vaurien to say the blessing."

He proceeded to load his plate. "Is that really the preacher's name?" His frame began to shake as he chortled silently. "Well, from childhood I've been taught that God is good, and so I can't imagine being punished for fighting off the pangs of hunger."

"Mr. *Laudermilk!*" Elvira's face showed he had genuinely shocked her this time.

He brushed some whipped cream from his mustache, speaking with a full heart and mouth, "I'm at my weakest when faced with temptation." He waved a hand at the feast prepared by the Women's Prayer Group in an apparent effort to place the real blame at their doorstep.

"Oh my," said Elvira East in despair.

The preacher raised both of his hands high above his head and commanded firmly, "Let us bow our heads." The churchyard, with close to forty people in it, became still except for children who resisted their parents' restraining hands, and two dogs that whipped around the edge of the building, one after the other. They went to the ground, snarling ferociously in mock combat while a little girl's penetrating high voice squealed with excitement. The words of Reverend Vaurien increased in volume in order that his flock might hear him.

Grace having been pronounced, a long line took place at the table. Almost all of those present joined it, but in the shadows near the church two men spoke to one another apart from the crowd.

"So the deal came through?"

Judge Hoskins, a stick-thin man in his forties with wispy hair and a grizzled mustache, peeled off his coat and folded it carefully on a short bench nearby as he waited patiently for Julian Haynes to answer him. The judge coughed and took out a handkerchief, holding it to his mouth a moment.

The two made an interesting contrast to one another. The banker, a powerful-looking man in the prime of life, had an olive complexion, a shock of dull black hair, and a closely trimmed mustache. A person would have to guess at the color of his eyes, for he kept them slitted, somehow managing to see quite well from between almost closed lids. As a youngster, cruel children had called him "Lizard Eyes," but no one dared mock him now. Besides, he had learned to smile, displaying a disarming expanse of blunt shining teeth. This evening he wore a white

shirt, a string tie, and a slightly wrinkled dark suit in spite of the warmth.

At last Haynes said, "I've agreed to deliver ten thousand head made up of one- and two-year-old steers and heifers to the XIT this year and a like amount next at a fixed price."

"They didn't wonder about a banker making an offer of that size?"

"The XIT's interested in just one thing—low prices. If they thought about it at all, they would have figured me to be some kind of middle-man."

The judge fought back another cough, took a difficult breath, and observed, "Well, in a way, that's about what you are." He smiled grimly before asking, "How much?"

"Fourteen dollars a head."

Hoskins shook his head. "Sounds low. Can you make money on that basis?"

Julian Haynes nodded. "Each note the Merchants State Bank has for loans I've been making to ranchers gives me the right to accelerate the due date—where the debt will be payable *in full* right away if a single interest payment is missed. There's not a doubt in my mind that they'll all default on those, and you know damn well the ranchers won't be able to pay the total amount of their debts. So, when that comes to pass, the bank will foreclose on their herds. In some cases we'll get their land, too."

"With Sheriff Baxter's and my help," Judge Hoskins put in dryly.

After a pause Haynes nodded and said, "Right." Then he continued, "Of course, I've got to have a place to take the cattle to separate the one- and two-year-olds for the drive north to the panhandle. And I'll need quite a bit of land for the breeding stock that I'll hold."

"Which is why you bought that big ranch from Jameson and his kinfolk."

"Well, that entered into it. What happened is that the Jamesons' note on their property came due, so I got it for about thirty cents on the dollar—based on a very conservative evaluation."

"I kind of figured you stole that land," Hoskins said, a thin smile on his lips.

"No," Haynes replied in frosty tones, "I took it in partial satisfaction of a past-due note. If a man gets in a bind and can't handle his obligations, that's no concern of mine."

"But now you've got to figure a way to get water so the ranch will be usable."

"That's correct," Haynes replied. "And I look forward to some good times ahead, for my arrangement with the XIT over the next two years is bigger than any single cattle sale agreement in the history of the state of Texas. Of course, mine is just one deal of many they're making. I learned from a man who works at City National Bank in Dallas that Colonel C. C. Slaughter has also contracted to deliver ten thousand steers and heifers to the XIT. It's my understanding that their management's planning to buy well over a *hundred thousand* head in the next two years. They're already building special pens for branding; and they're hiring top cowhands from all over."

"Hard to imagine folks with that kind of ready cash," Judge Hoskins said. He put both hands on the small of his back and arched it with an expression of pain on his face.

"Oh, they've got the money all right. The XIT is a syndicate, as you know, made up of Chicago people who received title to three million acres on the west side of the Texas panhandle in exchange for footing the entire bill for the state capitol building in Austin. They've got possession of the land now, and they're paying a king's ransom to fence it. A sheepherder named J. M. Shannon, and Ben Griffith—you may be acquainted with him—have a contract to fence the south part of the ranch, and they could both become rich men before it's over.

"To make a long story short, the XIT owners have got to put cattle on those empty three million acres. They'll have no trouble financing their stock purchases since God knows they bought the land at prices you couldn't touch these days, so they've got plenty of collateral if they should need it. But my hunch is that it won't come to that because there's a lot of money represented on the syndicate. For all I know, they're as strong as the group from Dundee, Scotland, that put together the Matador ranch up toward Ballard Springs. That's a pretty fair parallel, come to think of it. The investors in the Chicago combine have surely watched what Murdo Mackenzie has been able to do on the Matador with a great deal of interest."

"You kind of passed over your problem about the lack of water on the Jameson spread. I hear that Tom English refused to sell any of his land on the North Concho. And that's your only hope."

"No," Julian Haynes said, "I haven't overlooked anything. I know exactly how I'm going to handle that."

Haynes, the judge reflected, knew how to handle most situations. It still amazed him how swiftly and surely the banker had moved into a

position of strength. Almost like a professional gambler, Hoskins mused, dealing cards to a bunch of clumsy amateurs.

When Julian Haynes first arrived in Santa Rita he had joined the church and he made it a point to attend every public function that took place in the county. Perhaps owing to the natural tendency people have to try to get friendly with men of influence, the banker soon was seen as a high-minded pillar of the community. On Hoskins's arrival, he followed his friend's example. "How did we ever get along without them?" was the stock phrase that now made the rounds where people got together in the few populated areas in the immensity of Tom Green County.

"Better join the line," Judge Hoskins said, looking over his shoulder.

"Damn," the banker said, "that fat man is going back again. There won't be anything left."

"That's Calvin Laudermilk," the judge remarked. "Works for Tom English on that horse ranch he owns not far from town. Understand they're selling a good many mules and work horses to the drayage companies that run between here and Colorado City," he added, referring in passing to the town far to the north which had now been reached by the Texas and Pacific Railroad.

As the two men approached the depleted table, Calvin took one last plate of provisions over to a quilt which Elvira had placed upon the ground under an old mesquite tree. Lanterns hung from the rough-barked tree's stark branches, casting a festive glow upon the dark black sap stain bleeding down its trunk. The last shades of color faded from the layered bands of washed-out lavender hanging above the western horizon, and the total darkness of night closed around the churchyard's island of gaiety.

A sudden wind ruffled the feathery leaves of the old tree and then a gust blew a whirl of sand and dust through the startled assembly. It passed, leaving a complete calm, but all the lanterns and the candles in their protective cocoons made of stiff colored paper had been blown out.

Several ladies hurried into the church, where they lit coal-oil lamps. Then someone in the sanctuary began to play the piano, keeping her right foot firmly placed on the loud pedal so one note ran into and over the next one. Seven or eight of the members of the Women's Prayer Group could be heard singing. All of the voices blended except for one quavering falsetto that rose above the others, singing a half note off-key.

" 'Let us gather at the river, the beautiful, the beautiful river . . .' "
The strains seemed far off as people straggled inside to listen.

"We must leave," Calvin said to Elvira forcefully, taking her firmly by
the elbow.

"Oh, do we have to?"

"Yes. I have something to discuss with you."

Shadows covered the confusion which filled Elvira East's long-nosed
but not unattractive face.

As they rode in the buggy back to her brother's house, Calvin said, "I
would like your permission to call upon you regularly."

At first she did not reply but then she said with great seriousness,
"Nothing would give me greater pleasure, Mr. Laudermilk. Do you
think you should ask my brother's permission?"

"No, I don't think that's necessary."

"I'll discuss the matter with him, if it's all right with you," she said
shyly. "However, before I do, there is something very important to me
that we need to consider."

Something in her voice made him turn to face her as she posed her
question.

"You *have* been baptized, haven't you?"

"Well, not exactly."

Her mouth opened in horror. Five minutes passed with only the
plodding hoofbeats of the mare breaking the tense silence.

Calvin cleared his throat, desperate to break the awkward silence. "It
isn't that I'm not a religious man, Elvira." Parenthetically, he added, "I
hope you don't mind my using your given name, Miss East." Holding
the reins firmly and addressing his words directly at the mare's bedrag-
gled tail, he said, "I make it a regular practice to spend a quiet hour at
least once a week with my spiritual counselor." He did not add that this
person was his friend Tuck Bowlegs, the ordinarily drunken Indian
outcast who lived south of town.

Elvira looked at him with rapt eyes. "I might have known," she said
simply.

"The two of us," Calvin went on, warming to his topic, "seek guidance in God's open world where there is no sign of greed or man's
hatefulness. *That* is my temple." He closed his eyes, and happy memo-
ries came to him of sitting by the river with Tuck, sharing a bottle of
tequila.

"How beautiful," Elvira murmured.

"And tomorrow I will go down upon my knees with him to ask what I should do about this business of getting baptized."

Beaming from ear to ear, Elvira seemed to be at the edge of embracing him, but of course she didn't. "This is music to my ears, Mr. Laudermilk. You know the real reason why you haven't been baptized, don't you?"

"Why, no—I suppose I don't," Calvin replied with some confusion.

"You are basically a very shy man."

"That is true," he agreed emphatically.

"Gracious, all of this is working out so wonderfully well that I can hardly believe it. Reverend Vaurien is holding a revival meeting next Saturday and Sunday. They've made arrangements for it near the community of Christoval on the South Concho. So we can just ride out there in the buggy and you can get baptized where not a single one of your acquaintances here in town will see you."

"Surely you'll permit me to continue worshiping in my own way?"

"Come now, Mr. Laudermilk, don't act like a fraidy cat."

Calvin snorted with considerable impatience. "I ain't afraid of *nothin',*" he said emphatically.

# THREE

DUST DEVILS whirled sand and leaves in irregular spirals high into the air like miniature tornadoes and caused the tired horse pulling the buckboard to shy off to one side, drawing his head back in alarm. The constant whirring sound of locust songs came from the trees on either side of the rutted trail as Proctor Joab and Ed Bates warily approached the Tom English house on his Lower Ranch.

Bates tied the horse after they stopped, muttering, "I always prefer bargaining on my home ground—wish he'd agreed to come to the bank."

"He said he wouldn't do that."

Bates shrugged. "This looks to me to be a waste of time."

"We'll see," said Joab. He was a smooth-skinned man with a saturnine face and a pencil-thin dark mustache, dressed in a suit with a cravat at his neck.

Moments later, a dumpy Mexican woman with an Indian look ushered them into the house where she showed them to seats in the parlor. "Wait here," she said, wasting no words.

"He turned us down flat the last time," Bates said.

"We've got a better offer now."

Tom English walked into the room, and the two men rose, eyes fixed on him. The rancher's fresh white shirt made his dark tan stand out in contrast. Smiling easily, he said, "You fellows don't give up, do you?" He made a gesture for them to be reseated and took a chair facing them. He wore an old pair of scarred and scraped brown boots, no spurs, and no guns. From the dampness of his hair, from his freshly shaven appearance, it seemed that he had cleaned up for the meeting.

"Mr. Haynes asked us to give you his regards," Proctor Joab began. "And he told me, off to one side, that he always respects a man who knows how to negotiate."

"I'm not negotiating," Tom said.

"We've got quite an offer here." Joab pulled an envelope from his inside coat pocket and held it in an outstretched hand.

Tom took the envelope and put it unopened on a deep-grained red oak table beside his chair. "You get right to the point," he said, "and I guess that's what some would call the gringo way. It puts me in mind of a time, a few years back, when I thought about buying some cattle down in Mexico to put on the Circle X, a ranch we've got on the Rio Grande, not all that far from Langtry. Well, the seller had me come to his ranch in the state of Chihuahua. After I got there he spent a full three days showing me around while he talked in circles about one thing and then another. But that's the Mexican way; they think it's rude to be direct. So, after all this, he finally got around to how much he wanted for his stock, and we found we were too far apart to agree to a deal. It sounds like a great waste of time, and I guess it was, but at least I felt I'd made a friend. He came up to see me after that and I sold *him* some cattle. The Hereford breed fascinated him, although I don't know that they'll do well on his range. The point is, it's just that folks may not always get together the first time they try to do business."

"Aren't you even going to look at how much we're willing to pay?"

Tom shook his head.

"How about a lease arrangement—or an easement? All Mr. Haynes is askin' is a way to water his stock."

"The thing Haynes wants doesn't make sense. The old Jameson ranch that he got hold of must be twenty miles from the river. His cattle can't just go back and forth, for God's sake. Once a herd gets through my fences to water, they'll start grazing my grass. He's bound to have thought of this. His best bet is to rig some windmills and stock tanks. Has he tried drilling for water?"

"He has," Bates said, "but with no luck."

"I'm sorry to hear it, but I'm not going to change my mind."

"Our files down at the Merchants State Bank show that you own some four hundred and forty-eight thousand acres in Texas—we don't know what you've got in Montana, Mr. English—and we're only talking about a ten-mile stretch along the river, give or take a little."

"Your boss has his eye on the place where the Lazy E got started," Tom said. "Besides that, I'm not in the business of selling land."

The two visitors stood up. Joab held out a hand which Tom took briefly. "Julian Haynes could be an important friend. You sure you won't change your mind?"

"I'm certain about it."

After the two men from town had left, a very pretty woman with an inquiring look in her large brown eyes came into the room. Sally English wore an often washed faded blue dress that fit snugly about her waist. After the baby's birth she'd not gone back to her former weight as she had in Rebecca's case, a matter that troubled her. She rose to her full five feet one inches of height—full breasts pushed out, stomach pulled severely in—as she held her breath and looked in the mirror. Her eyes met her husband's and both of them broke into laughter at the same time. She knew without any doubt that he was fully aware of exactly what she'd been thinking. She asked him, "What did they want?"

"The same thing as last time."

Her musical laugh sounded again, and she said, "They don't know you very well."

She spoke to him of their daughter. Rebecca had remained behind at the headquarters ranch in the care of Lupe Acosta, old Santiago's wife. "She's still upset—says you promised her there'd be no more gunfights."

"I know." Turning to his wife, he said, "But you understand, don't you?"

She didn't answer him directly. With an abrupt movement, she put her arms around him and buried her head against his shoulder. "I don't know what I'd do if anything ever happened to you."

"Don't talk about things like that."

"I can't help but worry. You used to keep what you called your 'Mexican cavalry' around you. They used to laugh about the way they looked, armed to the teeth the way they were, but everyone knew you never went anywhere without them—and for a long time we didn't have any trouble."

"A man can't live his whole life surrounded by a bunch of bodyguards."

"I understand that, but . . ." Her voice trailed off. She moved away from him and looked out the window. "Maybe we should go away somewhere."

"I've run off twice, and trouble followed me. Seems like things got worse instead of better."

She didn't answer.

The baby began to cry in the other room. Probably hungry. Sally, with a wry smile, turned to the summons and left him alone.

He awaited her return, lost in thought. The dream had come again the last two nights. Even during the day it seemed so real that it caused icy chills to run up his spine. Pictures from it floated through his mind.

He faced a gunslinger and, in that split second when both men some-how *knew* the time had come, he'd gone for his guns—but his hands seemed so slow, in spite of his trying to force them to hurry. He realized he'd be too late at the instant that the fingers of his right hand touched the butt of his Colt. And, looking up, he stared into the black mouth of a barrel pointed at his eyes. Then he'd jerked awake, trembling like a child.

Long years of living with the dream had taught him the only solution that seemed to work. That morning he'd strapped on his wide cartridge belt with two low-hanging holsters and checked the cylinders of his left Colt and then the right. After this, he had saddled his young horse and ridden to the deep ravine several miles from the house where he prac-ticed.

Standing in the midst of a scattering of brass shells left there from earlier sessions, he'd faced his pretended enemy: a helpless much-scarred tree. First one gun, then the other whipped into his hand. Reloading, he'd turned a second time and then, as if to slaughter the nightmare threat, he'd cut loose with both handguns simultaneously, creating a cannonade that echoed wildly in the startled air. He felt his heart race and through the gunsmoke watched the bark fly from the wounded trunk. Tom stood, transfixed by the sight, and then he relaxed —even though his ears kept ringing.

Deliberately he slid cartridges into his weapons once again before holstering them. Then he started to swing up to the saddle. His snort-ing horse spun in an agitated circle the moment the toe of his left boot pushed down on the stirrup. Tom held the reins short in his left hand and also caught hold of the wiry mane with it. As the lunging animal whirled, he grabbed the saddle horn with his right and managed to get astride. Then, as the spooked young bay skittered about, his probing boot finally found the right stirrup and in a moment he succeeded in gaining control. He lengthened the reins, giving the cow pony his head, and welcomed the rush of wind in his face as his scrambling mount settled into a rocking lope.

Tom thought about the dream and about his routine practice and the urgent ride back to the corral as he waited for Sally to return. Uneasy, missing the weight of his guns, he stood in the safety of his parlor.

He recalled the words of Calvin Laudermilk when he'd asked, "How many does that make, anyway?" Tom hadn't answered although he couldn't possibly forget. He lived constantly with the sickening knowl-edge that he'd killed thirty-four men. And he'd caused the death of

others who had died directly because of him, even though it hadn't been his gun that put them in their graves.

When Sally came back through the door he said to her, "You know I'll be wearing my guns for a while, but it won't be forever."

She didn't answer.

He wondered if she knew he'd started drinking again, and decided she probably did. Tom English, considered to be one of the most dangerous men of his time, said, "Would you mind coming over here and holding me?"

Sally shook her head and began to walk toward him, tears filling her eyes.

No one in Santa Rita had ever seen anything like it. The new banker, Julian Haynes, not only had a private office apart from the main part of the bank, but it even had a small anteroom before it where people waited their turn to see him.

Sheriff Reuben Baxter sat there in a soft upholstered chair, feeling, in spite of the cushions, decidedly uncomfortable. He looked at his boots, hoping he hadn't tracked anything in, and then became aware of a plant with broad green leaves which sprouted five feet tall out of a heavy dull red ceramic pot with a geometric pattern encircling it. An oriental rug almost covered the floor, giving the waiting room a sense of opulence; and this was enhanced by an oil portrait of a woman with a pronounced nose and an eternally unfocused stare. A clock hung on the paneled wall, ticking audibly, as its pendulum swayed rhythmically from side to side.

Judge T. J. Hoskins opened the office door and made a beckoning motion with his head. "Come on in."

"Hello, Sheriff," Julian Haynes said to the man entering his office. Haynes sat in a black leather chair behind his wide desk. "The judge and I've been pondering our options. First, though, tell me what happened yesterday."

"You mean taking that shot-up corpse to the bar? About what you'd expect. Mostly local drunks and a few drifters there. Nobody there who amounts to anything and, naturally, not a soul recognized the dead man."

"That isn't what I had in mind. Did they get upset?"

"Damn right they did. Couldn't understand why a man like Tom English, who's known to be one hell of a shot, would deliberately mutilate a man the way he did. People all over town are talking about it."

Haynes glanced through slitted eyes at Judge Hoskins, checking his reaction.

A slight tic became visible in the left side of the judge's face. He put his hand up and began to massage it with his fingers before speaking. "It may be a little late to be having second thoughts, Julian, but before we go too far I think we ought to make sure this is what you want to do. You might be setting off a chain of events with right serious consequences."

"Of course I am. About as serious as they can get as far as English is concerned."

"He's got some mighty powerful friends," Judge Hoskins insisted. "It may be true that last night some loafers and drunks got stirred up, but don't forget that English is highly respected here. He's partners with Max Hall in a wool warehouse and some real estate over south of the river," Judge Hoskins said, referring to the owner of the First National Bank, the only competition that the bank owned by Julian Haynes had. "Not long ago Hall and English donated a school site to the city. The men around here who count for anything appreciate that, though there won't be a school over there for many a long year, if ever. Nothing but a dry mesquite flat right now, located just to the west of Fort Concho. But you know all of this."

The banker meticulously arranged several stacks of paper on his desk, aligning them with great care. "There's bound to be some who resent him. After all, here's a man who's known far and wide as a pistolero. He's nothin' more nor less than a killer, and I for one can't imagine how he's managed to live this long. Add to that the fact that he married a rich woman and, what with one thing and another, he's taken over neighboring ranches until he's one of the biggest landholders in the state of Texas. How do you think this sits with the ordinary citizen? Put yourself in the position of a man who works like hell for a dollar a day. He looks at English and sees someone who started out as a kid horse wrangler and now is worth a fortune. You know damn well that they have to ask themselves, 'How is it possible for an honest man to do that?' "

The banker finished touching the objects on his desk and leaned back in his chair. "You know, it's the most natural thing in the world for poor men to hate a rich one. They may stand a little in awe of him, but if that rich man can be shown to be a common murderer, that ought to put a sense of outrage in the place of that 'awe' I was talkin' about."

"You may have a point," Sheriff Baxter said, joining in the conversa-

tion with his superiors, "but by and large he's respected. Has a nice family. It's true he married old man Clarke's daughter, but they've never tried to lord it over other people. English is known to work the same as his men, in fact a little harder. And everyone I've talked to who's acquainted with the man seems to like him."

"Reuben," Haynes said, using the first name that he knew Sheriff Baxter couldn't stand, "when you're dealing with a mob, their likes or dislikes can vary from one minute to the next. I want you to pay close attention to what I've got to say now. Tom English, a notorious gun-slinger—in fact a legendary one if you read the pulp magazines—has shot a stranger who rode onto his ranch. We have no proof that the victim was even armed. Two cowboys who work for English brought the body into town, dropped it off at Noah and Japheth Massie's under-taking parlor. After that, Tom English had his lawyer come over to your office and say that this was a real unfortunate thing. Now, having said all of that, I want you to think about something: if a worker in this town or a cowboy should go out and kill somebody—and then send word to us that he was sorry that he'd done it—would that be the end of the matter?"

"Why, hell no," the sheriff spluttered.

"And don't the laws in this country cover *all* men, rich and poor alike?"

"You know the answer to that. What are you leadin' up to?"

"Can't you figure that out? I'm disappointed in you, Sheriff. In my opinion, you don't have a choice in the matter. You're going to have to arrest the man who confessed to the shooting of that poor stranger. So far as I can see, the dead man's only offense was that he trespassed on another man's land."

"Are you out of your mind? You think I'm fool enough to go onto the Lazy E and try to arrest Tom English? You're bound to have heard the same stories that I have. There's one in particular that makes my blood run cold. They say that one day in Black Horse, Montana, he went up against three men who were waiting for him out in the street. Now picture this: those three had their weapons drawn while his were hol-stered; but Tom English closed on them anyway and all of a sudden he went for his guns—and in less than a heartbeat all three men were dead on the ground. Not one of them had even managed to get a shot off." Baxter shuddered. "Can you imagine?"

The sheriff stood up and began to pace from one side of the office to

another. "No, sir," he emphasized, stopping in front of Julian Haynes, "not me. I ain't *that* tired of livin'."

The judge broke in. "Who ever said you had to go alone?"

"They ain't a soul within a hundred miles who'd sign on to help me in a situation like this."

Judge Hoskins showed his irritation. "How about the Texas Rangers, couldn't . . ."

"No chance," Sheriff Baxter cut in. "In the first place, John Robert Hale is off in the big bend country, and in the second, Hale just happens to be one of the best friends that English has."

Julian Haynes looked pained. "You're creating a problem where none exists. Damn it, Reuben, pay attention to me. I have no intention of sending you out to challenge a man like English. He's a man who'll follow his lawyer's advice, so all you need to do is tell Jedediah Jackson to have his client come to your office and give a statement of the facts. Call it a coroner's inquest or something like that. And once there, alone with his lawyer, you can place him under arrest. After that we'll call a trial so fast it'll make his head swim. If I do say so myself, that plan is a marvel of simplicity."

"I can't see the point of it, Mr. Haynes," Baxter expostulated, growing red in the face. "He'll claim self-defense, and the folks in Santa Rita will turn him loose. And after that happens he's liable to come looking for *me*."

Judge Hoskins cleared his throat before saying, "At my request Doc Starret examined the body and made a report to me. In answer to a direct question, the doctor admitted that any one of the four bullets would have been fatal. When this comes to trial I'll bring that point out. Since we don't have a regular prosecuting attorney, it'll be my job as judge to bring out any evidence that might show malice on the part of the accused."

Sheriff Baxter frowned. "You mean try him without a jury? Can you do that?"

"Well, stranger things have happened, but we won't need to," Haynes said smoothly. "We've already worked things out. Judge, maybe you can clear things up for Reuben."

"We'll have a jury of his peers," T. J. Hoskins said in his dry way. "In fact, we've already got the jury panel in mind. It makes great good sense to Julian and me to use a selection from those people who saw the body last night in the Concho Street Saloon. That's the best evidence the state has, but unfortunately cadavers don't hold up well during the

summertime—it won't keep a few days for others to view it. So what men could be better prepared to make a decision?"

"Christ, Judge," Baxter said, "them barflies can't serve on a jury. Not a one of 'em owns property, and ain't that a requirement?"

"We're not going to get hung up on fine points and technicalities if they stand in the way of justice being served."

Haynes chuckled dryly. "Well said, Judge." He swiveled about to face the sheriff. "Reuben, send word to Jedediah Jackson to have his client in your office Monday morning to answer some routine questions. Then put him under arrest."

"I don't know . . ."

The banker cut off his protest with an impatient gesture. "It's out of your hands after that, Sheriff. We're going to have a fair trial that ought to be over before suppertime."

Judge Hoskins listened carefully as he cleaned his fingernails with a pocket knife. The tic rippled again across his left cheek but this time he ignored it.

A sweltering airless heat seemed to rise from the broad river. It had rained heavily the night before and the swollen channel churned with brown waves. Sticks and foam twisted in the muddy current.

Earnest Vaurien, on this Sunday morning, looked with some anxiety at the South Concho behind him but then turned a beaming face upon the men and women and children upon the bank above him. There must be, the preacher thought, at least twenty-five grown-ups who had come to witness the baptismal ceremony. More than he'd had at his revival tent near the community of Christoval the night before.

Off to one side an open-topped shelter with canvas walls had been hurriedly erected to be used for donning the baptismal robes.

Reverend Vaurien looked at the enormous man hanging back with the spinster Elvira East behind the others. Even from a distance he could see that the fat man was perturbed. Better get started before he backed out, the minister of the gospel decided.

"Brother Laudermilk," his rich voice pealed, "stand beside me while I ask the Almighty's blessing on this gathering."

With much urging from Miss East and a few others in the group, the oversized man made his deliberate way through the small throng. Then, taking his stand beside Vaurien, who all of a sudden looked like a dwarf, he husked, "Preacher, I'm prepared to stand this only if you're a mighty fast talker. Forget your sermons and let's get in the river."

Ignoring the pale-faced sweating giant, Reverend Vaurien proceeded directly to his strong point, which was scaring his congregation witless with the promise of eternal damnation.

"You have all turned your backs on salvation," he thundered. "You're nothing but a bunch of muley, swaybacked, hidebound, stiff-necked sinners. And what will be your recompense? The Lord is a wrathful God. You will answer for your shortcomings—unless you *repent*. And as a sign of this you must be washed in the blood of the lamb."

Calvin glared at his tormentor, then looked down at the mud at his feet glumly.

"Bow your heads," the preacher ordered in ringing tones. The people standing in their Sunday best clamped their eyes shut as they ducked their heads obediently. A few mothers had to hiss at their children, but soon even the youngsters stood in a downcast and prayerful attitude.

"Thou knowest us better than we know ourselves."

"Yes, Lord," the congregation responded.

An uprooted small tree swept down the river, turning in the coiling brown ripples. A young boy cried out and pointed toward it, but his father growled at him to hush.

"Help us turn away from our own selfishness and concentrate on Thee."

"Yes, Lord."

A singsong give-and-take developed over the next ten minutes, and a number of the people began to look as though they'd been hypnotized. At last Reverend Vaurien said, with a terrible frown of concentration upon his face, "Hear our prayer, O Lord."

He looked upon his flock with judgmental eyes and demanded, "Raise your hand if you want to be saved."

The scattered individuals, shifting uneasily from one muddy foot to another, looked out of the corners of their eyes at their fellow worshipers. One by one, hands went up. Mothers caught at their children, tugging at their arms and scolding them. Soon every single worshiper had his hand raised high.

"And *now*," Reverend Vaurien declared, "raise your hand once more if you are prepared to join our brother Calvin Laudermilk in the holy sacrament of baptism."

The preacher's eyes roved back and forth, first slowly, then rapidly. With a note of temper in his voice he said, "All of you held up a hand, giving public witness that you want to be saved. Those who've already

been baptized certainly don't need to do it again. But I know good and well that there are at least six of you—and you know who you are—who *ain't* been baptized, so unless you're prepared to roast in hell for eternity, you better get your tails down here with this good man."

He glared balefully and then, raising his arms to the heavens as if to ask the Almighty what he should do with these recalcitrant backsliders, he turned to Calvin and said snappishly, "Well, at least I plan to save *your* everlasting soul."

Recovering his equilibrium, he said with dignity, "Come forward, Brother Laudermilk, and enter with me the tent of preparation."

With that he led Calvin with great dignity to the open-topped shelter. "We'll be right back," he called over his shoulder as he disappeared from the congregation's sight.

Once inside, the preacher said in a conversational way, "No use getting your good clothes wet. Take off those boots and then strip down to your underwear."

Without hesitation the Right Reverend Earnest Vaurien yanked off his shoes and socks and began to remove his outer garments. Calvin followed his example and in a moment stood in his best pair of long underwear, awaiting further instructions. He wore long johns even in the summer and argued that, far from making him hot, they helped matters considerably since they soaked up the sweat, enabling passing breezes to cool him.

The preacher took one robe and tossed another to Calvin. These had been made by the Women's Prayer Group from cotton sheets by the simple expedient of cutting holes in the center and stitching them so they wouldn't fray. Calvin watched the preacher poke his head into the hole and then smooth the sheet down over his legs. Calvin did the same but, owing to his bulk and the width of his shoulders, the fabric didn't reach his knees. Then the two white-clad men walked barefooted past the flap in the canvas wall and appeared once more before the faithful.

The preacher, not one to forget a grievance, cried out as the two men made their way into the water, "Those of you who held up your hands in false witness, the ones who did not come forward joyfully to participate in this sacrament, have just slapped Jesus Christ in the face."

A sharp intake of breath sounded throughout the throng at the awful statement. Several young people visibly flinched, their bloodless cheeks suddenly pale.

"We'll be here one more day," the preacher said, pleased at the reac-

tion, "so you'll have one last chance to avoid the dreadful torment of being turned upon a spit over the flames of hellfire down through the sands of time."

Apparently satisfied by his turn of phrase, he said to Calvin as the two stepped cautiously into the pressing current, "What is your Christian name, Brother Laudermilk?"

"You know damn good and well it's Calvin," came back the snarling reply.

The faithful upon the bank looked down at their pastor and the monstrous man beside him, their white sheets turning dark in the murky torrent and spreading out downstream. Fascinated by the sight, they seemed to be in rapture.

By the time the two had reached a point where the river ran waist deep on Calvin, and up to Earnest Vaurien's chest, the preacher chose to stop and declaim, "Brother Laudermilk, it's clear to me that demons have taken possession of you. In this purification ceremony I will exorcise them. You will emerge reborn and pure—as pure as an infant."

As he pronounced these words the two men were pressed by a force of the current and they began to topple sideways, going off the underwater ledge upon which they'd been standing.

Both of them sank instantly from sight, but a minute later two separate heads bobbed up and could be seen in flashes, gasping for air before disappearing again. The preacher surfaced, clawed out at the floundering form near him, and started to howl out, "Calvin!" but the river choked off his cry.

The astounded worshipers on the bank ran beside the surging South Concho as they saw their pastor and the fat man surface time and again, only to go under the muddy waves, twisting and turning as they became more entangled in their baptismal robes. At the point of drowning, each managed to rip off his sheet and make it with great difficulty to shallow water.

The people rushed up close to pull them in, but Earnest Vaurien, on his hands and knees in the thick mud of the bank, cried out, "We haven't finished. Stand back!"

He looked as if he might be in a state of apoplexy at this point, for he had leaped to the conclusion that the dark hand of the Devil had been involved, that Satan's dread presence had invaded Calvin to assist the demons he now felt sure inhabited that gross body. Mindful of the story of Jacob, who wrestled virtually all of one night with the Devil, Vaurien

watched Calvin Laudermilk striding out of the water in his soaked long underwear. These clung to his gargantuan belly and thighs.

Without warning, as Calvin left the river, Reverend Vaurien tackled him, throwing the off-balance hulk of a man down with a splat upon the slick mud. With that the preacher began to pummel Calvin with might and main, determined to drive out the Devil and his demons.

Calvin struggled for breath, his sagging cask of a body heaving from his exertions. As he came to his senses he felt a battering, a pulling and shoving, and as he looked about in amazement, he saw the blood-red-dened face of the preacher, eyes wide and glaring. A flood of resentment surged within Calvin's breast. Then, fed up by this treatment, he said to himself, "I'd as soon not be a Christian if this is the kind of initiation they require."

As this decision formed, all restraints snapped. He rose upright, feet propped wide apart, knees bent, and grasped the waist of his struggling antagonist with hamlike hands. He raised Reverend Vaurien high above his head and with a mighty heave threw him far out into the swirling waters of the swollen river.

Then, before the paralyzed throng, Calvin strode to the robing tent, recovered his clothing and his boots, and stalked without putting them on toward the spinster Elvira East. She stood there as he approached, glassy-eyed, staring at the clinging long wet underwear which outlined in stark detail the enormous drooping belly, the bulging crotch, and the tree-trunk legs of her suitor.

The two hastened to the buggy where Calvin hurriedly dressed, suddenly mindful of his appearance. Then they drove on the trail to Santa Rita to the north, with Calvin railing vehemently about the preacher who had, so far as he could tell, gone completely mad the moment he found himself in the water. "I came within an inch of breakin' his damn neck," he fumed.

At this moment Elvira broke her long silence. "Mr. Laudermilk," she said shakily, "given the circumstances, it is clear to me that we must get married right away."

Calvin clucked to the horse and they jounced along. "What was that, my dear?" he asked, reaching back and patting her on the shoulder protectively, gradually calming after his rage. He often became furious but these attacks were of short duration. He spoke again to his companion. "I'm afraid I didn't hear you, Elvira. Got water in my ears."

Elvira had in her protected life seen nothing more of the male form

than a rare undiapered baby or pictures of cherubs. Almost choking with emotion, she said in a trembling but quite determined voice, "My honor has been compromised. We must be married immediately."

"Great God," Calvin exclaimed upon this Sabbath day.

# FOUR

THE BUCKBOARD SWAYED, causing Elvira to slide on the worn seat until her hip bumped against Calvin's. The dusty black horse pulling them picked up speed going downhill into a dry draw, with Calvin flicking the reins to encourage him, and then slowed as he leaned into the traces and, with muscles straining, powered up the steep slope of the opposite side.

Elvira shifted as far away as she could when they reached level ground. "I've known dark days, like when Pap finally passed on to his reward." She sighed deeply as she spoke, a fierce look upon her face. "But up till now I've never been downright mortified before. You have *shamed* me in front of Reverend Vaurien and the entire Baptist congregation. How can I ever face a one of them again?"

She snuffled into her handkerchief for a time as her companion stared dead ahead with fixed-jaw intensity.

"How *could* you, Calvin? If I live to be ninety, I'll never live this down. After inviting you to our church, to have you pick Reverend Vaurien up and throw him in the river!" Her brow darkened with anger, and then she began to sob again.

Calvin pressed his lips together, refusing to defend himself.

Elvira blurted out, "Now you'll *never* get baptized."

"Hawgwash," Calvin snorted. "Bullcorn," he added, exhausting his supply of polite expletives. "You know as well as I do that to get christened . . ."

" 'Baptized' is the word," Elvira interrupted sharply, frost in her tone.

"All right, whatever label you want to hang on it. The only requirement is to go down to the water. Some churches sprinkle and others immerse, and there ain't a doubt in all God's good green earth that I got myself immersed. The preacher is to say your name, and I heard him holler 'Calvin' at the top of his voice whilst we was goin' under. All of which leads me to this point: if I need to hire Lawyer Jackson to fight

my case, or if I have to rassle with your full board of deacons, I'll do it, for there's no question but that I've been baptized fair and square. And once is all it takes. I ain't *never* goin' through such a thing again."

The horse's tail raised and Elvira turned her head, staring off to one side as though totally unaware of what went on directly before her.

"The trouble with you, Elvira, is that you're scared of anything that's *natural*. You can't go through life living in a playlike world. If you're upset because you saw me in my underclothes . . ."

*"Mr. Laudermilk!"*

"That's what all this foofaraw is about." Suddenly sounding miserable, he added, "Or maybe it's not. Could be that the real reason you're trying to pick this fight is that you saw me coming out of the water, half drownded, and instead of feeling sorry for me, all you can think of is that I'm fatter than you'd figured. You're upset about my appearance."

In shocked surprise, Elvira whirled toward him. "You mustn't think that for a moment. My word, such a thought never entered my mind. You're a fine figure of a man, it's just that . . ." But then, unable to continue, her face crimsoned and she looked away.

Mollified, Calvin said reluctantly, "I'm sorry if I embarrassed you."

"Thank you," she responded almost inaudibly. "The fact is, I can't believe I made that comment about marriage." She bit her lip and then continued. "It was just that I felt—and still do—that there's no other honorable course of action open to us. On the other hand, it's out of the question—what with your refusing to get properly baptized."

"Don't nag at me, woman," Calvin rumbled. "The ceremony, while not as stylish as you might have liked, did in fact take place."

"I'm not so sure about that."

Calvin clenched his teeth as he began to consider the things he did not like about Elvira East, beginning with her friends—those women in the Baptist Church with their pious ways and their tedious, obedient husbands. Also, he could not abide a bossy woman, and Elvira had that tendency. Not to mention the clear fact that she disapproved of just about everything about him. To top it off, the very idea of marriage set off alarm bells which rang as if a sexton were signaling a community emergency from a resonant belfry. As the metallic sounds subsided a picture formed, and he saw himself backed into a corner of a narrow living room with squalling babies on the floor and a wife crying out orders from the kitchen.

He said to himself, "If matters have reached this sorry state before I've even gotten well acquainted with her—they can only get worse with

the passage of time. I believe I have made a great mistake; thank God I found out before things went too far."

Elvira's suddenly weak voice intruded on his reverie. She spoke while holding a hand to her forehead. "I think I'm going to faint."

Calvin pulled the buggy to a stop. He helped her step down to the ground, and as he did she seemed to slip, falling into his powerful arms.

Calvin felt her prominent bosom pressing softly against him, a circumstance causing a stream of confusing but nonetheless pleasant sensations to flow through him.

"Oh, Mr. Laudermilk," Elvira said weakly, holding to him, "what *shall* we do?"

Calvin cleared his voice. "Well, the first thing we might consider is to sit down in the shade over yonder until you get to feelin' better."

As they walked to the grove of live-oak trees, he heard a warning voice from deep within himself that said, *"Be very careful, Calvin."*

"We could always go back to Christoval," Elvira suggested. "The revival goes on through tomorrow."

*"Never,"* Calvin said firmly.


Jedediah Jackson, seventy-four years old and a widower, had come to West Texas, he always explained, for reasons of his health. A distinguished lawyer from Nacogdoches in East Texas, he took pride in his reputation for astuteness and didn't want anyone to think he'd chosen to live in this godforsaken remoteness of his own free will.

Jackson had thinning gray hair and a completely white mustache which he had neglected to trim, and now it drooped several inches below his mouth on either side. A network of fine wrinkles covered his still handsome face. He had a wide forehead, intelligent-appearing blue-green eyes, and an aquiline, aristocratic nose.

He stood with his back to his visitor on this late Monday morning, looking with satisfaction at the new bookcases which lined his walls. He slid his worn copy of *The Common Law* by Oliver Wendell Holmes, Jr., into a slot open at the end of the leather-bound set of Blackstone's *Commentaries* and returned to his desk, where he sat down to admire his recent acquisition. Each shelf had a wood-framed glass door that pulled down to protect his precious books from dust. An amazingly simple metal apparatus permitted him to raise a door and slide it back out of the way. Newfangled perhaps, but practical. The bulky bookcases had been ordered through Massie's furniture store from the Globe-Wernicke Company of Cincinnati, Ohio, and they'd finally ar-

rived on the freight wagon the previous week. With loving pleasure he'd spent Saturday and Sunday arranging the numerous volumes of his law library in them.

Jackson leaned back in his chair, then took off his eyeglasses and held them by their gold wire earpieces as he looked across the desk and addressed Tom English.

"A hearing of this sort isn't out of the ordinary. I see no reason to be alarmed."

"I'm not alarmed exactly, more like bothered. The thing is, I don't trust the new sheriff."

"I suggest that we call on Sheriff Baxter and get this over," the old lawyer said, rising to his feet. He put his glasses on and took his hat from a rack by the door. Then he and Tom left together.

Tom's spurs made jingling noises and his boot heels thumped the board sidewalk as the two men made their way past Westbrook's General Store, then stepped down and crossed the dusty rutted road.

Tom felt the weight of his Colts, each one nestled in a leather holster which he kept supple with regular applications of pale yellow neat's-foot oil. He felt a nervous tingle go up the back of his neck and, looking around, saw a curtain drawn aside in a window of the Merchants State Bank. A dark figure could barely be seen standing behind it, observing his passage.

They walked to the unnamed road which paralleled Concho Street in the little town, and proceeded down it until they reached the sheriff's office. Once inside, Tom found himself in familiar surroundings. He wondered how many hours he'd spent there with Ben Jordan—before the old lawman had been killed.

Sheriff Baxter greeted the visitors absently. "Got some papers for you to fill out, Mr. English. Your lawyer gave us his version of the shooting, but we'd like you to write down for us just exactly what happened. Oh," he added as if it were a second thought, "would you mind hanging those guns of yours up on the wall?"

When Tom didn't answer at first, Baxter said, "It's a rule we follow—I'm sure you understand." He hid his nervousness with an attempted smile as he watched Tom reluctantly unbuckle his wide gun belt and then suspend it with his Colts from a sturdy peg.

After this, Baxter took a deep relieved breath. "Be back in just a minute," he said, leaving through a door which led to the other room of the modest one-story building.

"Has he got somebody locked up in that old jail cell?" Tom asked, nodding in the direction the sheriff had gone.

"Not that I know of," Jackson answered. "It hasn't been used for that purpose since the new ones got built. But it seems to me that the sheriff's acting a bit peculiarly." His glasses had slid down his nose and he looked over them at his client, a speculative expression on his face. Then he sat down in a straight chair with a leather seat.

"Might as well relax, Tom."

"In your profession you learn to be patient, I guess."

The lawyer smiled as he adjusted his glasses with his thumb and forefinger. "That's right." Jackson heard the interior door open and glanced up—with the smile gradually fading from his face.

Sheriff Baxter entered the room holding a double-barreled shotgun with both hammers cocked. Behind him stood the deputy with an out-stretched Smith & Wesson .44. At the same time, a hatless person with a shock of sandy orange hair and a face so pale that his freckles looked painted on it burst in through the front door holding a Winchester rifle pointed at the two men, who bolted upright from their seats.

"Hands above your head, English," the sheriff called out. "I'm arresting you for murder."

The jail had at one time been a house used by a man named Abe Koenigheim before his fortune improved and he'd been able to move to a better place. He'd built it out of limestone blocks with a heavy tin roof, a practice followed by many members of the German community who moved to this part of the state. When Abe sold the house to the city, they added a shedded-off frame section to it, increasing its size by almost a third, and that became the sheriff's office.

The original stone dwelling had been a two-room house with a privy out back, and it remained much the same as always except that the dividing wall had been torn out when the new iron bars arrived. They'd come in wooden crates by rail from Pittsburgh to Fort Worth—this was back before the Texas and Pacific had reached Colorado City—and had then proceeded by wagon freight to Santa Rita. These bars made up two sides of the rectangular cell, and the stone outer walls of the building made up the other sides. Only two barred windows gave light to the dim interior, since all the other windows and doors had been filled with irregular stone blocks cemented together with a mortar made of lime and sand and water which had itself turned as hard as rock. As a result, the only entrance to the jail was through the frame addition built for

the sheriff's office. Outside the cell the rest of Abe's old house served as
a storage area for odds and ends. A pair of discarded boots. An old rope.
Boxes of papers. A broken chair.

The wide fireplace where Abe had cooked his meals lay in the storage
area and not within the jail cell so people wouldn't be tempted to try to
drop things down the chimney to prisoners. Fires laid in this hearth
provided the only heat during cold spells in the winter, but since most
of the warmth rushed up through the flue, men in the old jail came
close to freezing, which was one of the reasons for building a new one.

The recently constructed courthouse in the center of the square
across the road from the sheriff's office had several cells in it, providing
a temporary home for the drunks who made up the normal jail popula-
tion in Santa Rita. Accordingly, Tom English found himself alone.

He looked through the two-foot-square window in the old jail across
the dirt street at the courthouse. The structure had been built up about
three feet above ground level and had stone steps ascending to an
abbreviated porch before its impressive front doors. A poorly maintained gravel walkway led from the steps to the road where a long
hitching rail made of cedar posts had been sunk solidly in the ground
with a series of rails nailed on top of them. Bushes planted around the
courthouse had died, their pathetic brittle limbs rising in crooked
clumps along the walls. No one had thought how they might be provided with water. However, on the east side of the courthouse some
stubborn chinaberry trees survived near a shallow draw filled with tall
Johnson grass and shinnery.

At one side of the front walk, in the hard bare dirt of the grounds,
stood a flagpole made from a single tall pine log brought in with difficulty from East Texas. At the moment no flag flew from it. On either
side of the pole two smoothbore cannons from the early days of the
Civil War had been placed at angles. Each rested between a pair of
slanted wheels that would never turn again—rim iron peeling away, dry
rot in the crumbling spokes. A small pyramid of rusting cannonballs lay
beside one of the cannons, a vague reminder of the bloody conflict more
than twenty years in the past.

Tom felt a tentative breath of fresh air on his face as he turned from
the window and faced the stifling heat of the poorly ventilated cell. Old
smells of human waste and sweat and despair hung within the room.
He began to pace back and forth. The cell would be, he calculated,
about twelve feet long and ten feet wide. Once it had held as many as
five or six hungover cowboys after payday Saturday nights, but now it

had been set up for a single person. A cot with stained ticking over a
thin mattress had been placed at one end with a chamber pot under it.
He had no sheets and not even a blanket to fold into a scratchy pillow.

Tom walked back and forth, restless as a cat, waiting for his lawyer,
remembering the outrage of his arrest. He'd been speechless as strangers grasped his arms and propelled him into the cell, slamming the
heavy door shut behind him with a reverberating clang.

Sheriff Baxter, as he locked him in with a long key, had said in his
deep voice, "You're gonna pay dear for what you done." Then he
laughed coldly before adding, "I'm told that many call you the meanest
man in West Texas, but you don't look so mean to me."

Almost two hours had passed. Over and over Tom asked himself,
"What in hell is going on? When is Jedediah going to get me out of
here?"

The door which connected the room containing the dusty storage
area and jail with the sheriff's office swung open. Tom stood in shadows
as Jedediah Jackson entered, squinting as he sought to adjust his eyes to
the gloom. A second man brushed past him.

The deputy—Tom had heard the others call him Ernie—unlocked
the cell door to permit the old lawyer to enter and then relocked it.
After this he dragged from the assorted junk behind him a chair with
one broken leg and sat in it, propping himself with his feet. Then he
proceeded to stare at them.

Jackson turned about with a pained expression on his face. "I plan to
speak privately with my client."

The deputy named Ernie had simply been curious. He shrugged and
said, "Suit yourself." With that he left.

"There's to be a trial."

Outside some dogs barked. A cat yowled. Then silence fell again.

"When?"

"To my surprise, this afternoon. I've raised all manner of hell, Tom,
and told them this haste is in and of itself cause for reversible error. A
defendant has an absolute right to what we call 'due process of law.'
The lack of time to prepare a defense denies that."

The lawyer moved to the cot, sat on its edge, and said, "I've taken a
handful of motions and writs to our local 'judge,'" pronouncing this last
word with studied disdain. "To no avail. If I had even a few days, I'd be
able to build a case, assemble character witnesses, maybe even learn a
little about that stranger who tried to shoot you in cold blood."

"But we don't have a few days."

"That's right." Jackson rose to his feet and moved to the window where he examined the freshly whitewashed exterior of the new courthouse. Then, as if bracing himself for battle, he squared his shoulders.

"There's a good bit to be said for the jury system. The average man has a good sense of right and wrong—and of fairness. When we go to trial the members of the jury will realize that the judge and sheriff, for some reason that absolutely escapes me, are trying to railroad you."

"So I'm to be tried for murder."

"Yes."

"What's the worst thing that might happen?"

"It's too early to think about that, but I'd say, in a situation like yours —where the defendant is a man who's never even been charged with a crime before, who has acted in self-defense—there might be no more than some time in jail. If we're terribly unlucky, that might turn into something a lot more serious, of course. I'm talking about the state penitentiary."

"Good Lord."

"I don't think it'll come to that. As I say, the very fact of their haste makes me certain that our appeal to a higher court will be granted. So, after the appeals process, I feel sure the case will be remanded for retrial, although my expectation would be for the appeals court to exonerate you entirely after a full review of the record."

Tom turned away and hardly listened as his old friend began to say, "When I get you on the stand I want you to explain how that stranger followed you. And then . . ."

Julian Haynes crossed the deep blue Persian rug in his private office, striding over to the mahogany sideboard against the wall. He touched the cut-glass decanter of sherry but changed his mind and uncorked a clear bottle of sour mash Kentucky bourbon, part of a case of this whiskey which he'd ordered specially. After pouring out a measure with the precision of a chemist, he sipped from it, nodded approvingly, and then turned about, facing Sheriff Baxter and Judge T. J. Hoskins.

He had been speaking of various bank customers, acting as if this were an ordinary day. "We're seeing more and more ranchers who are turning away from cattle to sheep. Less risk, for one thing, what with a steady market for wool. And you'll not find a cattleman who hasn't suffered financially due to the way beef prices always seem to fluctuate. One of their headaches, of course, for those of them who ranch within ten or fifteen miles from a town or community, is the serious problem

they have with the damn dogs. Seems like everyone in West Texas owns dogs. These get to running in packs, and they learn quickly how easy it is to kill sheep."

Haynes looked pleasantly at his guests as he sat down behind his desk. He had not offered either of them a drink; they didn't expect it.

"There's just no way to break a sheep-killing dog from the habit," Haynes stated reasonably. "Once they've got the taste for blood, you have no choice but to kill them. Isn't that so, Reuben?"

The sheriff squirmed at the use of this name, but he acknowledged the truth of the banker's statement.

"Which brings us to the case of Tom English. He has the taste for blood, has shot God knows how many men, and we can't allow this to go on. Are we in agreement?"

"We got him throwed in jail," the sheriff said cheerfully. "They tell me that this is the first time such a thing ever happened to him—and you never saw a man so mad. He'll think twice before he goes after anybody else."

Haynes took some time before he spoke again. He sipped from his whiskey before stating coldly, "It's not nearly enough. The son of a bitch is a homicidal maniac; we've got to protect our citizens."

Judge Hoskins looked uneasily at the banker. "You haven't told me exactly just what you have in mind, Julian."

"I want you to hang him."

# FIVE

JUDGE HOSKINS looked down at the milling crowd from his judicial bench in the new courthouse. Every chair had been filled and, in the rear, men on foot craned their necks as they crowded for a vantage point. The room rustled with the sounds of dozens of simultaneous conversations, of laughter, of coughing. Here and there he saw a few women, sunbonneted heads close together but not talking. Apparently uneasy at being in the center of such a crush of sweating men, they showed their excitement in the way they looked about, their eyes darting nervously.

Outside the building, he knew, the seven new deputies stood guard. Five more of the hardened gunfighters brought in from El Paso and New Mexico mingled with the crowd, down there right now in the midst of them. He stared into the jostling throng but couldn't figure out which ones they might be. "At any rate," he thought, "it's a damn good idea to have them handy—just in case. Some of those crazy Mexicans who work for Tom English might take it in their heads to try to break him free." But then he dismissed the thought. The speed of the trial was such that no one would have had time to make such a plan. And after today, he reassured himself, they'd have even more reinforcements. All the arrangements for this had been set in motion.

"I have to hand it to Julian Haynes," the judge said to himself. "He seems to think of everything."

The frame courthouse had windows along both sides to provide light and ventilation. Aside from these, it looked something like an undersized barn, with heavy beams and rafters showing above the heads of the people. Late afternoon sunshine probed over the heads of the chattering throng, and dust motes danced unnoticed in the streaks of light.

A few men sat in the back of the room silently, their serious faces damp with perspiration. But all the rest had given in to the atmosphere of expectant excitement, as if they'd gathered for a square dance or

other social occasion, and a confusion of voices fluttered throughout the room.

Jack Orly, the orange-headed man who had helped capture the defendant, stood near the judge's side and called repeatedly and uselessly, "Order. Order in the court." Orly looked at the judge with a helpless expression on his perpetually sunburned, freckled face, arching his sandy eyebrows and shrugging his narrow shoulders.

With deliberation the judge raised a gavel and banged it on the hardwood surface, causing a sharp percussive ringing to sound throughout the courtroom. He glanced at the already impaneled jury on his left and then glowered straight ahead, hammering his gavel as if trying to drive tenpenny nails as he sought to silence the intensely curious onlookers who still jockeyed for position behind the balustered railing. On the inside of this, Jedediah Jackson took his position next to Max Hall and Doc Starret at a narrow table stained so dark it was almost black, while across from them Tom English sat between Sheriff Baxter and Ernie Dugger, the deputy who'd been assigned to guard him in the old jail.

Baxter had a shotgun lying across his lap. Tom leaned forward awkwardly, and only those near the railing could see the reason why: his manacled hands had been chained to shackles around his ankles.

Jedediah Jackson approached the bench. "Judge, I represent the defendant, as you know, and I'd like to ask you to unchain him."

"We're taking no chances that some friend of Tom English might throw him a six-gun, Counselor."

The crowd fell silent, straining to hear every word, afraid they might miss something. Only an occasional cough or hawking noise came from them now.

"Please take note of my objection. You're treating him as you might a wild animal."

"Well," Judge Hoskins drawled, conscious that he had the full attention of the audience, "as far as I'm concerned, he's one hell of a lot more dangerous than any animal I ever run across. Be that as it may, I'll take note of your objection, just like all them others you made about the good men we got servin' on this jury."

As Jackson reseated himself, Doc Starret leaned over to him and whispered, "I notice that the judge uses pretty good grammar as a rule, but when he makes a point for the jury's benefit, he talks just as any of them might. Gets right down to their level. Don't underestimate him."

Before Jackson could reply, the judge brought the court to order by striking his gavel once more.

T. J. Hoskins cleared his throat and said in a loud voice, "The court of Tom Green County is in session to try Tom English for the murder of John Doe, which is the name we'll use for the poor son of a bitch he killed."

Jedediah Jackson sprang to his feet, exploding, *"Damn it,* your honor, you can't say such things to the jury. In my forty-five years of practice, I've never heard of a judge arriving at a conclusion of guilt at the outset of a case to be heard before him. At this time let it be noted that I make an emphatic objection to your sitting on the bench in this trial. You've shown in advance that you're prejudiced against my client—who, like any other man in the United States, is innocent until proven guilty beyond a reasonable doubt. I ask you to declare a mistrial unless you're prepared to rule on my motion for a summary judgment of *innocent.* You are fully aware that there's not a shred of evidence to support the charges against Tom English."

"I've heard *enough* of your God damn objections, you hear me? Any more of 'em and I'll have your tail thrown out, and the defendant can take his chances without you." He glanced as he spoke at the men in the jury box, and several of them snorted with laughter.

Hoskins said, "Let's get on with this trial." With that, he rose from his chair, stepped down from the raised dais to the floor, and walked over to face the jury. The twelve men sitting there examined him with varying degrees of attention. Some looked wary while others among them slouched down in their seats, apparently suffering equally from hangover and curiosity regarding what might be going on.

Max Hall leaned over to rumble to Jedediah Jackson in a low voice which nonetheless carried, "It would be hard to find a more disreputable group of misfits than they've put on that jury."

The judge heard this and glared at Max. "I reckon," he drawled, "that, by your standards as a banker, an ordinary worker ain't fit to sit on the jury when a rich man is gettin' tried. Is that what you're complainin' about?"

Max's face darkened and he started to answer but Jackson silenced him.

With a grim smile, the judge faced the filthy, unshaven men in the jury box once more. "Gentlemen of the jury, your job is to determine the facts in the case of the State of Texas against Tom English. We're trying him for murder, and we'll get on with that in a few minutes. Since we don't have a prosecuting attorney in Santa Rita, it don't seem fair for the defendant to be the only side represented by a lawyer, so

I'm going to make sure you get all the information you need so you can make your decision. Before we continue, let me make it clear to you that I am *not* a lawyer myself." In an aside he added, "Never knew one I could trust to tell you the truth." Several jury members chuckled at the remark.

Hoskins seemed to be enjoying himself. "I'm just an ordinary man like any one of you. But I've been around a lot of lawyers, and since they have a way of making all these objections, and saying things we don't completely understand, it's my belief that you need someone to keep things simple for you.

"And what we've got here is a *very* simple matter. A real unfortunate stranger rode his horse by mistake onto the Lazy E ranch that is owned by Tom English. Now, English is known far and wide to be the fastest and deadliest gunfighter in Texas, so you know perfectly well that this poor waddy would never have tried to go up against him with a rifle at ten feet or less. That's about how far away he was from his killer when he got shot, according to Doc Starret, who's sittin' over there." Hoskins pointed to the doctor as he paused dramatically.

"If the dead man had been of a mind to kill English, he'd-a taken a shot at him from a distance with his rifle. But he didn't. He rode up close, probably to talk. And then it happened."

The spectators hunched forward, listening intently as the judge spoke.

"The defendant shot him four times, and—again I'm using information given me by Doc Starret—any *one* of those four shots would have been enough to kill him. In my book, that shows that English did it out of pure meanness, which ought to be enough to prove malicious intent on the part of the defendant."

He wheeled about and demanded, "Ain't that right, Doc?"

The doctor half rose to his feet. "Wait until the whole story gets told and then . . ."

"Sit back down. It ain't your turn to talk." He grinned as he heard laughter come from the jury. "On the other hand, if I'm wrong, Doc, and if that cowboy died of something other than gunshot wounds, of course you need to get up and explain what might have caused him to depart from this vale of tears." Again a few men in the audience and several on the jury snickered.

Hoskins looked at the defendant and said, "Tom English is called the meanest man in West Texas. He has now killed thirty-four people, and I say to you that this state of affairs can't continue."

He examined the jury and saw that they didn't seem to be impressed. So he asked them, "Did any of you take a look at the remains of the victim when the sheriff tried to find out if anyone knew him?"

Several men spoke out in the affirmative.

"Well, now," the judge said, "this is interesting. How many of you saw that butchered-up corpse?"

One by one they raised their arms.

"A terrible sight. As county judge, I had the awful duty to view it myself. It would appear to me that you boys have a better idea of exactly what happened to him than anybody could possibly have who hadn't seen it with his own eyes."

The men on the jury showed they agreed by nodding again as they pulled their hands down.

"Any doubt in your minds about what went on?"

Several of the men said, "No."

The judge went back to his place on the bench.

"You got anything to say, Counselor?"

Jedediah Jackson stood up, a severe look on his patrician face. "I've brought Dr. Starret and Max Hall, two of Santa Rita's leading citizens, as character witnesses to testify on behalf of the defendant. After that, I'll put Tom English on the stand to tell us exactly what occurred."

"No use wasting any more of the court's time," the judge said coldly, "since he's already confessed."

"Under the circumstances, I hereby move for a mistrial on the grounds that . . ."

"Silence," Judge Hoskins thundered his interruption, "or I'll jail you for contempt of court."

The judge took a moment to gain control of himself and then addressed the jury once again, although forgetting his slightly exaggerated accent for a moment. "Tom English has confessed to his guilt—he shot and killed the victim. That's not in issue. Everyone knows that he practices with his handguns constantly, and I guess he can't resist finding a human target every once in a while. After he killed the stranger, he had men who worked for him *sneak* the body into town."

The judge waited a moment for his words to make an impression. "Let me emphasize that he didn't come in and make a statement, or let the sheriff or any other authority know there'd even *been* a killing. Not at first he didn't. English had his men deliver the body to Noah Massie's undertaking parlor."

Leaning back in his chair, the judge asked, "Gentlemen, does that

sound to you like something a man would do who'd acted in self-defense? If one of *you* killed someone while defending yourself, would you send the body over to the undertaker and try to hide what happened from the law? *Hell, no,* you wouldn't!" The judge answered his own rhetorical question. "You'd go right off the bat to the sheriff and tell him everything that happened. Isn't that right?"

Hoskins nodded his head, watching the twelve pairs of eyes fixed on his. It seemed certain that he had them under his spell. "Then what happened next? Well, maybe as an afterthought, Tom English had his lawyer tell Sheriff Baxter some weak story about being forced to defend his life. That's his *only* argument. You either believe it or you don't. No use wasting time for him and his golden-tongued lawyer to say the same thing in half a dozen different ways. That's the whole defense in a nutshell.

"But, does that make sense? Let me ask you a question. If a bushwhacker wanted to let off a shot at Tom English, and if the bushwhacker had a rifle while English only packed a six-shooter, how would he go about it? Would he ride up at close range to take him on—or would he gun his victim down from a safe distance? You see? When you realize that cowboy couldn't possibly have threatened harm to English, then an argument of self-defense is pitifully weak, isn't it?"

He fell back into the vernacular. "Hell, they ain't no doubt at all about it. Tom English felt like killin' somebody, and this poor stranger just came by at the wrong time. English musta had fun with that miserable cowboy—shot him *twice* in the belly, for Christ's sake, once in the chest, and then split his head wide open. Are we goin' to let him get away with that?"

*"Enough* of this inflammatory talk!" Jedediah Jackson roared.

"Sheriff, right after the trial, take that man into custody," the judge demanded in a satisfied tone of voice. "He's in contempt and has to pay a fine of twenty dollars or I'll let him rot in jail."

"This is nothing more than a kangaroo court," Jackson said, contempt etched on his features. "I swear before God that any judgment made today will be set aside, and as for your threats, I'll die before paying a cent of your damned fine."

"Have it your way," the judge said, winking at the jury. They laughed.

Hoskins banged his gavel time and again. "Let's have some order in here. Gentlemen of the jury, do you find Tom English to be guilty of murder?"

The unshaven men whispered to one another. One of them said, "We sure do, Judge."

A tumult broke out, but Hoskins stopped it by saying, "Get the defendant on his feet so I can pronounce the sentence."

With an effort, the sheriff helped Tom rise. He couldn't stand upright since the chain which fastened his hands to his feet was only a few feet long.

An angry hum, apparently from the friends of Tom English, began to grow in the courtroom.

Judge Hoskins sat without saying a word, a scowl covering his face as he glared at the people seated before him. Gradually, a hush sank over them.

*"Tom English, having been found guilty of the crime of murder, I hereby sentence you to be hanged by the neck until you are dead.* And may God have mercy on your soul."

A woman's piercing scream split the air, and then pandemonium broke loose.

Calvin Laudermilk occupied a rugged chair, his back to the wall, facing out toward the other patrons. From this, his regular table, he had long made a practice of welcoming the approach of night. His ponderous belly sagged over his unseen belt as if a great, soft watermelon were inside his shirt, causing it to strain against every button. His sweat-stained hat sat straight on his head, its wide brim not cocked to one side or the other. Calvin sat with an erect back as he leaned forward slightly with some ceremony and poured golden liquid from the bottle at his elbow into his waiting glass. Then, as he tasted it—with a wag of his head, a whistling intake of breath, and a slight but appreciative wince— he observed John Hope, the laconic owner of the bar, steeling himself in the effort not to be unpleasant to his customers.

John rarely spoke of personal matters but on one occasion admitted that he'd been on his way to San Antonio when he lost the trail. At last, after wandering a few days, he'd come upon the community called Santa Rita on the banks of the Concho River and decided to build his place of business there. The scarcity of people particularly attracted him. He gave no further explanation of the name he'd chosen for his establishment. Calvin assumed he made this unaccustomed excuse so people wouldn't search for some philosophic reason for his calling it the Lost Hope Saloon.

John Hope stood behind the bar wearing a white apron and with his

sleeves rolled up over muscular, hairy arms. He served drinks without answering the comments made to him by his customers, looking pained by all the convivial drinkers who intruded on his privacy and insisted on spending money for his whiskey.

The townspeople knew better than to approach Calvin when he drank with his hat square on his head. Though normally a man of peace and good humor, there had been a few notably violent exceptions. As one of the town drunks expressed it, "When that big sonuvabitch is on the prod, I wouldn't git within ten paces of him."

Calvin sat alone and thought grimly of his problems. He had long since come to terms with life and its promises and disappointments. He held strong and simple opinions on most things which he considered to be of importance. Few arguments could be made to him which he couldn't dismiss with a simple word or phrase. He lived with the firm conviction that he could cope with any form of stressful situation, and until today he had thought that nothing humankind might do could possibly surprise him.

It struck him that he had, in a way, an advantage, for he'd long observed his fellow creatures from a distance. Since childhood many had considered him to be some sort of freak, owing to his size. This, he felt convinced, made him unusually impressionable and receptive. Calvin knew that the world looked upon him as some sort of gross caricature, when in truth he *knew* he had more sensitivity than just about anyone.

He had erected a wall of defenses to the slights and open insults offered to those of ample proportions. Even so, it invariably hurt his feelings when people showed surprise that he appeared at mealtimes acting famished. "Fat people get just as hungry as skinny ones," he would protest, striving to make them understand. "We get as cold as any bone-thin stripling because," he would argue, "our nerves are on the outside, same as yours."

If the truth were known, Calvin had a rather low opinion of his fellow man except for certain ones who somehow managed to pass the strenuous test imposed by his intuition.

When he'd had a drink or two he often would at the outset become depressed, saying to himself, "I'm livin' in a cruel, lonely world . . ." But then his dependable defense would surface and he would phrase his own answer, ". . . yet no more so than the next man. We're all in the same sorry fix."

Tonight no such reliable thought came to mind, and he sank deeper

into his depression. He had been taught that justice would always triumph in the end, but after what had happened today, Calvin's faith in this had been badly shaken.

Max Hall wound his way through the roistering cowboys and townspeople, all of them involved in reliving the spectacle of the incredible trial of Tom English. Their eyes shone with a mixture of revulsion at the imminent spectacle of a human being twisting at the end of a rope and an open lust to see such a sight.

Max sat beside his hulking friend, neither of them speaking at first.

Calvin finally broke the silence. "I recall the stories of that range war, the one when Tom brought in those hard cases from Durango in Old Mexico to give him a hand."

"There'll be no time for him to get help from that far away."

"There *has* to be something we can do."

"I hope so. I paid Jedediah Jackson's twenty-dollar fine to get him out of jail. He protested at first but then agreed that he'd be of a great deal more use on the outside than locked up. Then I bundled up the old gentleman with some pillows and a down comforter for him to lean against in Cele's buggy—it's got good springs—and sent him on his way to Austin. Cele," Max added, speaking of his wife, "packed him a hamper full of sandwiches that will last until he gets to Menard. Emilio Escobar—you may know him, he's worked for us several years—is driving. He hitched that big chestnut of mine to the traces. With luck, our lawyer friend will be there in three or four days. I'll grant you, it concerns me for someone his age to make such a long trip, but he insisted on going. Says he has some contacts in the capital, and he thinks he can get help out here to put a stop to this, even if it means they have to send the Rangers in. Just hope they don't get here too late."

Max must have come into the Lost Hope Saloon looking for Calvin, for he normally stayed away from such places. As president of the First National Bank, he took care to protect his reputation. Borrowing Calvin's glass, he took a small sip from it, shuddered, and added, "Incidentally, Jedediah tried to send off some telegrams, but the wires must be down. No messages have come in or gone out all day. Hell of a time for that kind of trouble, though it's happened before."

"Speaking of Rangers, what are our chances of locating John Robert Hale?"

"As you no doubt heard, he's off in the big bend country somewhere. There was trouble out toward Alpine at a little place called Marathon. Some Mescaleros killed two of old man Harte's cowboys and stole three

or four of his horses. Well, you may have heard the stories about
Harte."

Calvin nodded. Everyone knew a host of tales regarding the eccentric
elderly rancher. Speaking thoughtfully, he observed, "Shootin' those
cowhands was one thing, but them Indians made a terrible mistake
stealin' Mr. Harte's horses. I hear the old skinflint has a most profound
respect for private property, particularly his own.

"The last time something like this happened, he chased the rustlers
all the way across the Mexican border and then clear up into New
Mexico Territory. Spent eight weeks and covered over five hundred
miles just to get back a few unbroken fillies."

"Did you hear what he did to the rustlers when he caught them?"
Max asked.

"I don't want to talk about it—don't have the stomach for it," Calvin
said, an involuntary twinge making him close his eyes. "I only hope John
Robert gets out there in time—or old man Harte may eliminate the
entire Apache nation. Maybe the Chiricahuas and Lipans too, unless
they get out of his way."

"It could take close to a week or two to find John Robert. We've sent
Jim Boy Irons, who can track him down if anybody can, but unless we're
mighty lucky, he can't get back here in time. From the way this trial
went today, the hanging could be over by this time tomorrow."

Calvin flinched. "God a'mighty, will they move that fast?"

"What do you think?"

Calvin drank deeply and refilled his glass. "My first thought was to
grab my guns and search out Santiago Acosta. Tom has a lot of loyal
cowboys workin' for him, and those Mexican hands on his ranch up
toward Villa Plata have a considerable amount of experience with gunplay."

"There's not a chance to break him out of that stone jail. Not with all
the guards they've got."

"That's why I said that was my *first* idea. It has required years of
beefsteaks and potatoes to build this up," he said, patting his paunch,
"and the thought of bullets punchin' holes through it pains me more
than I can say. But Santiago's men aren't going to worry about such
things the way I might. You've got to realize that Tom English gave
them a lot of pride. The original Lazy E has always had a Mexican
foreman—and every cowboy on it is Mexican, too. Besides that, they've
come through some miraculously tight places with Tom before. That
includes that standoff at Three Points when the Dawsons had them far

outnumbered. And the same thing up in Montana, when Tom took out after the Doggett gang. The thing you've got to realize is those men *know,* they know damn good and well that if they were in jail waiting to be hanged, Tom English would go through hell and back to save them."

"You may be right," Max said.

"I know I am. Old Santiago and Benito and the rest of them won't stand by while they hang Tom English."

Max shook his head, concern showing on his face. "They'll get themselves slaughtered. From what I hear, the sheriff has twelve hired guns in town with more on the way. He's been talking freely about this, saying that it's a temporary thing—that he's sworn to maintain the peace—and that as soon as English is hanged the threat to Santa Rita will pass. He says that after the execution he'll send his extra deputies packing, just as soon as the town gets back to normal."

Calvin said, "We have *got* to think of somethin' to head this off." He glared about him in a state of confusion: comforted on the one hand by the familiar surroundings and smell of stale, spilled beer, and frustrated on the other by his feelings of furious helplessness.

Thinking out loud, Calvin asked, "They lettin' anyone visit with Tom?"

"No, they're not. Doc Starret and I tried to get in, but they turned us away. Looks like a fortress over there; I saw armed men posted all around the sheriff's office and the old jail."

Max pulled a cigar from an inside coat pocket and rolled it in his fingers next to his ear. Satisfied with its freshness, he snipped off the tip of one end with a penknife, put this in his mouth, and scratched a kitchen match on the sole of his shoe. After lighting his cigar and puffing thoughtfully upon it, he said, wisps of blue-white smoke coming from his mouth with every word, "My hunch is that Julian Haynes is behind all this. All he wants, so far as I can tell, is title to some land on the North Concho River so he can make full use of the Jameson ranch. Maybe I should go over and talk to him, tell him that we need to work things out so that we'll still have a town here after this week. If he goes through with putting Tom to death, all hell is going to break loose—it'll top anything that even Haynes might anticipate."

He chewed thoughtfully on his cigar. "So, I have an idea that might get things defused: I could offer to talk Tom into selling him the land he wants in exchange for letting him go."

"Tom would never stand for that."

"He might—if I get the chance to get into his cell and explain what

I'm thinking about. You see, I asked Jedediah about it, and he said that a contract signed under duress—like signing an agreement with a pistol at your head—is unenforceable under the law."

"I expect Julian Haynes is smart enough to know that," Calvin said. "To my mind, this won't work."

"It's worth a try," Max insisted.

"If I see a dog coming down the road, frothin' at the mouth, snarlin' and showin' his teeth at me, I'm not goin' to lean down and rub his ears," Calvin protested. "By which I mean to say, when you're dealin' with someone like Haynes, sweet reason is somethin' that's a waste of time."

"You have any better idea?"

"I believe I do," Calvin said. The image he so often projected, his good-old-boy attitude and accent, dissolved as he concentrated intently upon the problem. "You know, I used to pride myself on my ability to play chess. While the game can be a very complicated pursuit, some of its principles are extremely simple. When threatened, you have three courses to follow: attack, run, or do something devious. While the first two choices don't seem to offer us a great deal, there's something to be said for the third. And, bearing this in mind, I have an old friend who has the appearance of being a very simple fellow, but when it comes to slyness, he takes the cake."

"How much have you had to drink?"

"Not enough," responded Calvin with a pained expression, a storm cloud gathering on his brow.

In spite of his years, Santiago Acosta was clearly in charge. He slipped a bridle on the paint horse he'd roped in the corral and then flipped a worn striped blanket on his back. Then he looped his saddle up and over, letting it flop down, stirrups and girth swinging down. He adjusted it with a practiced yank on the horn, reached under the horse for the girth, cinched it up tight, and flapped the stirrup leathers and fenders back in place. Then he pulled out his saddle gun, a Model 73 Winchester with a scarred stock. He cranked a center-fire cartridge into the chamber with the combination lever and trigger guard, and then carefully slid the rifle back in the saddle scabbard.

When he faced about he saw his son Benito already in the saddle on his sturdy bay. He wore two cartridge belts crisscrossed on his chest, and he also wore two six-guns. Pepe Moya came from the house carry-

ing a ten-gauge shotgun. He mounted his horse holding it, since he already had a rifle on his saddle.

Luis Batalla stood up in his stirrups, obviously anxious to get moving. Then he settled back, holding his skittish horse in check. Moya walked his pony alongside him, and the two spoke in low tones. Behind them, Juan Suarez sat his mount, holding to a lead rope attached to the halter on a long-legged sorrel stallion, one of the prize animals descended from the Kentucky thoroughbreds Tom had imported. The sorrel had some quarter-horse blood and appeared somewhat stockier than a pure-bred might. He had a blaze face and the cowboys called him Bandana. The smoothly muscled stallion would be, if everything worked out well, the horse that would carry Tom English to freedom.

Santiago stepped into his saddle, nodded to the others, and then they moved off, the hollow thudding of hoofbeats sounding muffled in the dryness of the dirt.

"What time do you think we'll get there?" Benito asked his father.

"About four in the morning," Santiago answered.

Saddles creaked. In the distance a coyote howled and, closer at hand, another one made a yipping noise.

"They'll be surprised, won't they?" Benito asked.

"I hope so," Santiago answered.

# SIX

THE FIVE MEN entered the town's north side stealthily, riding stirrup to stirrup in a ragged line. When they passed the scattered houses, dogs ran out, barking and lunging at the horses' hooves. At one point the riders stopped to talk, and Luis Batalla suggested that they tie their mounts and proceed on foot. All of them knew their only chance lay in the element of surprise, but Benito argued that they'd need to be able to get quickly into their saddles after breaking Tom free.

Their plan, such as it was, involved a run southwest into Mexico. In the confusion that would follow the jailbreak, the desperate cowboys thought they had a good chance to get away. Once in open country, they felt certain no men alive could catch them.

The thought of getting across the border came naturally. They'd go to Durango where most of them had family. They'd be safe there.

When they got near, they pulled up. The creaking of leather stopped; a sudden wind whisked by their faces; and then only the sound of their heartbeats filled their ears.

The stallion suddenly began to whinny, fluttering his nostrils and pawing at the earth.

"Can't you keep that horse quiet?" Benito whispered to Juan Suarez.

Juan dismounted and put his hand on the softness of the big animal's nose and talked to him in a low voice, trying to calm him.

Santiago, also on foot by now, said, "Follow me." He had made no speeches, even when they first heard the news from town. He, like all the others, knew deep down inside himself what had to be done.

All the cowboys stepped down, tying their reins to the hitching post in front of the new courthouse. They saw no signs of anyone awake, much less standing guard at the old jail attached to the sheriff's office.

The moon had disappeared behind a cloud hanging low in the sky. Yet they could easily make out the outlines of the buildings around them. The five men drew their weapons and stalked forward silently.

At that moment they saw movement on either side of the sheriff's office: six men materialized out of the gloom at their left, eight more on the right. Several rifles could be seen, and they heard the sliding sound of oiled steel as levers pumped shells into firing chambers.

A voice from among the men guarding the jail rang out: "Drop them guns—and do it now!"

Santiago Acosta and Luis Batalla walked in advance of the others and kept going forward. Pepe Moya slid off to the right, holding his cocked shotgun in both hands. Juan Suarez slowed down and then came to a stop, bending his knees and pointing a six-gun with each hand. Benito Acosta circled around to the left of his father and Luis.

"We're here for Tom English," Santiago called out.

"We got you outmanned, Meskin," someone yelled back. "Back off."

Benito cocked the hammer of his long-barreled Colt with the thumb of his right hand and leveled it toward his closest adversary. "Get out of our way," he said in his heavily accented speech, "and you'll live to collect the money they're payin' you."

A double-barreled shotgun edged out of the window in the sheriff's office, muzzle wavering at first, then steadied on the sill. A flare of flame licked out as the explosion ripped the night, and blood and bone erupted from Santiago's shoulder. The second barrel boomed as Santiago fell, hitting him in the head and neck, tearing part of his skull away.

The cowboys charged past their fallen leader, guns firing at the defenders, who fell back hurriedly before their fury. Luis saw Pepe spin down and lie still, his arms and legs outspread. He froze at the sight and then felt himself jarred backward as a mist of scarlet sprayed from his left side. A bullet plowed through his right knee, splitting through the bone, and he felt himself toppling forward. He tried to wrench himself to a sitting position but then a hail of shots slammed him down.

Benito's two guns had spat their dozen slugs, and he flung himself behind a wooden water trough. Bullets ricocheted, and several threw splinters and dust into his face as he fought to reload.

A man screamed hoarsely, over and over, from just in front of the sheriff's office. His howls diminished and turned into a gargled moaning. Two silent heaps lay on top of one another next to the stricken man, and off to the left, three other forms lay still upon the crusted dirt.

Juan Suarez dove to cover next to Benito as bullets shrieked and whined immediately above them. Juan raised just enough to see over the

top of the trough and squeezed off three quick shots. Then he dropped
back as a fusillade answered him.

The defenders had retreated to either side of the stone building and
they pumped a steady stream of pistol and rifle shots from the shadows.
A bullet hit a steel pipe at one end of the trough and it screamed off like
a banshee. Time and again the shotgun from inside the building
boomed its hollow, ringing explosion.

"The others are dead," Juan yelled to Benito. "Let's get out of this
trap."

"No," Benito screamed, raising up to fire his reloaded six-guns. Instantly he jerked backward as if he'd been roped off a running horse.
Before he struck the ground, other bullets hit him. He rolled over, out
in the road with no protection. The moon came out from behind the
cloud and in the silvered light Juan recoiled at the sight: Benito's legs
kicked frantically and then began to quiver.

A single rifle barked, making Benito's body jump. The rifle cracked
sharply three more times, spanking cloth and blood into the air. Then
the body lay as still as a rag doll in a spreading puddle of red paint.

"I give up," Juan yelled, hugging the dirt behind the sheltering water
trough.

"Throw your guns out in the street," someone yelled.

Frantically Juan followed the instructions.

"Now, stand up real slow, with your hands up."

With jerky movements, Juan complied, stretching his arms rigidly
above his head as high as they could reach. Numbed, he rose to his
knees and then to his feet. He stared blankly at the eight remaining
men. Off to one side, he heard the awful sounds of moaning made by
one of his fallen enemies. Closer at hand, he could make out—down
upon the stained earth in front of him—a moonlight-washed face with
sightless eyes staring at a sky which now lightened in the east.

Juan waited, feeling his heart jolt in his chest as he saw a tall man
before him who raised a rifle to his shoulder. He turned his head,
looking at the growing light along the horizon as hope drained away.
Then he closed his eyes.

The man with the rifle sighted down it carefully, then touched its
hair trigger. As Juan went down, while the echo of the shot still rever-
berated, the other survivors emptied their weapons at him. Inflamed by
rage and fear and the heat of battle, they reloaded and fired into his
lifeless body again and again.

Sheriff Baxter, the double-barreled shotgun in his hand, came out of

his office, looking around warily. Acrid waves of gunsmoke and the sickening smell of blood filled the air. He looked at first one and then another of the hired gunfighters, gazing into their pale, excited faces. Finally he spoke. "I *told* you they'd come tonight. It was a by-God certainty." His voice shook with emotion and triumph.

He paced out and stared at the fallen attackers. "These'd be the ones they used to call the 'Meskin Cavalry'—the gunslingers Tom English had to guard his back all those years."

The sheriff raised his head, his mouth slightly open, his eyes gleaming. "All five of 'em down. We killed ever' damn one of them bastards!"

A bearded man leaned down, feeling for a pulse, moving among the fallen defenders. He ignored the felled Mexicans behind him. Hunkering down on his boot heels, he husked out, "All dead with the exception of this one."

The sheriff approached and, looking down, said, "That's Jack Orly."

The redhead lay on his back, a froth at his wide-stretched mouth as he fought for breath, making awful noises. The bearded man beside him shifted his weight and went to one knee as he tried to check the extent of Orly's injuries.

"Well, I don't know," he said, standing up and cleaning the slippery blood from his hands by rubbing them on his pants legs. "Looks to me to be a suckin' chest wound; hit in the lungs, it appears. Doubt if there's much to do for him."

"Ernie," Sheriff Baxter directed, "you and a couple of others get hold of Jack and carry him over to Doc Starret's—roust him out of bed. You know where Doc lives. See what he can do."

Turning to those who remained, he said, pride showing in his voice, "You done *real* good, boys. Real good. You've earned the bonus we promised—and besides that, you'll collect the money we'd-a payed those who got hit. You'll divvy up the dead men's shares. Me and Judge Hoskins are goin' to see to it that you're well taken care of. Now, come on in here, and we'll have a drink to settle our nerves."

None of them glanced at the small window at the front of the jail where Tom English stood, his hands gripping the bars tightly.

"Hell of a rainstorm Saturday night—some fifteen or twenty miles south of here."

Max Hall sat at his desk behind the wooden divider that separated it from the open area. Although sole owner of the First National Bank, he had no private office. He thought that being accessible to his customers,

sitting as he did immediately next to the tellers' cages, was good for business. Calvin Laudermilk occupied the chair across from him and made no attempt to respond to the banker's attempt at conversation.

"But we didn't get a drop of moisture out of all of that. I went outside and saw the lightning off in the distance. Can't imagine how we missed it."

"I'm usually as ready as the next man to hold a heartfelt discussion about the lack of rain, Max. But right now we've got something a little more important to consider."

"I know, Calvin."

"Has anyone seen him?" Calvin didn't have to indicate that he spoke of Tom English. The impending threat of Tom's death by hanging left all his friends sharing the same sickness, the same knee-jerk reaction of denial.

"Sally tried but got turned away. Sheriff Hoskins and his men aren't lettin' anyone within fifty yards of the old jail. Naturally, Sally's beside herself—I've never seen her this way." He began to curse in a low, emphatic tone.

Calvin interrupted these helpless oaths. "Where is she now?"

"At my house with Cele," Max said, mentioning his wife.

Six men rode up outside and tied their horses to the array of hitching posts lining the sidewalk. They gathered in a knot, talking grimly, then came inside the bank.

Max rose to greet them. "We won't stand on ceremony, boys," he said, waving a hand at chairs in a semicircle around his desk.

Each man had a weathered look, faces and necks looking as rough as mesquite bark. They had tough, callused hands and, strangely enough, several had eyes red from tears. Calvin couldn't tell if these were caused by grief or rage—or both. Most of them limped a little from old injuries, and all except Scott Baker sat warily in the banker's place of business.

Scott had been there many times, owing to his duties as general manager of all of the ranches Tom English owned in the state of Texas. In fact, when Tom had tried to run away from trouble, changing his name and moving to Montana, Scott and Max Hall had for more than a year had total responsibility for all of the English financial and ranching affairs.

Scott concentrated on rolling a cigarette, brown bits of tobacco drifting to his lap in the process, then licked and sealed it with a practiced flourish. On lighting the somewhat bent cigarette, he automatically cupped his hands as he always did to keep the wind from blowing out

the match, although of course this wasn't necessary when sitting in a chair instead of a saddle.

Avoiding the matter most on his mind, Scott said, "We managed to get our hands on the Lazy E horses—all of them, including that stud of Tom's. Fella workin' for the sheriff tried to keep us from takin' them, but I told him that he didn't want to get the name of bein' a horse thief —not so long as one of these days he might find himself ridin' alone."

The other men laughed more than his remark warranted. A crack seemed to form in the icy control all of them appeared to be under.

Then Scott said, "We've been out to the cemetery to pay our last respects."

Calvin's jaw rippled almost imperceptibly. He'd gone there too, earlier in the day, after hearing what had happened the night before. He'd seen the fresh dirt and torn caliche covering a mound above a large square hole, the common grave for his Mexican friends: Benito and Santiago, Luis, Pepe, and Juan. Buried without benefit of a funeral service of any kind.

Osie Black's voice had a tendency to carry, Calvin recalled as the gnarled foreman rose to his feet, obviously preparing to say something. Calvin decided that he must have gotten in the habit of hollering in the vast windy spaces where he'd spent most of his life, and he followed this practice even when he found himself inside. Osie boomed, "Baxter and his hired killers dug a shallow grave and threw our friends in it without a single casket." His voice shook with indignation and its reverberations reached the rafters, causing the bank tellers to look toward him in alarm. Osie continued, "We'll go there later on and cover them with rocks to keep the coyotes out. But before that happens, them bastards are goin' to have to pay for what they done."

An electric tension filled the room until Scott Baker said quietly, "Easy, boys, let's settle down and think this thing out." .

Ted Carrothers commented, "The sheriff and his men sure as hell rushed things, Scott. They must have wanted to get Benito and his men underground before any of their friends showed up."

Calvin pulled his head back into its supporting collar of chins and spent a moment fighting against the revulsion that welled up within him before he asked, "Does anybody know the name of that Catholic priest who shows up every six months or so to hold a communion service and hear confession?"

"I think he's from San Antonio," Scott volunteered. "Don't know his name or how to get in touch with him."

"Maybe he can hold a special graveside service of some sort the next time he's out this way," Calvin said. The others nodded in vague agreement. There seemed to be an unspoken consensus that the very serious fact of death should be observed with formality.

Calvin looked to one side at Joe Burnett, foreman of the Circle X ranch on the Mexican border more than a hundred and seventy miles away. He knew that Joe was present by pure coincidence. His mother, who had once taught school in Sherwood, a small community west of Santa Rita on the road to Ozona, had fallen and broken a hip. At the age of seventy-eight she lived alone with no living relatives other than Joe, her only surviving child. He'd come to find someone to care for her.

Joe looked exhausted, for he'd ridden straight through, changing horses at ranches along the way where he knew people. He had made the four-day trip in less than forty-eight hours, with only a few catnaps along the way.

Next to Burnett sat Jim Farr, foreman of the former Clarke family ranch. Ted Carrothers, who ran the West ranch, and Osie Black, foreman of the East ranch, sat behind the others. Calvin Laudermilk had received instructions from Scott Baker to attend this meeting since he, with the active help of Ed Mac Bascom, ran the Lower Ranch, the one formerly owned by Jason Field.

Max addressed himself to Baker, the ranking man present. "Who do you plan to put in charge of the Lazy E?" he asked, referring to the ten-section ranch on the North Concho formerly run by Santiago Acosta with the help of the others who had died the night before.

Turner Hopewell had taken a chair next to Calvin. He had long been foreman for Hester Trace, the good-looking widow who owned the ranch just to the north of the Lazy E. He said, "I sent Ira Turnbull and Severn Laycon down to ride fence and look after the stock. If the need arises, Asa Coltrane is out of bed and able to sit a horse again," he said, referring to another cowboy from the Trace ranch.

"Damn nice of you, Turner." Scott Baker slid his chair around so he could face Hopewell. "I haven't any idea who to send on a permanent basis. Could your boys help out for a spell?"

"Tom's always lent us a hand when we needed it," Hopewell responded with an abbreviated nod of his head.

A silence fell over the group. Finally Max Hall broke it. "I've been out to see the colonel at Fort Concho. He agreed that the conviction for murder looks like it's clear out of line, but maintains that his hands are

tied. There's no hope from the cavalry. They won't touch civilian matters."

"Well," Jim Farr remarked, "reckon we'll have to take things in our own hands."

"Benito and Santiago already tried that," Scott Baker said dryly. "They ended up dead—along with Luis and Pepe and the kid, Juan Suarez. Last thing I heard is that Sheriff Hoskins has reinforcements on the way and has armed guards posted. They've put out the word that, at the first sign of a gathering of men who look like they plan to rescue Tom, they'll shoot him on the spot."

"That beats hangin' at any rate," Turner Hopewell observed.

The stern-faced men looked at Baker for advice and guidance.

He couldn't think of any to give them.

Calvin Laudermilk rose to his feet. "I find it hard to concentrate in town," he said as he stalked away. Without another word he left the bank.

Calvin rode Sully, his great dappled gray Percheron, with long stirrups, knees scarcely bent. He leaned back slightly and pointed his mount into a sea of broomweed. Its presence mystified him. Some years they'd have none at all while, during others, they'd be besieged by the growth. The clutching, bushy plants spread for miles, reaching higher than a man's waist. Sully ignored the obstacles, plowing into the dried weeds like an oceangoing vessel cresting through waves.

The bulky horse lurched sideways, causing Calvin to grasp the saddlehorn in surprise, and at the same instant he heard a high sharp buzzing, the gut-wrenching sound of a coiled rattlesnake. He'd almost ridden on top of one. Taking a deep breath, he spurred Sully sharply, sitting firmly in the jarring saddle as they jolted out of harm's way.

He emerged from the broomweed and rode through rolling land with occasional prairie dog towns. When one came in sight he circled it carefully, for a horse could easily go down if a hoof fell into one of their holes.

From the rumbling in his stomach as well as the position of the sun, Calvin realized that he had in his haste missed his noon meal. "I must be terribly preoccupied," he said to himself, "to have allowed such a thing to happen."

A short time later he angled west of the trail and headed for the distant South Concho River, aiming at a particular stand of native pecan trees which towered above the rest.

Calvin smiled as he recalled having told Elvira East of his regular practice of spending a quiet hour with his spiritual counselor, seeking guidance in God's open world. "Well," he told himself, "that's almost true. It's on the edge of truth, anyway, and most things men say don't hit it dead center."

He pulled up his horse at a wretched fishing shack which lay a few hundred yards above the riverbank. Large surrounding trees drooped their dark leaves, providing welcome shade. He saw no signs of any occupant.

*"Hello,"* Calvin bellowed. He looked one way and then the other. A soft breeze moved tree limbs, and one of them made a scratching noise as it clawed the primitive wooden roof of the shelter. Aside from these, he heard no other sounds.

Calvin put all his substantial weight in his left stirrup, causing Sully to sidestep slightly, then stepped down to the ground with a number of grunts and groans. After tying his horse securely, he loosened the cinch several notches to enable Sully to breathe more easily, jostled the saddle by its horn, then stumped to the shack.

When he reached its front, he saw his great and good friend, Tuck Bowlegs, hunkered down, cleaning fish with an old hunting knife that had been sharpened so often that its razor edge had been honed on a blade which tapered from not more than a quarter of an inch in width to its wickedly sharp point.

"Hello, Fat Man," Tuck said without looking up.

"Hello, Rude Son of a Bitch," Calvin retorted gruffly, mimicking Tuck's manner of speech. He added, "I'm starvin'."

"You always say that," Tuck replied. "Began cleanin' these fish ten minutes ago when I heard that buffalo you ride knockin' down mesquite trees on your way in."

"I can't abide an upstart, but what can you expect from an infidel?"

Calvin sat down cross-legged upon the ground and tugged a saddle behind him to serve as a backrest. He sighed with contentment, looked around sharply, then smiled and leaned over to one side and with a smooth motion pulled an aged leather bag into his lap. It had once been decorated with beads, although most of them had long since fallen off. He withdrew a half-full bottle of mescal, inspected its contents, and winced at the sight of what looked like a fat whitish grubworm curled at the bottom of the suspicious-looking liquid. He closed his eyes expressively, knowing that by now Tuck would be watching him, and pawed in

the bag again. The next effort rewarded him with the sight of a bottle of tequila.

Calvin made a guttural noise, clearing his throat in anticipation, as he uncorked it, tentatively held it to his lips, and then, throwing caution to the winds, gulped down a fiery mouthful.

"Jehoshaphat," he wailed, baring his teeth and drawing in a huge gasp of air. "I don't believe I'll ever become accustomed to the taste of this stuff. Although, to my everlasting credit, let it be known that I'll continue to try."

Tuck Bowlegs shook his head. The son of a Seminole Indian who had taken a Comanche woman as his wife, he had lived around white men for many years. But he had never understood a single one of them. They talked unceasingly without saying anything. He had listened carefully to their comments and had been forced to this conclusion.

Tuck considered the white man's attitude about working to be another oddity of their race. His woman, Jimmie, who served as a cook at John Hope's saloon in Santa Rita, earned enough for the two of them to live in what he considered to be comfort. Accordingly, Tuck saw no reason to work, although he did hunt and fish—because he enjoyed doing that—thereby occasionally providing food for the table. White men often accused him of laziness, of vagrancy, and worse. But in his estimation those who labored unnecessarily—when they already had food and shelter—possessed a terribly foolish set of values. He had once spent five minutes or more puzzling about this. It seemed that white men worked so that others wouldn't be able to say to them that they *didn't* work. They all apparently wanted to be like everyone else. Tuck, for his part, didn't mind being different. He enjoyed watching the slow and lazy passage of days and even years. If he had not had to exert himself during these periods, he considered it a stroke of good fortune.

Tuck knew, of course, that food and shelter alone were not all there was in life. However, now that he'd learned to trade fish for mescal and tequila, he couldn't think of anything else that a reasonable man might want.

If Tuck had any problems at all, they lay in having to deal with the peculiarities of mankind.

Ever since he'd gotten in so much trouble for riding naked down Concho Street, racing his horse while howling Comanche war cries and terrorizing the settlers, he'd promised Jimmie that when he had a serious urge to drink strong spirits he'd do it out of town. So, for the past ten years, he had been spending more and more time at the fishing

camp, since these urges seemed to arrive with more frequency than when he was younger. Probably due to the increasing pressures brought about by changing times.

In addition to his failure to understand white men, Tuck couldn't understand Mexicans or, for that matter, Indians. He did, however, understand his woman Jimmie.

Jimmie had been a widow when he met her, having formerly been married to a buffalo soldier at the fort. They attended to one another's simple needs in a straightforward fashion without wasting time on conversation. And neither of them gave a hoot in hell that their union had not been sanctified by any clergyman. Such a thing in fact never occurred to either of them. Jimmie was a mixture of African, Indian, and God knows what else. She had a Negro's dark skin, an Indian's straight jet-black hair, and didn't say sixteen words a month. But when she spoke, she went right to the point, as she had only the night before after Tuck had traded for the bottles now in Calvin's capacious lap. She had looked at the tequila and mescal and then at Tuck and had said quite simply, "Go." And he went.

Calvin experimented with another sip of tequila. "I expect you heard what they're fixin' to do to Tom English."

Tuck made it a point not to respond when Calvin asked a question to which Calvin already either knew the answer or should know it.

The silence grew until Calvin couldn't bear it. "And you probably know how five of Tom's men got theirselves killed tryin' to bust him out of jail."

Branches scratched across the shack's roof, and limbs groaned as they rubbed against one another.

"Well, I've made many an unkind remark behind your back and to your face, Tuck, but I know that, aside from being fairly useless when it comes to most things, you're the kind of man I want backin' me up when I break Tom out of jail."

Calvin had seen Tuck in action before. Quick pictures flooded his mind, recollections of what he termed "the Great South Concho Fish Fight," and the even deadlier time when he and Tuck and Tom English had gone up against that pack of outlaws at the Jason Quest ranch near Knickerbocker.

Tuck reached over and pulled the tequila away from Calvin. He stuffed it away in the old leather bag before saying, "If we're goin' after him tonight, we better do it sober."

# SEVEN

TUCK BOWLEGS slung a saddle blanket over the sharp spine of his off mule, the one Calvin called Jug. Tuck saw no purpose in giving names to animals, but it didn't bother him that Calvin should do so. He normally traveled in a wagon after harnessing a team of two mules to it —with Jug hitched up on the right side from the driver's viewpoint. Tuck appreciated the advantages of driving a wagon whenever he was fortunate enough to down a big buck deer. It took a rare horse and an even rarer mule to stand for a deer to be tied on its back; and to drag it with a rope would ruin the meat. He kept a sadly tattered saddle at his fishing camp, however, for cases such as this one when he found the need to ride. He swung it onto the mule's back and cinched it in place.

After this, Tuck slid a handful of wide-barbed deer arrows with dog-wood shafts into a lightweight quiver and then pushed into it a short thick cedar bow which hadn't been strung. Its strong, wiry cord dangled loosely. Then he pulled the quiver over his head and made an adjust-ment so it would hang comfortably on his back.

Calvin Laudermilk sat on his bulky plow horse, waiting impatiently while all these preparations took place. Finally Tuck stepped into his saddle and the two men reined their mounts about, heading toward Santa Rita.

In the darkness of early evening Calvin said, "My plan, when I come up with it, will prove to be a masterpiece."

Tuck grunted noncommittally. He had a walnut-colored hatchet of a face, with a strong-beaked nose. Deep furrows ran from it to either side of a thin-lipped, downturned mouth. An old leather headband re-strained black hair threaded through with gray. Despite his years, his body had stayed hard and lean. He could still run for hours when on the trail of a wounded deer or antelope, a point of pride with him which, of course, he never mentioned.

Tuck enjoyed an essentially solitary life in the immense territory that

had been the hunting ground of the Comanche until some twenty or thirty years before when the white man began to encroach upon it. He lived on this limitless land, using his fishing camp as a point of departure, except for such times as he felt the need for his woman in Santa Rita. However, after a short time in town he'd become uneasy. Jimmie had an unvarying method for dealing with this symptom: she sent him on his way.

The two rode in silence until Calvin asked, "Why didn't I think of this before? All we need to do is get some guns and ammunition into Tom's hands. I'll guarantee you, all of Sheriff Hoskins's men will hightail it out of there when that happens. They'd sooner stay in a closet with a rabid pit bull than in a building with Tom English once he's got a pistol in his hand.

"Now, Tuck, pay me close heed. This is what we'll do: while Tom flushes them like quail, you and I'll be waiting behind cover to pick them off. What do you think about that?"

They rode in a growing silence.

Calvin said, "Of course, there are eight of them, plus the sheriff, who lived through the fight last night. That's nine against three of us, not counting the reinforcements I heard the sheriff had on the way. Might be five or six more, for all I know. Could be fourteen or fifteen of 'em."

They rode without speaking for another mile or two. Then Calvin said, "I know you're wonderin' how in hell we're goin' to get close enough to slip some guns to Tom. I guess you're right, Tuck. That might not be such a good idea."

Calvin tugged thoughtfully at the ends of his mustache with his free right hand before beginning anew. "Well, how about this? We'll get some oily rags, put them on a few of your arrows, set them on fire, and you shoot them onto the roof of the jail where they've got Tom. They'll have to pull him out when the jail goes up in flames, and we'll gun 'em in their tracks when they come runnin' out. I'll let you use my Winchester, it ought to be more accurate than that old Spencer of yours, and I'll go borrow the scatter-gun John Hope keeps behind his bar. Nothin' like the sound of a scatter-gun to sow the seeds of terror in the hearts of villains. Then, in the confusion, we'll grab hold of Tom and make our getaway."

Sully plodded along with singular dignity while Jug kept up with a hitching gait. Calvin looked at his companion thoughtfully. "You don't like that either," he said, scowling. "Guess you got a point—they'd just

let Tom burn. Well, *you* come up with something, if you're so damn smart!"

An owl hooted mournfully from a shadowed stand of trees.

Tuck finally spoke. "The old jail has a tin roof, anyway."

When the two men arrived in Santa Rita, Calvin thought of a scheme which he liked. They left their mounts at the Elkhorn wagon yard, made arrangements for a third horse to be saddled and held ready for Tom to use, then walked down the road dubbed Chadbourne Street past the new construction where they picked up several tools which the workers had left on the site. Calvin seized a crowbar, while Tuck grasped a pickax and carried it down at his side.

The two men retreated, crossed Chadbourne, and went behind Rector's Saddle Shop, which faced on Concho. They slipped through scrub oak and Johnson grass which lay in back of the line of buildings on Concho Street and those facing the other direction on the next block to the north. Bending forward, they crept past the rear of the sturdy limestone structure which held Tom English prisoner and the shed off to the west side of it which served as the sheriff's office. Through the gloom they made out the shadowed figures of several men standing guard. One of them lit a cigarette, and for an instant they saw a patch of yellow light flare about his face. Then only a red point of light showed where he stood.

A broad dirt street with deep ruts down the middle of it divided the courthouse on the north side from the scattered buildings on the south —the sheriff's office with its attached jail and, not far away, the frame seed store with its shingled roof.

Calvin and Tuck circled about the store, then tried the windows and doors. Finding all of them securely fastened, Calvin picked up a rock and with a certain delicacy cracked a windowpane. Since only a vacant lot separated Twohig's Feed and Seed Store from the old jail, Calvin held his breath after breaking the window glass on the far side. When no notice seemed to have been taken, he opened the window and with a prodigious effort wriggled through it. He felt his way into the storage room on the side nearest the jail, with Tuck following close behind him.

"Got to make some space," Calvin said, leaning down to begin work.

Dust clouded the air as the two men threw feed sacks to one side to clear room. They spent twenty minutes struggling to drag the inventory out of the way, sweating as they pulled and tugged at heavy burlap bags.

The storage area had a dirt floor, Calvin was pleased to notice. "Perfect, just perfect, Tuck. We got here unnoticed with our tools; now

we're all set to dig a tunnel." He stood with one hand outstretched and
said, "We'll go down five feet, then start diggin' underground thataway."
He pointed toward the jail, which lay on the other side of a small vacant
piece of property. "I stepped it off," he added, "and we'll need to go
about forty-five paces west, then dig straight up and we'll find ourselves
in Tom's cell." Calvin began to chuckle. "I can just see the look on his
face when I stick my head in and say, 'Wake up, old son, it's time to get
out of here.' "

The moon had risen and its light streamed through the window.
Tuck raised his pickax and swung it down forcefully. The steel point of
the ax rang out sharply as the tip struck stone. Tuck stood bolt upright
and then backed away. Calvin probed down and began to pound with
his crowbar into the rocky soil.

Tuck sat down on the feed bags to watch Calvin work by the light of
the moon. From outside they heard a group of men singing a marching
song, and then a crackling sound, like firearms in the distance. Calvin
and Tuck looked at each other, then shrugged this off. Some thirty
minutes later Calvin, sweat pouring from his face, and with a shirt as
wet as if he'd fallen in a lake, said, "This could take awhile, couldn't it?"

At last Tuck spoke up. "About two weeks," he agreed. The crackling
noise followed by cheering started again, and they stared at one another
without comprehension.

An hour later Calvin leaned on his crowbar, heaving for breath. He
stood in a slight depression, about four feet in diameter, perhaps two
feet in depth. "This is a terrible idea," he announced, clambering out
and throwing his iron crowbar down. "Seems to be a rock shelf just
under the ground here."

Tuck rose and peered through the window, then beckoned for Calvin
to join him. "Look," he said, pointing.

Calvin glanced over his shoulder and saw a number of people calling
out to one another. "Well, I'll be damned," he said.

"What's happening?" Tuck queried.

"I'd nearly forgotten," Calvin replied. "It's the Fourth of July, and
there's a big party scheduled out front of the courthouse—just like the
one they had last year."

Several people could be seen gathered about a small bonfire. One of
them lit a long sliver of kindling wood and advanced, holding the flam-
ing stick in his outstretched hand. While others called encouragement,
he leaned down and touched it to a fuse. Then he retreated, hesitated,

started to return to touch the fuse again, when a string of firecrackers exploded merrily.

People squealed and yelled and laughed. In the flickering light of the bonfire they could see the man who had touched off the fuse. He stopped in mid-flight, abashed and grinning.

"No wonder they didn't hear you bangin' that crowbar in the rocks," Tuck commented.

"Marvelous!" Calvin exclaimed. "They have created a diversion. The very thing we need. Quickly, Tuck, come with me."

"I hope this idea is better than the others," the Indian muttered.

A short time later the two made a run for the high weeds and scrub oaks behind Twohig's store. They hid their rifles and Tuck's bow and arrows there before making a long detour which led them to Concho Street, where they broke into Westbrook's General Store. Throwing caution to the winds, they found a coal-oil lantern, lit it, and carried it with them as they searched for provisions.

"I know it's here," Calvin fumed, "I've seen it before." Then a great sigh of satisfaction escaped him. "Ah," he breathed.

After this he wandered at random, picking up a small item at one counter and a collection of coarse cotton pillowcases at another.

He placed four silver dollars on the counter. "Since I don't know the prices, I'll have to estimate how much to pay." With a wink he added, "I'm always rich as Croesus during the week after payday, then I'm poor as Job's turkey for the rest of the month."

He shook his head as though struggling with the injustice of life. "Often I cry out to the Almighty and ask, 'Why? *Why?*' But the Lord merely replies, 'You don't really want to know the answer—you just want to start an argument.'"

Tuck's mouth pulled down in an evident show of disgust at his friend's meaningless chatter.

Calvin strode with purposeful strides, with a keg tucked under his right arm and his other purchases held firmly in his left hand. "Come on, Tuck, we've got some more shoppin' to do."

They walked half a block west to the Concho Street Saloon, pausing there while Calvin put his burden down upon the sidewalk next to the frame wall. "I would never leave an unguarded bottle on a table, but in this lazy town the useful things you pick up in hardware stores are as safe from thievery as if they was in a bank."

The two men stepped through the batwing doors and saw that few

customers remained. These sat around a table at one end playing cards.
So engrossed were they in their game that they didn't even glance up.

"My friend," Calvin said to Chesley Upshaw, the bartender, "the
whole town seems to be celebrating our nation's independence. They're
out in front of the courthouse setting off fireworks."

The bartender didn't take his eyes from his work, continuing to dry
off a number of glasses with a frayed dish towel. He grumbled, "To my
mind the Fourth of July is nothin' but a damn Yankee holiday now. I had
a good crowd startin' out tonight, expected some brisk trade, but a
couple of hours ago almost everybody wandered off outside like a bunch
of little kids." Raising his head, he bespied Calvin's companion, and his
mild gaze changed instantly into a glare of shocked surprise.

"Jesus Christ! Git that Injun out of here before someone sees him."

"This is my friend, Tuck Bowlegs, and he's with me."

"I don't want no trouble in here, Calvin."

"Nor do I. Especially not on a national holiday. Tuck is just as Ameri-
can as you or me, Chesley, and maybe more so. And he and I have
decided to take some refreshments to the party that's going on."

"I could use the business," Chesley observed, deciding to make no
further protests about a savage being in the saloon in spite of strict
unwritten rules about such things.

After deliberating gravely, Calvin went to the rear of the establishment and came back dragging a large metal washtub. After this, he
deposited a stack of silver dollars on the bar and began making his
selections. He began by pouring five quarts of tequila into the tub. After
this, for flavor, Calvin opened a large can of cherries and emptied them
and their juice into the liquor. Getting into the spirit of the occasion, he
suggested a bottle of rum and one of whiskey. With a proper base
established, they half filled the washtub with warm sudsy amber beer
from a barrel which stood at the end of the bar.

"We'll need a coffee cup to use for a ladle, and a bunch of glasses,"
Calvin directed.

The poker players had left their game, falling prey to curiosity. They
approached, watching with interest as Calvin stood over the mixture,
stirring it occasionally with a broom handle.

"What on earth are you doin'?" one of them asked.

Calvin replied, "Well, hell, what does it look like? I'm inventin' a new
drink. Don't you get tired of the same thing all the time?"

The questioner looked at Calvin blankly and then, after some hesita-

tion, accepted the offer of a coffee cup filled with the concoction. Tentatively, he tasted it.

The man jerked back as though stung, then wheezed in a particularly strained manner as if on the verge of losing his voice, "I think it needs a little somethin' else. Tastes like sheep dip."

"Maybe some more cherry juice?" Calvin inquired anxiously.

"No," the sampler replied after he recovered from a fit of coughing, "I don't think that would help it none."

Calvin took a generous swallow of his recipe, sucked in his cheeks, turned slightly purple, and said, "We got to do something, boys. I have too much invested now to let it go to waste."

With this, he went behind the bar and came back with a half-gallon jug of gin which Chesley Upshaw kept for a few special customers. Calvin pulled out more dollars from his pocket and put them on the bar before he poured this into the yeasty, malodorous brew. After stirring it vigorously, he ladled out a few inches into a heavy glass mug and inspected it. The brown flecks of foam on top of the evil-looking liquid had turned to olive drab. Calvin eyed it suspiciously before taking a cautious sip.

"Now *that's* more like it," he rumbled triumphantly as a beatific smile spread all over his face. "The gin has smoothed it out."

With the help of the poker players, Calvin lugged the big tub out back and put it on a two-wheeled handcart in the alley. Chesley used the rickety handcart to haul off trash, and it worked perfectly for this new purpose.

"Roll it right over to the courthouse, boys, and take great care with the potholes—don't spill a drop. And," he reminded them, "don't forget the coffee cup and the glasses. Me and Tuck are goin' to pick up a few more things for the party and we'll meet you there."

A short time later Calvin emerged from behind Twohig's Feed and Seed Store carrying his rifle and a small wooden keg as well as his other purchases. Tuck Bowlegs followed a few footsteps back with his old Spencer rifle in the crook of his arm and a bristling quiver on his back.

The ten or twelve men who'd been in front of the courthouse had run out of fireworks, and they greeted the prospect of free drinks with gusto.

Calvin, taking on the role of host with enthusiasm, served them flamboyantly, handing each man a brimming glass as he announced, "Boys, this is what I call Courthouse Punch. If you drink enough of this you'll be as sly as a lawyer and mean as a judge."

All of the celebrants welcomed his offers. After their first stunned reactions, they became silent, apparently reacting as boys do to dares: "If you can do it, I can too." But after that, with their senses cauterized, the second glasses went down more easily. Gradually they began to make a few whooping noises.

One cowboy warned his friends, "Look out for them cherry pits and stems, a man could choke to death on 'em."

Calvin scowled blackly at him, his feelings obviously hurt.

With Calvin's encouragement, several of the celebrants carried drinks to the guards who had gathered in front of the old jail, watching the noisy party across the dirt street. Before long, all but two of these had scuffed across the rutted way and joined the others surrounding the washtub.

Calvin pulled Tuck to one side and said, "Slip over while no one is payin' any attention and warn Tom to get in a corner over in the east end of his cell. Tell him to curl up in a ball, and for God's sake to keep clear of the window. Then come back and help me."

"Where's the sheriff?"

"Don't know, Tuck. They must have divided up so they can guard Tom in shifts. Apparently six are on duty now. Four are gettin' in a festive mood over here, so only two are takin' their jobs seriously."

Tuck faded back from the bonfire and the circle of men who stood holding glasses, wavering on their feet, and braying with laughter. He slipped through shadows and crossed the street.

Calvin pumped a round into the firing chamber of his Winchester and held it warily as he eyed the guards who stood with their backs to the jail. These men watched the crowd across the street with fascination.

"What's takin' him so long?" Calvin asked himself. But at that instant he saw Tuck creeping along the base of the limestone wall. He slipped rapidly to the window at the jail, raised his head up to its ledge a moment, and then dropped down and moved away and out of sight.

Calvin turned his attention to other matters. Taking up his parcel and the wooden keg, he walked to one of the two old cannons which sat on either side of the flagpole on the courthouse grounds. Hurriedly, he cracked open the keg's lid and poured a stream of black powder down the priming hole at the back of the piece. Then he pulled a long fuse from the articles he'd placed at his feet and pushed it into the priming hole.

Tuck joined him as he continued his preparations. Calvin very care-

fully uncocked his rifle and then knotted several pillowcases around the end of its barrel. Then he poured a copious quantity of black powder into the cannon's cylindrical muzzle, shoving and tamping it into place with the pillowcase-wrapped Winchester.

"You're puttin' way too much in it," Tuck observed.

"Don't lecture me about technical matters, you unlettered heathen. We won't get a second chance. It's goin' to take a powerful blow to knock that stone wall down. So stand back." With that he poured the remaining contents of the keg down the ancient cannon's round, rusted throat. After this he forced two pillowcases down the muzzle to hold the powder in place.

"Help me with this cannonball, Tuck. There we go—God a'mighty but it's a tight fit. I'll shove it . . ." A huge grunting noise caused by his effort interrupted his words, and then he concluded, "Think we got it —that's the way. Ah."

Calvin grasped the rear of the cannon with his massive arms and pulled it around. With the air of an expert he put his head down and sighted with one eye closed along the cast-iron barrel.

He backed away and said, "That's perfect, Tuck. I've aimed this piece right below the window. Now, in about two shakes of a lamb's tail, we'll show this town some *real* fireworks. The minute that we blow a hole in the jail, you and I'll shoot those two over yonder. While you hold off the others, I'll get Tom. And then we'll make a run for the horses!"

With that, he struck a match, held it to the fuse, and watched it begin to sputter. The long fuse glowed and fizzed and twisted as it burned. Calvin backed away instinctively some eight or ten yards, while Tuck went twice as far and crouched down with instinctive prudence behind a gnarled chinaberry tree.

A sheet of red and orange flame joined by an explosion unlike any heard before by those within earshot rent the night half in two. Or so it seemed to the men who miraculously survived it. The cannon exploded at the breech, splitting asunder; the wheels on each side went spinning wildly away; and then the remainder of the weapon flew straight up in the air at least six feet before careening back to earth. The rust-encrusted cannonball had not budged an inch from its spot within the bore where Calvin had forced it, and could be seen through a jagged split in the cannon's barrel.

Calvin felt himself lifted by the sheer force of the explosion and thrown backward with great violence. He landed on his broad rump and sprawled out wondering if he was dead.

He sat up, felt his arms and legs, and realized that he still had life. Yet not like that he'd had before, for now his ears rang as though he were himself the clapper in a cathedral bell ringing out vespers.

The cowboys and townspeople who'd been celebrating had thrown themselves in panic to the ground. One of them howled, "What in the name of all that's holy was *that?*"

The two stunned guards across the street retreated toward the jail until they reached a small wooden porch in front of it. They held their rifles before them with both hands.

By this time, Calvin had recovered his rifle. He ripped the pillowcase from it, banged it against his boot a few times to jar loose any foreign matter that might have lodged in the barrel, and hollered, "Let's go, Tuck. No more of these damn plans."

Tuck materialized out of the darkness at his elbow, saying, "I told you not to use so much powder." He sank to one knee and strung his bow.

"Damn your bones, just follow me," roared Calvin, as he lumbered toward the street.

A guard advanced toward them, raising a rifle to his shoulder. He came to a sudden stop, eyes wide, as a deer arrow whistled through the air just under his hands. It sounded as if someone had hit a watermelon with the flat side of an ax. A ripe "whap" sound. He spiraled about, dropping his rifle, putting both hands on the feathered shaft that protruded from his sternum, and fell to the ground with a look of perplexity upon his face.

The other guard's rifle boomed once and then Calvin's bullet splintered his arm. He fell back momentarily, drew a six-gun with the uninjured arm, but then a second slug from Calvin's Winchester caught him in the throat. He went over backward, kicking at the wall an instant before all movement ceased.

"Hurry, Fat Man. You waked up the whole town with that cannon."

"I know," Calvin gasped, too out of breath from running across the street to respond as he would have liked. He fumbled with the knob, ripped the door open, and burst into the sheriff's office.

Somehow they found the keys to the cell and released Tom, who rushed to the sheriff's desk. He had seen them put away his guns when they locked him away. Tom pulled open a drawer and grasped the cartridge belt and its two full holsters. Tuck and Calvin were at the door, yelling at him to forget his guns, that they didn't have a moment to spare, that all hell was about to break loose.

Tom English, eyes cold as frosted steel, ignored them. He took the

time to strap on his matched .45s, even pausing to fasten the tie-down thongs around his thighs before going out the door.

The cowboys and the sodden townspeople had gathered at a safe distance. The surviving guards, staggering from the effect of Calvin's punch, moved behind the other people for protection when they saw their feared prisoner had armed himself.

"We've got to stop 'em," one of them yelled. The other said, "I'm right behind you."

"Come on!" the first one hollered, his voice thick from drink. He made an effort to scurry to one side but tripped and fell in a heap.

Tom backed around the side of the sheriff's office. He heard Calvin call to him. "This way—we've got a horse for you over at the Elkhorn wagon yard."

Tuck said hurriedly to Calvin, "It's time to run, Fat Man," and with that loped away.

Calvin trotted a few steps and then settled for walking swiftly. "Impatient savage," he grumbled.

Off to the north they heard the muffled sound of horses' hooves clattering on the hardened earth.

# EIGHT

SHERIFF BAXTER rode the lead horse with seven mounted men careening behind him. His sorrel skidded into the turn from Chadbourne Street onto the lane leading to the blazing bonfire on the courthouse grounds—with the rider leaning toward the inside to hold his balance as he rounded the corner. As he pulled onto the straightaway he tugged out a six-gun with his right hand and, reaching the excited crowd, hauled back hard on his reins with his left. The sorrel's head almost came back in the rider's lap as the horse's stiff front legs helped him jolt to a jarring stop.

The other riders with Baxter swarmed upon the scene, veering to one side to keep from running into him, their mounts excited and capering sideways. One particularly cantankerous horse squealed and thudded kicks in the chest of another behind him.

The members of the drunken mob all seemed determined to be the first to tell their tales of what had happened, and several shouted at the sheriff at the same time.

"They murdered Les and Ben Jack," a thick-voiced man hollered. He staggered slightly as he came into the firelight.

One of the hired gunmen brought in from El Paso by Baxter and Judge Hoskins walked up close to the sheriff and began to make excuses.

"Ned and Billy and the rest of us fought from over here," he said, waving vaguely behind him.

The sheriff stared for a moment with no sign of emotion at the two bodies sprawled in front of his office. Then he faced the man who'd spoken to him last. "Did they bust Tom English loose?"

"They did," he lied, "but we put up one hell of a fight."

"How many men do they have? Did you recognize any of them?" The sheriff had difficulty controlling his horse owing to the drunks floundering around him.

"The fat man done it," a hoarse voice slurred out of the crowd, "him and that wild-assed Injun friend of his. Calvin Laudermilk and Tuck Bowlegs got ever'body drunk and then stormed the jail."

"There was nothin' we could do," another hired gunsel explained.

"You mean to say that you let *two* men get the best of you?"

"Christ a'mighty, Sheriff, they had a cannon."

Sheriff Reuben Baxter looked at the speaker with a mixture of confusion and disgust. "Which way did they go?"

"Yonder," he said, pointing past the jail. "They was runnin' toward Concho Street, but they can't git far on foot."

The remaining gunfighters who had served as guards had by this time straggled up near the sheriff's horse. He stared down coldly at them for an instant. Finally he spoke to the mounted men behind him. "Come on, boys, let's go."

Sheriff Baxter and the seven gunfighters didn't wait for the drunks. Wheeling their horses, they fanned out and began to ride up and down the few streets of downtown Santa Rita. After ten minutes of this, they went from door to door, rousting out people wherever they saw a light. Finally at the Elkhorn wagon yard they spoke to a boy of about eighteen named Junior Sims who had conquered his tendency to stammer by forcing himself to speak very slowly. He told them they'd just missed their quarry.

At the outset they had difficulty in communicating, since the sheriff yelled at the kid to talk faster, which brought on waves of stammers. Biting his lip, the sheriff forced himself to be patient and bade Junior Sims to tell the story in his own way.

With difficulty the young man explained that Calvin Laudermilk and the Indian, Tuck Bowlegs, had come for their mounts, a very large workhorse and a mule. He also said that they'd taken a rented horse, a paint.

"I did my dead level best to explain to Mr. Laudermilk that we didn't have no saddles or bridles for rent—they wanted them for the paint— but damned if he didn't take Mr. Yates's rig he'd left here, give me forty dollars for it, and said if old Yates wasn't happy with the price, he could talk to him later about it." The boy twitched as he added, "Ain't that somethin'?"

Then he said, repeating the question put to him, "Did I see Tom English? No, sir, I didn't, although there was someone waitin' for them outside whilst we talked."

The impatient men sat their lathered horses. These, after having

been rawhided up and down the street, first being spurred into a run and then pulled up short, now danced in circles nervously.

"Dad blame your hide," said Sheriff Reuben Baxter, a man who rarely cursed and who was proud of his temperate speech, "where in the God damned hell did they go?"

A razored line of dawn's light slit the slender space between the curving earth and eastern sky at the horizon, and then—ten minutes later—a paleness washed up from it. In the sullen darkness that clutched around Tuck Bowlegs's fishing camp, the crowded droop of leaf-laden branches of clustered pecan trees could be sensed but not seen. Gradually, their mass stood out, a different sort of blackness against the fading charcoal heavens.

A fire crackled as it hit sap pockets, snapping as dry mesquite wood gave in to yellow flames. The Indian sat on his haunches watching it without expression.

Calvin Laudermilk, propped against his saddle, slowly opened his eyes and groaned. Turning with difficulty, he extracted a turnip-sized old watch from his saddlebags and squinted at it, holding it sideways so the flickers from the fire would illuminate its hands.

"Five o'clock. I thank you for wakin' me up, Tuck. It wouldn't do for a man to sleep his life away. We must have tossed and turned here for a good four hours at least."

Tuck made no answer as he began to fry fillets of catfish which sizzled as they hit the pan.

Calvin reached for his boots and tugged them on, making puffing noises as he strained forward, sounding as if he were lifting great weights upon his shoulders.

"What have we here? Catfish? For breakfast? Great God, Tuck, have you sunk to that? Well, it's a mercy that you're not servin' us with prairie dog and rabbit stew. Someday, old friend, I'm goin' to take you to John Henry's café at the Taylor Hotel and get you a civilized breakfast." He closed his eyes as if in prayer. "I can just see a great platter laden down with thick-sliced ham and redeye gravy, of grits and eggs and steaming golden biscuits—fairly dripping with melted butter—and, to top it off, hot coffee in a mug." He winced and shook his great head. "These are thoughts which lead to madness."

Tom English walked from the darkness, leading his paint. Already saddled, the compact, muscular pony followed him docilely. Turning, he tied the reins to a tree branch and joined his companions.

"I guess you saw that your horse has one blue eye and one brown," Calvin observed.

Tom nodded with a slight smile. "Checked his teeth, looks to be around four or five years old. Hooves and legs in good shape, and from my standpoint, best of all, he has an easy trot."

Calvin broke in, "He ain't much, compared to those thoroughbreds and fine quarter horses you're accustomed to ridin'."

"He'll have to do for now."

After they had eaten, Tom said, "Jedediah Jackson has gone to Austin to try to get some law and order sent to Santa Rita. It's my understanding that he might even talk to the governor. But things have gotten complicated now."

"Well, yes, you might say that." Calvin huffed out the words. "We've shot two scamps who were part of the bunch plannin' to hang you—more than likely today or tomorrow. There wasn't, in my judgment, a hope in hell that we had the luxury of time—the luxury, that is to say, to wait around for the wheels of justice to turn. The old saying has it that the mills of God grind slowly, yet they grind exceeding small, which is perfectly satisfactory for philosophers, I suppose, but for an innocent man dangling at the end of a rope, that's small consolation."

"You have a point."

"There's another point, Tom, although you might look on it as a minor one. Now they probably plan to hang Tuck and me as well as you since the men we shot happened to be wearing deputy sheriff badges, even if they were, in truth, hired ne'er-do-wells."

Tuck grunted impatiently. He said, "That cowboy you shot by the river, the one who was goin' to bushwhack you?"

Tom waited for Tuck to continue; and Calvin fell into unaccustomed silence as he listened.

"Somebody sent him after you."

Calvin, eyes suddenly alight, said, "By God, it ain't true that Injuns don't have the capacity for rational thought. Tuck may have hit on something important. All this trouble got started by that drifter with the rifle who trailed you on the Lazy E. Of course, I guess it's a little late to be trying to figure out why he would do such a thing."

"I don't know, Calvin." Tom looked down, frowning slightly as he forced himself to bring back a memory that he had resolutely tried to erase. At last he spoke again.

"The stranger sat a worn-down horse—one that had a limp—it fa-

vored its right forefoot. I remember his face, his big hooked nose, a mustache that kind of hung down." Again he fell silent, lost in thought. Tom took a stick and knelt on one knee. Speaking softly, he said, "The horse had an unusual brand on its left hip. Couldn't make it out too well under all the caked lather, but as best I remember, it looked like this."

With that he drew a jagged line in the dirt floor of Tuck's cabin. Tom rose, and the three men stood looking down at the representation of the brand.

Tom glanced out the window. The sky turned furnace white in the east but still stayed dark blue above them. A strong south breeze stirred the leaves, but in spite of that perspiration already darkened Calvin's shirt. He wiped impatiently at a trickle which ran down his face. Taking out a large red bandana, he used it to swab his forehead. "Going to be a scorcher," he said. Then he asked, "Have you ever seen that brand before?"

"No, I can't say that I have."

Tuck said, "My father was a Seminole. He acted as a scout for the Dragoons, and later for the U.S. Cavalry. They came out here to fight the Comanche." Something that looked almost like a smile softened his face. "But my father didn't fight them much. He married one. When he died, my mother took me to where her tribe had run away—in New Mexico Territory. I lived there with the Comanche twenty years. We moved all the time, drug our lodges when we'd follow the game. But then, over by the Canadian River in the panhandle, the cavalry rounded us up. They put what was left of the tribe on a reservation in Oklahoma Territory. That's where I learned to speak English so good."

Calvin snorted at this, but Tuck ignored him.

"I signed on with an outfit that supplied beef to the reservation and rode with them for years. We'd go to South Texas, wind past Fort Concho on the way to Indian territory. On one of those trips, I met my woman here, so I stayed."

Calvin said, "That's the longest speech I've ever heard you make, old friend, and I'm delighted to know that you can talk so much good English, as you say. But what does that have to do with Tom's problem?"

Tuck Bowlegs looked at him with a pained expression. At last he replied, "I've made a few trips back to New Mexico Territory where I lived as a boy. The last time I went, maybe three years ago, I rode by Bitter Lake and Caprock and then I spent a night high up on one side of

Carrizo Peak. There's a mean town they call Lincoln southwest of that mountain. The Indians know to stay clear of it, and the Mexicans do too. So I circled around it, rode through rough country, and to the south of Lincoln is where I saw that brand," he said, pointing at the rough drawing made by Tom in the dirt. "I rode with old friends that day, and they told me that's the Bent Snake brand used by a man named Joe Hill."

"The name's familiar," Calvin said.

"A lot was written a few years back about the Lincoln County War—and some of it had to do with Joe Hill," Tom English observed.

While Tuck cleaned up after breakfast, Tom took canteens to the river and filled them. Calvin took this time to saddle Sully and Tuck's mule, Jug.

A short time later they stood together, preparing to mount. "Are we on our way to New Mexico?" Calvin asked Tom.

"I am," Tom English replied, "but more for the sake of curiosity than anything else. If I can find who sent that man after me, maybe I can figure this thing out. I've got to run somewhere, and I doubt that anyone would guess that I'd go in that direction. Most likely they'll figure that I've gone to my own place, the Circle X down on the border, or to that ranch I've got along with Hap Cunningham's boy to the north of Black Horse, Montana."

"You don't want our company?" Calvin asked.

"It's not that. I think it's important to know if we have any hope of help from the governor, or anyone else Jedediah's been able to talk to."

"Reckon Tuck and I ought to go to Austin to look for him?"

"No, Calvin. The pair of you would tend to stand out a little. After all, not too many big men on Percherons travel alongside of an Indian riding a mule. It wouldn't take any time at all before you'd get caught. No, I think the two of you should go to ground somewhere on the road back to Santa Rita from Austin. You know good and well that Jedediah will head back to town just as soon as he can. Find a safe place and keep an eye on the trail so you can intercept him as he passes by."

"When we find something out, how do we go about getting in touch with you?"

"Send a wire to the telegraph station in Lincoln. Use the name of Tom Germany, that's the one I used the last time I was on the run. Probably no one in New Mexico has heard of it."

"Sounds like as good a plan as any," Calvin said. "This'll give my friend Tuck and me a chance to scout out some of my old stompin'

grounds around Fort McKavitt. That's not so far from Menard, which is on Jedediah's way back from Austin. I have a friend named Edmund Bench who lives on land owned by Alex Allison. He'll take us in, or at least me. Don't know if he'll offer shelter to a wild Indian."

He sniggered momentarily, an odd sound coming from one so massive. Then he said, "Now, calm down, Tuck, I was just guyin' you. Old Edmund, if he's got any faults at all, it's that he likes *everyone*. I find that unnatural, but at the same time it's refreshing, and that's why we get on so well, since I don't like many men at all. We make a kind of balance.

"But the main reason I always search out Edmund when I'm anywhere near to him is that he's probably the finest cook in the Western Hemisphere. He learned his skills at his mother's knee. Also, since he's so particular about his kitchen, he won't let anyone in it while he works, so he's not like some people who pride themselves as cooks, the ones who put you to work dicing vegetables and skinning game and such as that."

Tom smiled. "Calvin, you should avoid him like the plague. The last thing you need is to be exposed to rich cooking. In fact, I was about to suggest that you might take this time while you're hiding out to go on a diet."

Calvin paled. "Good God, Tom, don't even joke about such a thing. The mere idea of a diet makes me desperately hungry."

"Fat Man's always hungry," Tuck Bowlegs snorted. "Complains all the time. 'Why don't you have bacon and butter?' That's what I hear every morning when he's out here."

"What in the *hell*," Calvin demanded with a show of exasperation, "does butter and bacon have to do with my weight? Every creature craves nourishment. There's no sin involved in a man's asking to have three meals a day."

Tuck raised his hand, and a fierceness crossed his face. With swift grace he moved twenty yards away, then called in a low voice, "Horses coming."

Without wasting words the three men seized their weapons and gear, then made their mounts ready.

Tuck ran back into his cabin and returned with a large bundle which he jammed in one of his saddlebags.

"We'll send you a wire in Lincoln, New Mexico," Calvin said.

Tom waved at his two friends and urged his paint into a quick trot through the tall pecan trees lying between the cabin and the South

Concho River. He headed his horse down into it, loosening the reins as the paint sank until only his head showed—along with his tangled tail flowing out behind.

Tom held his horse's mane and with gentle slaps to his neck guided him to the far shore. Water surged up to his chest and for a moment he worried about his ammunition, but then realized that he'd been soaked many times before. With modern, metal-cased cartridges, his weapons would fire.

The paint labored out of the water on the slippery mud at the water's edge, then lunged up the steep bank with Tom leaning forward and gathering his reins. The cowpony, responding to the touch of spurs, bounded over the crest and, on reaching the flat country on the other side, lengthened his stride into a run. Tom slowed this rush and for a short time sat a rocking lope before pulling back into a long traveling trot, heading west toward the Mexican border. He planned to angle northwest once he came close to the Rio Grande.

"Stay here," Tuck said. He and Calvin had stopped in a stand of hackberry and mesquite trees. Both dismounted and Calvin held the two sets of reins in one hand. Jug, Tuck's placid mule, stood stolidly, long ears perked forward. Sully, Calvin's oversized draft horse, put his head out and began to wrench leaves off a mesquite.

A gust of wind rattled the branches. It had grown steadily stronger as the sun rose, and now it bent the treetops toward the north.

Calvin watched Tuck with a puzzled expression. "By damn, if you ain't one strange Injun. What in thunder are you doing?"

Tuck didn't answer. He picked up a slender four-foot-long, dead tree limb from the ground, broke off the small branches from it, then returned to the side of his mule. He opened a saddlebag, took out a dark, greasy clump of rags and a long strip of rawhide. Moments later he had tied the rags to the end of the stick.

Looking up at Calvin, he said, "I brought these from the cabin. Poured coal oil on them."

While Calvin looked at him blankly, Tuck struck a long wooden kitchen match on a stone and carefully lit the rags. In an instant a sharp rush of flames flared out from the torch.

Tuck burst out of the thicket, running gracefully with long strides, and began to draw the firebrand in his hand along the top of the waist-high sea of dry brown broomweed. The wind whipped the small bright flecks of fire, thousands of sparks whirled through the air, and then a

strange rushing, crackling noise began, building in intensity like a distant storm of fireworks mixed with the roar of a train.

Tuck ran tirelessly in a wide arc, right arm holding the streaming bright orange torch, which streaked backward across the spreading feathery heads of the stiff, clutching weeds. He ran almost a mile, threw the torch into the burgeoning firestorm, and then circled around and began striding smoothly back toward Calvin: head steady, not bobbing, arms pumping as his legs plowed through the dried growth. Tuck seemed to glide off to one side of a climbing flared wall of flame which hurled spirals of red and orange and yellow in the air, dark smoke climbing now, the prairie glowing strangely.

Smoke billowed, and the whipping wind threw spark showers and embers and whirling gusts of smoke and brilliant flashes into the sky.

Slowing as he reached Calvin's side, Tuck gasped out, bending over, hands on his knees, "That ought to slow them down."

Then Tuck clambered upon his mule, Calvin with great groans and grunting made his creaking way into his saddle, and the two rode toward the east. The huge man and his whipcord-lean friend cast glances to their left toward the boiling dark smoke until they ascended a small rise. Drawing to a halt, they faced about and gazed with astonishment at the sight before them: a crescent-shaped prairie fire moving at a surprisingly rapid pace southward. In the enveloping pocket of this fire they saw the dark figures of eight mounted men, racing frantically away —lashing their horses as they fled in a frenzy, seeking escape from the pursuing flames.

"Well, I'll be damned," said Calvin Laudermilk. "You had that planned all along, you wily savage."

# NINE

THE PAINT with one brown eye and one blue moved easily, but wheezed. Short of wind after no more than an hour at this pace. But at least, Tom English thought, looking at the bright side, he had an easy trot. The unfamiliar saddle had that old-fashioned high flat cantle that caught him in the small of his back, and he couldn't get comfortable. "If I'm going to be on this trail for long, I need to make some changes," he remarked, half to himself and partly, in a conversational tone, to the bobbing head of his horse.

Earlier he had looked behind him and seen the sky black with smoke, and he'd stopped a moment, staring at the strange distant sight with mixed feelings. All ranchers dread prairie fires. Sometimes, when carelessness around a campfire started one, the cowboys fought it with whatever came to hand.

But this time he knew what must have happened. It would have been Tuck's doing, an old Comanche trick, a way to block off pursuers so he and Calvin could get away from Sheriff Reuben Baxter and his hired honchos.

Tom directed his pony at a slower trot through the scattered brush in the short-grass country on the flat. Far off to his right he could make out the two knobs that people in Santa Rita called "the twin mountains," although folks from Colorado and West Virginia who'd moved to Texas, hearing this, would laugh until tears came into their eyes.

A few miles farther on he forded another river, finding it shallow enough to get across on the gravel bed, and feeling thankful for this circumstance. His clothes had dried out soon enough in the hot south wind and fierce sunlight but his boots were only now getting where they didn't have that clammy feeling.

He kept thinking: "God, I hate being on the run again." The thought of leaving Sally without a farewell hug, an explanation, a chance to tell her how much he loved her, caused a physical pain which surprised

him, making him bend forward just an instant before he straightened in the saddle. Images of his lovely wife ran through his mind and then he thought of Ben, the baby, and, with sharp sadness, of Rebecca, his daughter who seemed almost grown, though of course she was just a girl still. He couldn't free himself from the memory of the shock he'd seen in her eyes after he'd had to shoot that drifter—the one who had thrown down on him with his rifle back on the Lazy E. He had promised Rebecca, he'd given her his word, that he'd never do such a thing again. And he had broken that vow. But it all seemed to have happened so fast.

As the paint scrambled down and through a dry, steep-sided arroyo, he had a mental conversation with himself. Excuses. Men always seem to be able to come up with mighty good explanations for whatever they do. Rebecca hadn't answered any of the ones Tom gave her. Just looked at him. Hadn't asked if he was serious about avoiding gunplay forever like he'd sworn to her, when she surely had heard the far-off sounds which echoed when he worked daily with his Colts. She hadn't asked, "Why pretend that because you don't strap on your guns you didn't have them with you anymore? Why were you carrying that six-gun in your saddlebag?" Well, she couldn't know about the nightmare he'd had since he was seventeen and all this hell broke out in his life. The one where his hands were slow as molasses as he stood helplessly looking at the muzzle of a .45 in the hands of a faceless killer.

Tom had learned through a good many years that the only way he could drive that terrible picture from his mind was to go out and practice. He took a deep breath as he rode along, saying to himself, "It's not the sort of thing I've ever tried to explain to Rebecca. Maybe if I'd treated her more like an adult and admitted to her something most men never do, the fact that they, the fathers, have the same kinds of fears that kids do. Things that they don't feel strong enough to handle. In fact, I rarely admit that sort of idea to myself. Anyway, when she left to go over to stay awhile with our neighbor, Hester Trace, she just looked at me, tears in her eyes, and rode away without a word.

"I'm not going to think any more about the way she left without saying good-bye," he said to himself. "And for another thing, at least for now, I won't think more than I have to about that poor devil who trailed me till I knew I had to do something to look helpless by the river. I didn't have a chance against a man on a ridge somewhere, hidden from sight, holding a rifle on me. I had to stand and look unarmed and draw him down closer so I'd have some kind of chance. Most times I've

planned things like that, almost instinctively, and the results aren't at all the way I thought they'd be, but this time he came on in. I suppose he was one of those mean ones who wanted to see me crawl before he gunned me down. But anyway, it didn't work out that way. So now I have no choice but to go into hiding.

"My greatest hope is that the Rangers or some law from Austin will come into play and get this whole mess straightened out. But if it doesn't, maybe I can come up with some kind of proof that I went up against a man deliberately sent out to kill me."

These thoughts coursed through his mind and some of them he spoke softly, not really aware that he was doing so. Tom felt the old saddle's tall cantle banging into his back like a slapping plank as he rode on a wind-broke paint starting on a terribly long journey clear up into the unknown broken land where Lincoln lay, a place in the New Mexico Territory he'd only heard about from others.

Tom's increasing anxiety had a whirling center he could locate exactly. He spoke out loud toward his horse's ears: "It runs from the center of my stomach up to a point just above my rib cage. If I could get some whiskey down on top of that, maybe I could get some relief. The rest of me feels just fine."

People who spent too much time alone, he decided, got into the bad habit of talking to themselves.

Tom left the main trail, forded a river, and went to the south of it, south of Sherwood heading west, riding between Dove Creek and Spring Creek, all of it claimed around 1864 by R. F. Tankersley in spite of swarms of horse- and cattle-stealing wild Indians, dead center in the hunting grounds of the Comanche. Tankersley decided that he was by God going to set up a cattle ranch in spite of that. "My Lord," Tom thought, "what a nerve that took."

The Tankersleys and their descendants, many of them Noelkes, lived on this broad land which old-timers said once had grass clear up to a man's stirrups, though that was surely not the case now.

After so many hours in the sun, without a meal at all, Tom began to feel lightheaded. He tried to while away the time by singing to himself. He never sang in the presence of others since he was aware of his lack of talent in this regard. But now his voice even grated on his own ears. "My mouth must be too dry," he reasoned. Then he began to think of an eccentric friend of his who lived not far away, alone in a Mexican shack. A man who told delightful yarns about his forebears. He grinned

as one of these came to mind, the tale the young man told about his daddy.

The old man was on a trail drive, sitting a "steeldust" horse, the first of the breeds from which some say the best of the quarter horses came. A recently hired young cowboy, perhaps thinking the old man was hard of hearing, said derisively to another youngster, "Wonder what that old son of a bitch thinks he's good for?"

At that very moment a feisty steer that had been causing trouble on the drive for days broke from the herd, heading toward the brush. The old man slammed his spurs into the big steeldust horse, careening after the racing steer, which zigzagged first left, then right, with the old man staying right behind him, making wrenching turns and circles, slamming over young mesquite trees and brush and through great patches of prickly pear.

The last time this same steer had made his break, six men had fought for over an hour, determined to hold him and get him turned and back to the main herd. But now they watched the ancient cowboy in amazement as his big mount flew like a racehorse across the rough ground. The old-timer whipped out his rope and, leaning forward like a nineteen-year-old might, standing in his stirrups, he whirled a hard flat loop around the fleeing animal's wide horns. The steeldust stud slid to a stop, and as the big steer hit the end of the rope, he turned an absolute flip in the air and came down with a resounding crash, almost killing him.

Without an instant's hesitation, old man Noelke flung himself from his horse, ran twenty yards forward, and slammed a boot into the nose of the downed and half-stunned beast. The old rancher bent over and flung dirt into the steer's eyes, kicked him a few more times for good measure, then retrieved his rope. He remounted, sitting there while the injured animal slowly rose, rear end swaying up first, followed by his head, and wobbled back to the herd. The old man rode behind, pulling in his rope, coiling it, and then tying it by his saddle strings where it belonged on the right front side of his saddle. As he drew within earshot of the young cowboys he said, without looking at them, "That's *one* thing this old son of a bitch can do."

At last Tom reached the windmill where he'd watered herds before. It was on the Chisholm Trail leading all the way to Dodge City, Kansas, and the discovery of this water had made passage on this flat ground, far from the rougher country near the river, a great deal easier. And, for the ranchers, it meant they could water their stock without walking

them half to death getting to Dove or Spring creeks. What had happened, long before, was that a couple of cowboys had found a hole in the flat prairie land. Out of curiosity one climbed down the hole, which twisted around. One stayed out, holding a rope, while the other fearfully descended, finding to his great surprise that it kept on going down. And then, to his everlasting amazement, he came upon an astounding discovery: an underground river! Here, in the desert, with no apparent water clear to the horizon in any direction.

Full of their discovery, they went back to their camp and took the foreman into their confidence. This worthy, being a cagey fellow, bought their knowledge with the promise of the magnificent sum of one hundred and fifty dollars—a fortune for cowboys working for thirty dollars a month.

No one had much use for this dried-out area which lay too far from water for any practical use. And so the foreman filed his claim and bought it. In a short time he got some backing and, with great difficulty, his "combine" purchased, and with teams of horses brought out, a large steam engine to the site. Great tanks made of stone were constructed, and then Mexicans were hired, and they began to lay waste with single and double-bitted axes to every tree that lay within twenty miles of the place in order to provide fuel for the steam-powered pump.

And that's when the big herds began to come through, sometimes as many as three or four thousand head of cattle would mill about, impatiently fighting for their chance at the water troughs and tanks. But then the wood for the steam-powered pump played out, and about that same time the railroad came to Colorado City, and the days of the cattle drives to Kansas died off. Besides, ranchers had begun to fence their pastures in some places, making the great cattle drives almost impossible.

The Noelkes ended up by buying out that quick-witted foreman who had purchased the property where the underground water lay, and so it meant they had a means of life at hand for their increasing herds. But now, with the advent of the windmill, they didn't have to try to fire up the hulking steam engine. This rusted away off to one side of the wooden tower of the windmill with its wooden blades which made a constant creaking noise, together with the repetitive sound of the sucker rod, heaving up and down.

Tom put down his saddle, having no bedroll or blanket, and slept a few hours beside the great stone tanks and far-spread watering troughs

where all those thousands of cattle had once milled about. And in less than a minute he fell into a dreamless sleep.

On the second day of his trip, Tom got an early start. He didn't know what time it was, just that he'd been feeling his way along in the dark for almost two hours when the welcome dawn spread a pink chalky shadow along the eastern horizon behind him, while he traveled toward the waiting blackness. Then, with the early morning shadows stretching strangely before him, he did his best to forget the hunger pangs that gripped his stomach.

During those hours a slow rage caught him by the throat. The one thing he'd made himself thrust off to one side was the brutal killing of his friends from the Lazy E. More like family than friends, really. For many years he'd trusted his and Sally's lives and all he had to them. Old Santiago Acosta had stood by him at the showdown at Three Points. Along with members of his family from Durango in Old Mexico, they'd held off the superior numbers of their enemies in the brief range war that followed. Santiago had stayed with him through thick and thin. Luis Batalla and Pepe Moya and Benito Acosta, Santiago's son, were with the bunch who rode up to help him when all hell broke loose at Black Horse, Montana. Juan Suarez had been with him as well through all those hard times. And now all five of them, riding in to get him away from the hangman's noose, had fallen into a trap laid for them—and had been butchered. They never had a chance. And he, Tom English, had been the bait used to lure them.

A shudder ran through his body and a hotness built within his head. "The men who planned this thing will answer to me," he said to himself. A razored flare ran through him and he said, "I'll be seeing the judge and the sheriff before this thing is over." For an instant he could see the remembered faces of T. J. Hoskins and Reuben Baxter, and then he shook his head. He had unconsciously reined his paint to a stop and almost turned around, but then he got control of himself and headed west again.

Late that afternoon Tom reached friendly landscape about fourteen miles west of Ozona. Earlier he had passed by the Turkey Roost ranch and rode for hours through Cyrus Lafayette Broome's spread. That old gentleman, a former Confederate officer, had returned after the war to the ruins of his plantation near Utica, Mississippi. Because of trouble he never discussed, which happened during the first year of Reconstruction, he and his wife had moved all the way to West Texas, staying some

of the time near Fort Concho, a while near Sherwood, and now had
made their way clear out here.

Seeing familiar sights, thinking of his friends in this isolated community, Tom fought off the temptation to go see them. His wife's older
sister had been married to a man from there before her death, so Tom
had a distant link as a sort of kinsman of one of the "insiders" in this
clannish town.

But even friends talked, and in any little town gossip was a thing that
spread like a contagious disease. If he were sighted by someone, the
word would spread into every nook and cranny of the village. No use
taking such a chance, and so he circled until he reached the ranchland
held by the Couch family. He saw Armand Couch's house in the distance, bunkhouse off to the left side, a barn and pens behind it. Smoke
came from the chimney, Florence would be cooking supper, and with a
sudden weakness, he pulled up before their place. Armand came out,
carrying a rifle, then a great smile crossed his face.

"Well, I'll be blessed if it ain't the meanest man in West Texas come
to see me. Get on down from there and come in the house."

Tom dismounted stiffly, tied his horse and loosened the girth, and
made ready to go inside. It always shook him when people addressed
him with this title. He'd got it a long, long time before when the gunfighter who had once borne that sinister nickname called him out into
the street. When the smoke cleared, only Tom had remained standing.
That was when his fame had begun to spread. And since those remote
days things had gotten completely out of hand. The newspapers and
the pulp fiction writers had published all manner of stories about him.
They couldn't imagine how that would affect his life, prompting ambitious gunslingers and even raw young kids he'd never met to try to draw
down on him. Not to mention inflaming the passions of his many enemies, the kinsmen and friends of those who had fallen before his guns.
Taking a deep breath, he ignored the form of salutation and circled
around behind his horse. Armand hadn't meant to cause him any concern by calling him that, he was only making fun, which was something
you had to expect from Armand Couch.

Armand's great horny hand surrounded that of his guest, and he
shook his welcome vigorously. "Howdy, Tom."

"Well, Armand, it's been a spell."

"Yes, it has. Last I heard, they were fixin' to hang you, old friend. Did
they change their minds?"

Tom walked into the house with Armand right behind him. "No," he

answered, "I'm afraid they haven't, so I'd be obliged if you didn't mention my passing by this way."

At that moment Florence, a bone-thin attractive woman, though she must have been close to forty, around Armand's age, came running in to hug her unexpected visitor. She chattered on about how she missed seeing Sally, asked about the kids, talked about hers, and brought Tom a big cup of coffee. Off to one side Armand pulled a bottle of rye whiskey from a cabinet and filled a glass for Tom.

He received these gratefully, taking alternative sips of coffee and swallows of that rye whiskey. On an empty stomach, it wasn't long until his head began to whirl.

Armand waved off his wife, who approached him with a cup and the big iron coffeepot, muttering that he had few enough times to celebrate things, and he intended to take full advantage of this occasion. Then, seating his tall frame comfortably in a heavy rocking chair, he sampled his whiskey with obvious satisfaction, winked at his wife, and turned toward Tom.

"Going back to Montana—or will you hole up down at your place on the border, at the Circle X? Or keep on going and ride into Old Mexico clear out of sight?"

"Haven't quite decided, Armand."

"Well, whichever way you're headed, you need to get better mounted. That paint sounds like a broke accordion. And the saddle looks like something my Aunt Josie would have thrown away. You got good credit with me so, by your leave, I'll let you pick through my remuda for a horse that'll get you where you want to go. And just by chance I have an extra saddle that ought to suit you just fine."

During supper they insisted that Tom stay with them in their home instead of in the bunkhouse. After a halfhearted argument, Tom willingly gave in; he was so tired by then that he didn't protest when Armand took his horse to the pens and unsaddled him. By the time Armand got back, Florence had led their guest to the small room which he would share with a sleeping baby boy, their latest addition, one they had named Bert. "He's the dearest thing I ever saw," Florence murmured, but Armand told her she said that about every one of the babies they'd ever had. But he sounded proud too and said, "I reckon I'll make a cowboy out of this tadpole."

The next morning early Tom shared a hearty breakfast with his hosts and then the men joined the cowboys at daybreak. The wrangler had brought in about thirty horses and they milled around the corral. Tom

took a perch on the top rail and looked them over. One in particular caught his eye: a dark bay with his head and tail carried high. He wasn't oversized, maybe a little over fifteen hands, but he had a deep wide chest and well-muscled sloping shoulders and strong hindquarters. A gelding, he had a white star-shaped patch on his forehead and looked alert. Fine big eyes, ears tipped forward, heavy neck held back; Tom couldn't keep his eyes off him.

"Oh, hell," Armand groaned, "you done what I most feared, you're going to run off with my new Morgan horse. I can't believe a friend would do such a thing to me."

When Tom protested that he sure wouldn't do that, Armand laughed out loud and said he was going to insist Tom take him all the same. "If you have to run for your life, I certainly hope you'll be able to get away, and with that Morgan you might be able to do it."

Tom insisted on paying for this animal and for the fine saddle, which had a bedroll with a poncho tied across the skirts behind it, as well as a Navajo saddle blanket. Over Armand's vigorous protests, Tom told him to go see Max Hall at the First National Bank the next time he went to Santa Rita. He gave Armand a note to take to Max, noting a generous price and requesting that the funds be paid out of the Lazy E account.

After that he went off to the side of his barn, hunkered down, and wrote a short letter to Sally. Armand would see that she got it. Tom wrote her that he was fine, that he'd get in touch, and then told her how much she meant to him. Tom sent his love to Rebecca and to the baby, Ben Westbrook English, thinking at the time what a long name that was for a little fellow. The letter couldn't say all he felt, but Sally would understand. And because she'd been with him through so many tight spots, he knew she had the nerves to stand this latest batch of problems.

When Tom returned to the corral two men were having a terrible time getting the Morgan saddled. His eyes rolled, and he pulled back and shied away. Finally one of the cowboys put a bandana over his eyes, hung on his neck, pulling his head down, and the other got the saddle on and cinched it tight.

Armand said, "Tom, it's a cool fresh mornin' and your new horse is feelin' frisky. He's actually half quarter horse, and it looks to me like that half is all riled up right now. Maybe we ought to let my bronc buster, ol' Muley Pike here, top him off for you." But Tom said he'd have to get acquainted with his new horse sooner or later, and since he

couldn't ask Muley Pike to ride along with him on his trip, he'd just as soon get the process started now.

Without hesitating, Tom stepped into the saddle, found his stirrups just as one of the boys pulled the bandana off, and the Morgan instantly reared straight up, almost falling backward, but Tom whacked him over the ears with his hat. And then the rodeo commenced, with the Morgan making prodigious, twisting leaps and bone-jarring landings on stiff legs. As he bucked, the bay made a high whistling noise, sounding almost like a scream, while he got spurs raked from his neck to his belly on every buck he made. And then he stopped, still bowed up and trembling, before finally relaxing.

All the men were laughing, and they looked with admiration at the way Tom sat the horse, solidly but with total balance, looking as if there wouldn't be a way in all the world that he might get thrown.

"Looks to me like that Morgan and you have come to some kind of compromise agreement," Armand said.

"I most certainly hope so," Tom replied, breathing heavily, "for I think this bay quit just before I did."

Then he rode around the corral with the horse acting as if nothing out of the ordinary had happened.

"He ain't been rode in a few weeks; he don't normally act that way," a cowboy said.

"What's his name?" Tom asked.

"Haven't come up with one," Armand answered. "With more than a hundred horses on the place, I find it hard to get a name for all of them. Been callin' him 'that Morgan bay,' although, as I said, he's got quarter-horse blood too."

Florence had prepared a large store of provisions for Tom to carry, along with two canteens of water, since he was riding into dry territory. He had sat at the breakfast table and talked in general about where the water lay, to the west and northwest, for he had rarely gone this direction. So now, feeling as prepared as he was likely to be, he grinned at all the men, said he hoped to see them in the future, and at last leaned over, shaking hands one last time with Armand. He waved at Florence, who had come out from the house, and rode off toward the rolling low hills lying to the west.

An old familiar feeling crawled up the back of his neck. He'd felt it many times before, and when it came he knew he was on the verge of danger, of real trouble.

# TEN

SALLY ENGLISH had lost weight, something she had wanted to do for some time, but now she didn't even notice it. Her cheekbones stood out, and her dress seemed to hang on her. Sitting in Cele Hall's living room, she picked up a cup of freshly brewed tea and noticed that her hand trembled. She watched the tremor, saw the tea almost spilling, but couldn't help it. Deliberately, she put the cup down carefully on the delicate table next to her chair.

Max came into his house and joined his wife and Sally. He had a drawn expression as he stalked in, his heavy footsteps jarring the floor. He faced away from them, standing before a large, dark mahogany sideboard with a carved decorative apron scalloped under its massive top, supported by elaborate curving cabriole legs ending in ball and claw feet. This was among the remnants of his heritage which Max's father had brought south.

Max poured a crystal glass full of amber whiskey from a decanter and drank deeply from it before sitting down.

"It came out the way we expected, Sally. I did my best to represent Tom, but they railroaded the damn thing through." He paused, embarrassed, and said, "Sorry about the language."

Sally smiled wanly, automatically, hardly thinking of his words, trying to show her appreciation for his support. She knew that Max would give his life for Tom, they'd been best friends for so long now. "What happened at the courthouse, Max? Tell me so I can understand."

"Julian Haynes brought in a lawyer from out of town, from Dallas. Some of the meanest lawyers in kingdom come live there, as we all know." Max slugged down another swallow, screwed up his face, and coughed.

"He filed a case claiming his client had a right of easement to the Concho. His lawyer said that, historically, the Dawsons and others west of the Concho had watered their herds there. The lawyer brought up all

sorts of cases as precedents. Now, for all I know, none of this was right. We didn't have a lawyer for our side; the only one in town is Jedediah Jackson and he's off to Austin, trying to get some help for Tom. Anyway, Judge Hoskins listened to him, then I got up and so did several others, and we did our best to argue that a man has the right to fence his ranch, there doesn't seem much doubt in anybody's mind as to that, but Hoskins said he had to go by the law, and in about ten minutes he said that he'd given full deliberation to the matter and was forced to agree with the Dallas lawyer."

Max stopped speaking, looking first at Cele and then at Sally before concluding, "To sum it up, the judge said Julian Haynes had the right of easement.

"Then I jumped up and said that maybe the Dawsons had watered their herds there, but that Tom English had long ago bought them out, and the ranches out west of the former Dawson land lay more than twenty miles away, that no herds could make it in to water from such a distance and then go back out. There sure as hell had been no historical practice of herds coming to water from way out yonder, so the lawyer's argument made no sense at all. Then I told the judge that what he was doing was the same as confiscating Tom English's private property, because those cattle belonging to Julian Haynes would come on the English ranches and eat their grass, and that didn't seem right at all."

Max, his tanned face turning dark with anger, looked at Cele and at Sally, eyes smoldering. "The judge just said to me, 'If there is a right of easement to get to water dating back historically to the Dawsons, there don't seem to be no reason to say that it don't belong to other folks the same as it did to them.' Then the Dallas lawyer began to talk about 'riparian' rights, whatever that means, and the limitations on them, and then he cited other cases, which might have had something to do with the situation or maybe they didn't, how should I know?"

Max gritted his teeth and poured himself another glass of whiskey at the sideboard. "But the upshot of all of this is that Judge Hoskins ruled in favor of Julian Haynes. It appears that Haynes, with all that dry land he foreclosed on out west of Tom's ranches, had to find some water. It turns out that he's got a contract, if you can believe this, to supply some ten thousand head of one- and two-year-old steers and heifers to the XIT up in the panhandle this coming year, and so his bank has started calling notes right and left, taking over ranches, accelerating due dates, doing all sorts of damn things.

"Haynes had them sign over their rights to their cattle when they

were getting what they thought was nothing but some temporary loans to tide them over, and now he has said that because they're behind on their interest payments he has clauses in their notes to accelerate them, which is another way of saying that the entire notes are immediately due and payable. Well, you know as well as I do that there is not a chance that those men can come up with all that money. They put those loans into feed and into buying livestock with the understanding that they would 'calve out,' which is to say, over time, they'd be able to pay off their debts. That's the way all of us bankers have had to work with cowmen, the way my bank does it, the only way it can possibly work in this country. Technically, it looks like Julian Haynes has the right to take over a lot of ranches and all those herds, but he's made some enemies all of a sudden who are fighting mad. Be that as it may, the big problem we've got is with his actually getting the right to use the Lazy E with some legal tricks as if it were his own—free of charge."

Max got control of himself, and his voice lowered somewhat in volume. "The foreman running the ranches for Haynes is a hard-nosed man from El Paso, the place where Haynes seems to get all his top hired hands, and that includes Judge Hoskins and Sheriff Baxter. The foreman is nothing more than a killer, a man named Eli Jones. Calvin Laudermilk knows him, and told me once that Eli always wears his shirt buttoned clear up to his throat in hot weather and cold so as to cover up his scales. I asked Calvin what he meant by that—you know Calvin—and he answered that this was because Eli is half reptile and the other half, which is human, is embarrassed about the fact."

Max laughed in spite of himself. "But that doesn't mean that he hasn't got a feared reputation. I understand that he and Haynes's other top men have recruited some fifty or sixty cowboys, most of them renegades, and all heavily armed. Haynes, I understand, has ordered Eli Jones to have his men bring those herds he foreclosed on to the old Jameson ranch he took over west of the Lazy E."

Max looked into Sally's eyes, noting their confusion, and continued. "After getting that court order saying he has an 'easement,' which is the legal term, I understand, meaning the right to cross another man's land, it would be my guess that he has men cutting your fences as we sit here talking. When his herds mix with Tom's and his men go in to drive them away and cut out the young ones for the drive north to the XIT, I don't see how they can keep from mixing in a lot of Lazy E cattle. It looks to me like the dadblamedest type of rustling, with an excuse that

it's legal because some judge from El Paso who works for Haynes has signed a piece of paper."

The three sat for a moment, then Sally asked, "What do you think we should do?"

"I've got to talk to Jedediah some way," Max said. "We're going to have to get some real lawmen to help us. Some of our friends are off toward Marfa trying to run down John Robert Hale. We need a Texas Ranger around here, and I got a rumor that he's out in that part of the state. In the meantime, we need to get word to Hester Trace to see if there is anything her cowboys can do to slow down Julian Haynes's men."

Max said to Sally, "You're acquainted with most of the cowboys who work for your neighbor, Hester Trace, I expect."

"Yes."

"There's one among them, Asa Coltrane, who has a past most don't know about."

"I know Asa Coltrane well. We had him on our place for a long time after that low-life Milo Studly shot him last year."

Max sat down beside his wife, his anger having cooled. He said, "I know all about that, Sally." He paused, taking time to light a cigar, a ceremony which he never rushed. As he did so he thought of Asa Coltrane. He was a fine-looking young fellow when he first rode into the Concho River Valley. Came from South Texas after running into trouble. The other cowboys used to call him "Pretty Boy" Coltrane, but after he flattened one or two of them they only said that behind his back. With time he got scarred up, the weather hardened him, and the years did too—so the men stopped using that old nickname.

Max said, "I'm sorry—got to thinking about Asa." He said to Sally, "I'm aware of the debt he owes to you and Tom for all you've done for him. He spent months on your place, living in Santiago Acosta's house, with Lupe Acosta and you nursing him during his recuperation. Needless to say, he got to be awfully close to the Acostas and the other Mexican ranch hands during that time."

Max paused a moment reflectively, saying softly, "I can't bring myself to believe that Santiago and those other fine men are dead. That has to prey on Asa's mind even more than mine—he spent so much more time with them."

The women waited for Max to collect himself as he chewed on his cigar. Finally he continued, "All I'm saying is that Asa Coltrane has

every reason to go out of his way to give us a hand. If he can do that, maybe he can delay things while we get help from other directions."

Sally nodded. "Asa's a good friend. I think the world of him and the other cowboys working at Hester's. Turner Hopewell, their foreman, and Severn Laycon and Ira Turnbull are the salt of the earth. I wouldn't be surprised if Blue wouldn't pitch in and help too." This last man, a freed former slave, not only served as cook at the Trace cattle camps and bunkhouse but also had turned into a fine cowhand, although he said he preferred to concentrate on his cooking.

Sally continued, "While I don't know what they can do to help, it wouldn't hurt to talk to them." She rose from her chair. "In fact, sitting around here won't do us any good. I'm going to ride for Hester's ranch tonight."

"Better wait for daylight," Cele implored, rising and going to her friend, touching her arm.

"Thanks, Cele, but I know I won't sleep a wink anyway." She moved toward the stairs to go to the guest room she'd been using. "I better change clothes," she said matter-of-factly. Then she added, "Don't worry. I was raised on horseback; besides, I know the country between here and the Lazy E like the back of my hand. Before breakfast tomorrow, I'll be at Hester's place. I'll be riding Tom's old horse Judge, and I doubt that anyone alive can catch me, even if they try."

Seeing that they couldn't dissuade her, Cele ran to the kitchen to prepare provisions for the trip. Sally would be riding just about thirty-two miles that night to reach the Lazy E headquarters, and then another eight before she got to the Trace ranch.

"You sure you don't want me to go with you?" Max inquired when she returned downstairs.

Sally laughed. "Max, you mean well and I love you like a brother, but a man your size—and one who spends his time behind a desk—would only slow me down. The best thing you can do is to get word to John Robert Hale. And you might send a telegram to Austin to try to get hold of Jedediah to let him know we need help real bad."

"They tell me the telegraph wire's still down," Max said, "but if so, I'll send a man north to Colorado City. There's bound to be one operating there."

A short time later the three friends went outside where Sally, without waiting for help, quickly saddled her horse. Wearing tight-fitting denim pants and a checkered shirt, and pulling down a curl-brimmed old cowboy hat around her ears, she looked more like a slender nineteen-

year-old boy than the mature mother of two children, although her full
breasts took away from this illusion. With a nod, she bade her friends
farewell and reined the big horse Judge around and spurred him into a
brisk trot.

Elvira East, a wrapper around her long dressing gown, opened the
front door late that night with an alarmed expression on her face. Then,
with a muffled cry of amazement, she put both hands to her cheeks.
"What on *earth*, Mr. Laudermilk! I can't believe my eyes."

"I had to turn about in mid-flight, my dear, for I had neglected to say
farewell to you."

She looked at him uncomprehendingly. "They say you committed
murder, you and that Indian, and that they plan to hunt you down and
hang you." Tears filled her eyes suddenly, and one of them rolled down
her face.

Calvin stumped forward and took her in his arms. "There, there, my
dear," he said, surprised and pleased at her reaction.

Enjoying the embrace, he pulled her enthusiastically to him, raising
her tearful face with one hand, and gently kissed her.

Trembling, she pulled away, touching her mouth with her fingers.
"Calvin," she said weakly, using his first name without thinking. This,
for Elvira, was a marked show of intimacy.

Calvin did not realize that she was on the trembling verge of casting
off a lifetime habit of restraint.

Without warning, the ample-bodied Elvira flung herself forward with
considerable energy, not to mention passion, and almost threw Calvin
off his balance, in spite of his having the bulk of about two natural men
inside his single frame.

In full retreat, with boot heels thumping mightily, Calvin left the
house, a great smile wreathing his face. He called over his shoulder,
"Farewell, my dear. Keep me in your thoughts." And to the waiting
figure, holding the reins to both of their mounts and fidgeting impatiently in the shadows of a nearby oak tree, he whispered, "Now, let's
get over to Miss Hattie's where I keep my emergency money, and then
get the hell out of here."

Tuck Bowlegs shook his head, totally mystified, and said, "You said
we had to get some cash to live on was why we had to turn around and
come back. I thought that was what you were doing in there."

"By no means," Calvin responded vaguely, still overwhelmed by his
own gallantry. "I was speaking to my 'light of love,' as the poets say."

Tuck grunted. Then he said as the two rode through the charcoal night, "That 'light of love' looked plenty heavy to me."

"I forgive you, Tuck," said Calvin. "Forgiveness is numbered among the various virtues that Christians have. It's only one of many things that make us superior to the heathen Chinee, the murderous Indians, and all of those sons of bitches who are chasin' us."

"Let's get the money," Tuck said. "No more talk."

Carefully the two men circled the scattered houses on the western side of the small village, then rode back east on a winding trail that more or less paralleled the dirt road called Concho Street. Reaching the rear of a well-proportioned white frame house, Calvin pulled Sully to a stop and said, "Here is where I do my private banking, Tuck. Come on in with me."

"In here?" Tuck asked, astounded.

"Surely," Calvin said, sounding hurt, "you aren't going to act like a prude, Tuck."

Tuck stood impassively, disdaining a reply.

"I mean, just because the ladies of the night who grace our town make this their lodging, I surely wouldn't think you'd be one of those close-minded chaps who'd hold their occupation against them."

"Indians, when they reach their man-stage, get their own lodge. After that, girls and women come see them." Tuck's eyes narrowed. He would never understand the white man. And this particular cultural peculiarity had always puzzled him. "All the time I spent with the Comanche, even on the reservation, we never had no places like this." He decided to think no more about it, banishing from his thoughts all questions which related to the industry of prostitution and why it seemed to thrive wherever the white man lived.

"You heathens don't understand that we civilized folks protect the gentler sex from being affected by nature's fierce appetites, which only strike the male of our species, and so by this means we let off steam, in a manner of speaking, and can be gracious and courteous to the fair ladies of our community who turn a blind eye to such places as this."

"Your money inside that place?"

"Yes."

Tuck tied Jug, his tired long-eared mule, to the same limb where the Percheron had his reins looped. "Don't forget that there are men around here somewhere planning on killin' us," Tuck said, following Calvin's lead around to the front of the house. The sounds of a piano tinkled faintly in the background.

"Jesus Christ," a woman's deep voice roared when they entered the door, "if it ain't my darlin' Calvin Laudermilk." The hefty female stood, arms akimbo, and examined him. She wore an off-the-shoulder gown revealing broad shoulders and a great slope of bosom with an awesome amount of cleavage dusted liberally with white powder which she displayed with obvious pride.

"Howdy, Miss Hattie," Calvin boomed, looking absolutely delighted. "What a great pleasure it is to see you."

"Thought they'd of hunted you down before now, honey, and I feared you'd departed for the hereafter. Come on in this house and sit down." Looking behind him, she spied Tuck and said, sputtering, "A lot of things go on in here—I ain't one for worryin' my head with right and wrong—but, hell's bells, Calvin, you got to know I have some hard and fast rules which I'll by God not break."

"Tuck is my great and good friend, Hattie. He is not disposed to enter into trade this evening in your establishment and is with me as my specially invited guest. I've told him of my fondness for you, and I'll appreciate your extending to him your far-famed cordiality."

"Calvin, you big ol' son of a bitch, you could charm the birds right out of the trees."

Moments later Tuck and Calvin found themselves seated side by side on a velvet settee, and they looked about at two young women, carelessly attired in loose-fitting dresses, slouched on the arms of chairs nearby, winking and grinning shamelessly.

Off beside the wall a black man played upon the upright piano, jangling from it a catchy tune, patting his foot, wagging his head, singing in a low voice, but they couldn't quite catch the words of the lyrics.

Miss Hattie brought them brimming beakers of foaming beer which Calvin gulped while Tuck, looking most uncomfortable, tasted tentatively.

"Hattie, my dear, I've left a stash in your room upstairs, and I'd be most obliged if you'd fetch it for me. As much as I like my time here, there are folks about who are flat unfriendly, and I'm going to have to be on my way."

"You wouldn't want to rest up just a spell with Nora May or Flippy, or both of them at once, would you?"

"Why of course I would, although they'd be second choice to you, old hon', but time is of the essence."

"I do like to hear you talk," the madam chuckled, her voice as low as a man's. "But I can understand your hurry, so I'll go get that sack of cash

you left with me for a rainy day. Just thought we might lighten your
load by taking a little out of that sack. Only two dollars; sure you won't
change your mind?"

"For both of them?"

Tuck growled, "For God's sake, Calvin."

"He's right," Calvin said to Miss Hattie, although reluctantly. "Besides, I have fallen in love and am fixin' to change my ways. I am also
facing a possibility which may require me to confess my sins, and I have
enough of them without adding to the list."

"Well, bless my soul," Miss Hattie said. "Fallen in love? That don't
sound like the Calvin I know, although you've always had a streak of
romance in you. When I think of Calvin Laudermilk it puts me in mind
of that workhorse you ride, a great big old handsome stud, and I don't
wonder that some woman would cast her eye on you. But when this
fancy falls away, you come on back here and we'll pick up right where
we left off. That is, if you should live that long, which don't seem likely,
now that I think about it."

Bare shoulders shaking with laughter, Miss Hattie swayed up the
stairs, broad hips wagging.

The music filled the air while Calvin finished off his beer and sig-
naled to Nora May for a refill. Then he said solemnly to Tuck, "I'm an
expert when it comes to judging fine whorehouse piano playing." And
then, with a barely perceptible wink, he added, "This is a natural talent
—not an acquired one."

Tuck sat nervously on the edge of the velvet settee. He drew out his
long sheath knife absently and began to whet its razor edge by sliding it
back and forth over the callused palm of his left hand. The young girl
named Flippy, seeing the black eyes of the Indian set fixedly upon her
tousled golden hair, began to back away and then, murmuring that all of
a sudden she felt puny, ran up the stairs toward safety.

Moments later, after Hattie brought Calvin his money, a clattering of
horses' hooves could be heard careening down the dirt road outside.

"With your leave, my dear," Calvin said, "my friend and I will depart
through your back door but we'll look forward to another more fulfilling
time together in the near future."

"Calvin," Miss Hattie said, alarm spreading across her features, "stop
talking and ride for your life!"

# ELEVEN

CALVIN AND TUCK slipped out of Santa Rita in the midnight blackness and rode on the south side of the river below the point where the North and South Concho came together, on the long meandering way of the main branch of the Concho toward its junction with the Colorado. After eight or ten miles they decided they were safe enough, hearing no sounds of pursuit, so they picked out a place to pass what was left of the night. A dark camp, no fire, and hard ground for a mattress. This last did not affect Tuck, who instantly fell asleep, but caused great concern to Calvin, who lay first on one side and then the other, swearing monotonously, cursing the fates that had placed him not only in danger but in such discomfort. However, when dawn broke, his humor improved.

They found a crossing, forded the river, and headed in a southeasterly direction. The longer they rode, the more Calvin's disposition improved. He was in fine fettle when at last they reached the range which he had once owned, rocky ground with rolling hills, not that far from Fort McKavett.

Calvin pulled to a stop and waved his hand in a princely gesture. "Once all of this belonged to me. Almost as far as the eye can see, if you're half blind. But it was *mine,* and I lived here for many years."

"Why didn't you keep it?"

"Tuck, you cannot imagine the difficulties I endured. Bought cattle high and sold them low—if they didn't die for lack of water. All nature conspired against me, not to mention the dastardly actions of unscrupulous cattle traders. I wasn't suited for the harsh environment where those men live."

"Who owns it now?"

"Well, all that over yonder was bought by J. J. Powell and his pretty twin sisters, and from this point on clear to the far horizon is under the control of Theron Cargile. And beyond that we've got a combination of

Raineys and Rusts who have the most of it." He waved an arm, adding, "And on west of there is the range of the Marches and young Compton. Of course, these families have been here over the years; I was just around for a brief while. A man of my disposition belongs in town where there are sociable folks around. It's a hard thing to live alone out on the prairie.

"It won't be far until we find Clear Creek, where old Fritzie used to live. Had him a goat he fed beer to, and the damn goat would get drunk and stumble all around the yard. Made old Fritz half die of laughter. Those of us forced to live in isolation have got to take our fun where we can find it."

They had ridden another two hours when Tuck raised a hand. "Two men on foot down there," the Indian said.

Tuck and Calvin pulled their horses up short and sat on the ridge, watching two figures down below, weapons in their hands, stalking through the shinnery and underbrush, past the cactus and over rocks.

After a moment a gentle smile crossed Calvin's face. "These are my former neighbors, Tuck. I'd like to say a word to them before we head on."

As they approached they saw two very tall, angular, large-boned men walking along, holding shotguns. Each wore a dirty canvas vest, dark with old dried bloodstains and a few wispy gray feathers stuck here and there. Both wore ancient hunting boots which they must have owned for many years; they were white with age and ragged, with a few peeling strips of leather hanging from them.

One of the hunters had darker hair and a large handsome head. He stopped and waited imperiously. The other, wearing a fairly narrow-brimmed cowboy hat, crumpled with age, the right side of the brim curled higher from where he'd handled it over the years, was also a large man but a bit leaner and with a thinner face than his companion. He too was a fine-looking man, but he had at this moment an attitude of severity. Neither of them smiled or said a single word. No sign of recognition or greeting came from them.

Effusively, Calvin Laudermilk said, "By God, it's good to see you. My old neighbors, out here as fearless as ever." Turning to Tuck, he explained, "Theron Cargile and Ephraim Rainey are dear friends of mine. They patrol the land and if attacked by doves or quail they fight them off. It's a never-ending battle, and you'd think the birds would have given up by now. They must bank on winning due to their great num-

bers. But even at this time of year, out of season, these old boys are out
to protect their properties from those feathered invaders."

The darker-haired man, the one with the great square face, said, "I
hardly recognized you, Calvin. Don't know I ever saw you when you
weren't in a chair or on a bar stool."

"Cargile, you friendly bastard, I knew you'd be glad to see me. This
here is Tuck Bowlegs, my companion, and we're on our way to get on
the trail to Menard so as to head off Jedediah Jackson, who's coming
back this way from Austin."

And then the tall man's face broke into a curl-lipped smile, and his
features lightened, and it was as if a stormy sky had been split by a shaft
of clearest sunlight. He began to laugh, deep tones coming clear from
his chest. "Calvin, you haven't changed a bit."

Rainey also smiled, the hardness vanishing from his fine blue eyes,
and he said, "Jessie and I came over to spend some time with Sass and
Theron Cargile. We'd all be happy to have you stop by and have a meal
with us."

"No time for that, I fear," Calvin responded. "My friend and I
wouldn't think of interrupting a serious hunt, so we'll be on our way."

The two laconic hunters, faces blank again, nodded and without a
word proceeded down a draw, eyes alert for any moving thing. Eager
for the kill.

As Calvin and Tuck rode on, Calvin babbled and Tuck kept his eyes
alertly open, looking for threats, turning frequently to look behind him.

"Those two are a pair," Calvin stated. "Never for the life of me could
I understand how they could tempt such fine-looking women to be their
wives. I marvel how men who barely say six words a day could have
managed to attract such delightful ladies. Theron Cargile is married to
little Sass Willoughby, who's not bigger than a minute and is pretty as a
picture. She's wasted her life out here with an old cowboy like him. She
ought to be in Philadelphia or New York or someplace big where there
would be society and she'd be appreciated.

"And Ephraim Rainey had the blind luck to wed Jessie Gordon, who
is descended from John Y. Rust. Jessie is one of God's finest and most
courageous creatures. No matter how much trouble she's ever had,
she's got so much love for all mankind that it absolutely glows. A lovely,
lovely woman. If you weren't a fearsome redskin I'd-a took you in to
meet them, but they're both too gentle to stand the sight of the likes of
you, and I chose to spare them the shock of such a confrontation."

"Fat Man, in a little while I'm goin' to catch a few catfish or bass and

cook them. If you'll stop makin' so much noise, I may let you have some."

"You understand exactly how to appeal to my better nature, Tuck. No one knows me better in all the world." With his stomach growling and his mouth watering, Calvin reined his big horse down the slope leading to Clear Creek.

Three of the men who worked for Hester Trace, the widow of Roy Trace, saddled their horses, checked their weapons, and prepared to leave the Lazy E, the collection of ranches put together over the years by Tom and Sally English. The Trace cowboys had been helping out most of the time lately on the ranch owned by their neighbors after the deaths of the five Mexican hands who had tried to break Tom out of jail. This circumstance had left this part of the Lazy E without a single cowboy to care for the stock.

Sally English had come in the dark of early morning, told them in brief terms about the pending invasion of the Lazy E by the great herds now assembled by Julian Haynes. And she explained the little she knew about the men Haynes had hired, laying emphasis on the fact that people in town said Eli Jones, the gunfighter, was heading them.

"We'll need help," Severn Laycon at last remarked, after a large gulp. And so they had ridden with Sally to the Trace ranch, some eight miles to the north.

After they arrived, Sally spent some time with her daughter Rebecca and with Hester, before coming out to talk to them again. "It's hard for me to ask you to take this risk, boys." Distress showed on her pretty face; her full lips parted as she hesitated before adding, "If Tom were here he'd think of something." She said, "I checked at the other ranches, hoping I could find some of our men, but all of them were out in cow camps somewhere, not a soul was around." She stopped, obviously feeling helpless.

And, of course, they had no choice about the matter. If trouble came to Trace land they one and all knew that Tom English would be the first to lend a hand. So, changing to fresh horses which they chose with great care, they slowly rode away—without an actual plan.

The foreman, Turner Hopewell, rode in front with Asa Coltrane by him. Behind them, sitting easily in their saddles, were slope-shouldered Blue, the ebony-faced former slave, carrying a long-barreled buffalo gun that weighed more than two Winchesters, and Severn Laycon, with a

six-shooter and his saddle gun, and at his side rode Ira Turnbull, also heavily armed.

Turner Hopewell, a man of middle age, looked troubled. "During the late trouble," he said in low tones to Asa Coltrane, "I rode with Hood's Texans. Through the glory years and later through horrors that most men can't even imagine. I was a private then, and since that time I've only met two others who bore that rank. Now, when I see veterans in town or in the bars, they all claim to have been lieutenants at the very least. Most claim to have been colonels. Jackson Sadler and I decided that he and I had been the only privates in the Confederate Army during the whole damn Civil War. So we set it up—made it formal. Gandy Chandler heard about it, said he'd been a private too, so now we've got what we call the Privates Club. Damned exclusive. Only us three members."

He rode without speaking for a long time. Then he said, "I ordinarily never speak about the war."

Asa nodded, knowing he'd never heard him mention it before.

Then Turner said, "The point is that I know something about going up against long odds—and there are some tricks you don't forget. We may need to bring one or two of them into play if things are like Miss Sally fears. But I hope to God she's wrong."

Asa didn't give him an answer, not that Turner expected one. Asa kept looking straight ahead, his weathered features, handsome as those of a carved Greek statue, stoic as he rode silently beside the foreman. Asa had a fine thin scar running through his left eyebrow. Another scar showed faintly on his left cheekbone. Out of sight was a great ragged red patch where a heavy forty-five slug had broken through his collarbone and a rib before lodging against his shoulder blade in his back. This had come about only the year before when in a poker game, for no good reason, a half-insane drifter named Milo Studly had tried to force a gunfight on friendly Severn Laycon. Asa had stepped between the men and coldly informed Studly that if he insisted on a showdown Asa would oblige him. Without warning, Milo had shot Asa down before he'd had a chance to arm himself.

Somehow Asa had lived through that. Big Lucy, Blue's wife, with the aid of Hester Trace, had taken him in a buggy to the Lazy E ranch headquarters. There, with Sally English acting as his nurse along with Lupe, Santiago Acosta's wife, and with the attention of old Doc Starret, Asa had pulled through. And for some months he had recuperated in the little house where Santiago and his family lived.

It had remained for Tom English to take revenge on Milo Studly, and it had happened in a most peculiar way. But this was something else that Asa didn't care to remember.

None of the cowboys in the wide and distant reaches of West Texas where men from time to time decide to move on, going from ranch to ranch, question another man's past. But word had come that Asa Coltrane had left South Texas under a cloud, had been on the run from the ranch which lay near the border not far from Reynosa in Old Mexico where he'd cowboyed ever since he was a kid. They knew that Asa had killed a man down there, but they respected his silence. The past should stay behind and not be mentioned.

Turner, breaking the tense silence, said, "Asa, whenever Sally English turns up you get right red in the face. She sure seems to have a strong effect on you."

Asa coughed and said that he, like all the rest, had a high regard for that lady. Then he clamped his mouth and Turner saw there'd be no more talk, that the conversation, if it could be called that, had ended.

The horse Asa had picked out, a sleepy sorrel called Dreamer, plodded along. Not by any means the fastest mount he could have roped and certainly not the best-looking, this red mare, even with her swayed back and ewe neck, had the most even disposition of any horse he'd ever ridden. He liked to hunt for wild turkeys down around the river, and for antelope and deer when these came into sight. And on these hunts he'd learned a singular thing about Dreamer: she didn't flinch at the sound of gunfire. There were not that many horses that wouldn't shy off, jumping sideways before skittering around, crowhopping, if a man fired while riding them, not to mention the majority that would— in the cowboy phrase—"break in two," which is to say, go into a fit of violent bucking at the first explosion of a six-gun or a rifle in the hands of a man on their backs.

"Gettin' on toward midmornin'," Ira Turnbull said conversationally. "Seems just like any other day."

"I wish to hell it was some other day." Severn Laycon looked miserable. "I got a fire in my belly. Don't like to say that I'm afraid or nothin' like that. Just that I've always felt that caution was a virtue. And here we are, goin' up against God knows how many men who are led by no less than Eli Jones, who, from what I hear, has no more kind feelin's than a rattlesnake might."

"Look at all that dust over to the west," Blue called out, reining his horse off to one side. "Maybe I better get up higher and take a look."

"Stay down, Blue," Turner Hopewell barked. "I want all you men to keep out of sight. We'll stay behind this line of hills until we're between them and the river. They'll be heading straight in."

The five men put their horses into a gallop, following Turner's lead. Ten minutes later he hauled back and his horse slid to a sudden stop.

"Ira," Turner drawled, looking completely calm now, "I'd like you to pull up some brush with your rope, a good bit of it, and ride to the south behind these hills. Stir up plenty of dust. And, Severn, you go back north, the way we came, about half a mile, doing the same thing. The instant that you hear the sound of that big Sharps gun of Blue's, dismount and run up to the top of the hill and fire a few shots. Ira, you do the same thing. When Blue lets off a shot, you cut loose too. I have no idea of how far off they may be, but if they're close, don't neither of you shoot to kill; these are warning shots to try to scare them off.

"After that, both of you run back to your horses and drag the brush on your ropes behind you, kick up all the dirt you can. About every hundred yards, get back up to the ridge and let off a shot or two—and then keep that up, going to and fro. The idea is to fool those men who're pushin' that herd and make 'em think we've got a lot more men than just the five of us."

As Ira and Severn pulled their ropes free, Turner led Blue and Asa Coltrane to a stand of mesquites where they quickly tied their reins. "Bring yourself a brace of some kind, Blue. Break off a forked branch if you can find one."

The three men crept carefully, bending over as they neared the summit, and then, going down to all fours, they crawled the last few yards to the top of the rise. When they peered over it they saw before them a wide valley stretching endlessly out of sight, and on it was a vast, milling herd of spotted cattle.

"There must be thousands of head out there," Blue observed.

The others didn't answer. In the distance they saw dozens of cowboys riding back and forth, waving their ropes or hats, keeping the herd gathered, while out in front of the cattle some six or eight men worked on foot, cutting the strands of barbed wire and rocking cedar fence posts from one side to the other, trying to work them out of the ground.

"Got here just in time," Turner Hopewell said conversationally. "Blue, you're always tellin' me what a good shot you are, and now I'm goin' to put you to the test. Set up that buffalo gun of yours and kick up some dirt around those fellas."

Blue carried his long, heavy Sharps with him and put it carefully to

one side. With a vigorous heave of his muscular shoulders he stuck the splintered dead branch of a mesquite tree in the hard dirt, shoving it down and tamping around it with his hands. Blue inspected the wooden fork he had put in place with a certain satisfaction. Then, using this as a substitute for a tripod, he picked up the Sharps rifle, inspected the muzzle to be sure it was not obstructed, and placed it in the Y of the broken branches.

"Allow for the south wind, Blue," Turner said, "and be sure not to hit anybody."

Blue lay on his belly, aiming down the barrel, twisting the knurled small nob so as to adjust his back sights for the distance. He'd worked with the gunsmith who'd made the sights for him, and had practiced long and hard in his youth with this old weapon which he'd bought second or third hand. In those days he'd learned his skill through necessity, for he had little money for bullets and depended on downing game in order to have food on the table for himself and his wife. Even now, as this flashed through his mind, he had to smile, thinking of Big Lucy. Then he concentrated on the men before him. Blue knew that the single-shot Sharps, with the heaviest black powder cartridge available anywhere, so far as he knew, was deadly up to and including a thousand yards. An unbelievable distance. Well over half a mile. The men before him were almost that distance away. He squinted down the sights and squeezed gently on the trigger.

The Sharps exploded with a metallic roar, leaping from its support and falling back. Seconds later, off to their left and from their right, they heard a rattle of rifle fire. The Winchesters carried by Ira Turnbull and Severn Laycon couldn't possibly reach far enough to do any damage, they didn't have near the range of the Sharps, but that wasn't what Turner Hopewell had in mind.

The men on foot in the distance jumped up from the fence, dropping their wire cutters, and—as Blue's Sharps blew its huge slug into the ground not half a yard from one of them—they broke and ran in a state of panic. Behind them, the other cowboys must not have heard anything above the bawling of the cattle, and they kept working, holding the herd in place, preparing to drive it through the cut fence toward the far-off water of the North Concho on the Lazy E.

Looking off to his right and then his left, Turner grinned, turning about, holding his rifle in an easy grip. "Ira and Severn look like they each got about a full company of men with them." And it was true that great clouds of dust rose behind them as their horses raced, dragging on

ropes the mass of shinnery and brush each man had managed to pull
from the ground. They kept firing their rifles and galloping back and
forth, getting into a certain rhythm, seeming to enjoy the dangerous
game they played.

Down on the flat they saw a man on a chestnut horse assembling his
cowboys, sending riders back around the herd. Soon all the cowboys left
the cattle to drift back away, and they rode forward warily, staying back
a few hundred yards behind the fence.

"We can't run this bluff much longer," Asa Coltrane said. "We'll have
to do something else pretty quick." With that he said, "I'll go try to
throw a scare on 'em, you never know when that might work. They
don't look any too sure of what they're doin'."

"Watch yourself" was all that Turner said. "At the first sign of real
trouble, head back this way. In the meantime, Blue will keep you covered while I get Ira and Severn with us behind those big boulders to my
left. That's where you'll find us."

"Got a handkerchief or something?" Asa asked. Turner went down
the hill and dug from his saddlebags a gray linen bandana he carried to
tie across his face for protection during sand or dust storms and handed
it to Asa. "Plan on a truce flag? Fixin' to talk to them a little?"

"It's a startin' point."

"Good luck," Turner said tersely as he mounted his horse and rode to
round up the other two men.

Asa stood beside his horse and pulled out his "Peacemaker," as many
called the single-action .44-40-caliber six-gun, the famous frontier
model designed by Colt back in 1873. He used the same metal cartridges in his Winchester Model 73 rifle. Holstering the Colt firmly, he
pulled his rifle from the boot or saddle scabbard, levered a shell into the
chamber, hearing only silence and the ominous sound of oiled steel
sliding as he flicked his right hand down and up. Then he tied the linen
bandana around the rifle barrel, out at the front sight, and, holding this
in his right hand, stepped into the saddle. His swaybacked thin-necked
mare didn't seem to notice the flagged rifle but plodded docilely forward as Asa neck-reined her, guiding her through a lower section between two hills.

Asa leaned forward as Dreamer's hooves struck stones and clattered
up the slope, and then leaned back as she slid and scrambled down the
other side, holding the rifle with its flag out to one side. Underneath his
hatbrim he could make out the cowboys who had gathered about their

leader, the man who rode forward now on his big chestnut horse, heading straight toward Asa.

The rider came up to the fence, with twenty or more armed men holding together in a threatening pack some thirty yards or so behind him. Many of them pulled out pistols and held them with their right hands, muzzles pointing up.

When Asa reached a point twenty yards away from the grim figure waiting on the big horse behind the fence, he pulled to a stop. His eyes locked with those of the other man.

At last the one facing him said in a deep bass voice, "You got that flag on your rifle for some reason, I reckon. What might it be?"

"None of your men is to cut our fence. That's about all I've got to say."

"Do you know who you're talkin' to, cowboy?"

Tension built between the two men, a quivering reality so evident that Asa felt that if he put out his hand he could feel it, could touch it in the air. He seemed to see a shimmering, as though he looked through heat waves, but then he saw more clearly. The man across from him had reddish-brown eyes, pig eyes, mean and narrow, that were set close together in his face above a squashed-out nose. Scars from some bad illness pocked his face.

Without thinking Asa said, "Mister, I sure don't want to hurt your feelin's but I don't believe I ever saw an uglier man."

His antagonist's face turned absolutely purple, and through gritted teeth he said, "You son of a bitch, you're talkin' to Eli Jones. I guess you've heard of me."

Asa said, "Yes, I've heard it said you're real hard on helpless drunks and men you've got half scared to death."

With a threatening softness, the ugly pox-scarred brute of a man whispered in such a way that the words carried: "But you're not scared? Is that right, sonny boy?" He spoke derisively—but as the words came out he shifted in his saddle and his right hand hovered near the butt of his six-gun.

"Well, with about forty men dug in up on those hills behind me, and with a man in charge as famous as Colonel Turner Hopewell, who rode with none other than General Hood in the late war, I hope you fellows don't make some kind of serious mistake."

Asa had roared these words, making sure that all within earshot heard them.

On the other side of the fence the furious man, his face working, his

mouth trembling, began to speak again. "So, you think I'm ugly, do you? You don't know what 'ugly' is, sonny," he said, using the diminutive again. "And all the time there you sit on that miserable swaybacked nag, my God, what kind of judge of looks can someone like you be? Hey?" He snorted out this last with something like a sneezing sound.

"I won't stand for anyone to insult my horse," Asa said calmly, pulling the bandana from his rifle barrel and stuffing it into his left saddlebag. Then, without a hint to indicate what he was about to do, he pulled Dreamer around sideways, with Eli Jones off his right shoulder, and with unexpected swiftness he stepped down from the saddle. At that same instant, standing completely protected behind his swaybacked, stolid sorrel mare, he placed the Winchester's barrel on the seat of the saddle and aimed it squarely at the man's chest.

Eli Jones made a bad mistake then. He'd always come out on top when faced with fresh-faced kids. And this mocking handsome son of a bitch across the fence raised such a flood of hatred in him that he couldn't still his hand. Lunging for the grip of his Colt, he got his fingers on it just as a .44 slug slammed into the direct center of his chest, knocking him backward. What had been Eli Jones slid off to the right side and the big chestnut horse rared straight up, waving his forefeet before lunging forward, and then leaping left and right, as the grotesque bundle with a boot caught in the stirrup flapped wildly about the leaping animal's feet. Wheezing out great breaths, the chestnut bucked, trying to free himself from its terrifying burden. With each leap the horse made, the body slapped up and down, vivid scarlet spraying from a gaping hole in the dead man's chest.

Before the shocked cowboys could react, Asa jumped back on his horse and hollered out, "We got forty men looking down their sights at you, boys. So get the hell away from our property."

With that he heard a distant boom from Blue's buffalo gun, followed by a kick of dirt which spurted immediately in front of one cowboy's horse that had started forward. The horse jumped sideways while the rider fought for control. Another boom, and another bullet hit only inches from the hooves of a second rider's horse.

While the cowboys pulled back, Asa called out, "Don't forget that you're up against Colonel Turner Hopewell and all his men, and they're holdin' the high ground."

Then he galloped away. But he didn't put his mare into a run, for he'd already seen the panicked men turn tail and flee. With Eli Jones,

their fearsome leader, down, it looked to Asa Coltrane that those men had lost their appetite for combat.

When he arrived at the boulders he saw the anxious faces of his friends. And then he said, "I'm sorry about what happened. There just wasn't no other way, or at least there wasn't any I could see. We had a few hard words, and it struck me that if I tried to ride away he'd likely shoot me in the back. Besides, he said some harsh things about my horse."

"He insulted your swaybacked mare?" Severn Laycon asked. "Well, I sure as hell will be careful in the future what I say about her; you can rest assured I'll never stand in judgment where she's concerned."

"To tell the truth, I'm right shook up," Asa said, and the absolute whiteness of his face bore this out. "I'm no quick-draw gunfighter, and while that Eli Jones may not have been half as fast as Tom English, he was likely twice as fast as me. So I had to do something different."

"He was a damn fool for drawing when you had the drop on him," Ira Turnbull said.

Asa didn't answer. Instead he turned to Blue and said in all seriousness, "That was some shootin' on your part, Blue. At least a thousand yards away, and you kept 'em scared off of me. Your bullets hit right next to their horses' feet—I wouldn't have thought it possible."

"I could have hit that man facin' you," Blue said.

"I know you could."

"Thing is," Blue said, "I didn't know about your situation."

"I didn't know myself. But things turned out about as well as we could have hoped, at least for now."

Blue's dark face creased into a broad smile and he chuckled, pleased by the compliments.

Asa faced the foreman and said, "Turner, as far as those men know, you were a colonel during the war. But I won't let on to Sadler and Chandler about your promotion, for they'd likely kick you out of their club."

# TWELVE

TOM ENGLISH guessed he must be in New Mexico by now. He rode in clear hot morning sunlight through grass-filled land with hardly any trees at all. This part of the territory must have had good rains that year. An hour later he stopped his horse in surprise as he reached a bluff and gazed down across a broad, deep valley. He knew he'd been crossing what many called a plateau, though you don't recognize it as such when on foot or horseback. It seems just like any other prairie land. But all of a sudden it had come to an end, and a great depression had been carved out of it, as if God had pushed in the side of the world, wondering if He ought to mold it in a different shape.

Tom sat there, marveling at the unexpected sight of the surface of the earth falling precipitously before him while a foolish idea slipped unbidden through his mind: that the Creator, above all, could give way to creative instincts whenever He felt like it. Then Tom felt uncomfortable at the impious thought.

On the far side of the basin he saw blue foothills and behind them craggy shapes of mountains. Real mountains, not like those in Concho country back in Texas. It made him think of the time he'd ridden into Montana Territory and gazed with awe at the northern Rockies. He winced at the recollection; it had been the first time he'd been on the run, calling himself Tom Germany. Well, once again he found himself using that alias, except he rode today in the territory of New Mexico.

Uncertain of his route, thinking he might have gone too far north while still in Texas, he rode in a southwesterly direction. Four days after discovering the sudden valley, during the early afternoon, he found a settlement and rode into it. A sleepy collection of shacks called San Antonio de Belén; not much to it, no place to stay, and the natives directed him, speaking Spanish, to another village not far off called Frisco. When he reached there at dusk he found a single wagon yard, the only one in town, where he put his horse. The boy looking after

things said that Tom could sleep in an empty stall if he wanted, and told him, "You can git yourself somethin' to eat in the bar down the road a piece."

After washing up as best he could, Tom walked down the dirty road, strewn with abandoned barrels and one slanted broken-down wagon with the left front wheel off of it.

He'd heard of Frisco; it was not far from the headquarters ranch of the legendary J. B. Slaughter, a cattleman who had vast holdings in the New Mexico and Arizona territories. He'd met Slaughter twice before: once in Fort Worth and another time at a bank in Dallas. They had talked about the price of cows, felt each other out, and at one time the older man had told Tom that any time he might wish to make a big reduction in any of his herds he, J. B. Slaughter, would offer him a fair price. Tom hadn't anything he wanted to sell at the time, but maybe that was the best way to get to know someone who might be of use in the future—when neither party wanted anything from the other.

At any rate, he recognized the famous Slaughter brand when he saw it on at least fifteen ponies hitched outside a much larger bar than you'd expect to find in a little place like Frisco. But then he realized that this would be the closest town to the Slaughter ranches, and he expected that it would surely be the watering hole for the eighty or ninety cowboys who would be needed to work on all those hundreds of thousands of acres.

Tom entered the saloon cautiously, looking at the rowdy cowpunchers who stood in a line at the long bar. At the first sight of a familiar face he was prepared to turn about and leave. It wouldn't do for men to recognize him. But they all looked to be strangers, and not that friendly either. So he sat down at a far table, caught the eye of a Mexican with an apron, and ordered the biggest steak they had—and in addition called for two whiskeys and a mug of beer.

"A lot of trail dust in my throat," he said under his breath, recognizing the self-deception. This was another vow he kept breaking, though he knew he didn't *have* to drink this whiskey, it was simply something that he *felt* like doing. Particularly when he got real tired, and he was by God tired now. Worn clear out, in fact.

A nice-looking youngster, one of the cowpunchers, wearing a foolish but amiable smile from having had a few drinks too many, ambled toward him, holding a bottle in one hand.

"Howdy, stranger," the young cowboy said, sitting down across the table from Tom. "Don't see too many travelers in these parts. It ain't on

the way to anywhere, so you can't be passing through. So I guess you
came to try to hire on at Mr. Slaughter's ranch. But let me tell you,
they'll work your tail off here. Yes, they will," he said, bobbing his head
up and down with a touch of self-pity. " 'Jump up, boys, it's nigh on
daylight, git yore boots on and let's saddle up'—that's what I hear just
about ever' mornin', and don't think that if there's work to be done on
Sunday you can rest then neither."

The youngster shook his head sorrowfully, and then he said, "But the
bright side is that once in a while we come in to Frisco and get dead
drunk, and that's kind of fun. Right now my head is all a-whirl, and the
floor looks tilted to me."

With an effort he focused on Tom's face. "Well, you ain't said a
word. Are you plannin' to sign on with us or not?"

Tom smiled. "I guess you're right in saying that people don't come
here on purpose if they're passing through, for I'm in Frisco because I'm
lost. My destination is a ranch south of Lincoln where I hope to get
work."

"Jesus Christ," the cowboy snorted, "you sure *are* lost. That's way to
hell and gone to the east of here. What outfit is it you're looking for?"

"The Joe Hill ranch. The Bent Snake brand is what they use."

"Can't say I know the brand, but I've heard mean things said of Joe
Hill, if he's the same one as that murderer who went in and out of the
Lincoln County War, the same one who had all that trouble in Texas,
around El Paso and other places. They say he and his gang rob banks
and stagecoaches, not to mention rustlin' cattle."

"A man can hear all manner of gossip," Tom replied. "The only thing
I've been told is that he runs a ranch and pays good wages."

"My friend," the young man said, drinking straight from the bottle
and then coughing as though he had lung fever, "you may be right. But
if it's a cattle ranch where you plan to end up, I feel I need to tell you
that a cowboy's life is a mournful one. I've a mind to render a song for
you which I often sing to all them wild longhorn cattle we got mixed in
with our Meskin and our shorthorn and our spotted cattle, for that song
has a way of soothin' them."

"I appreciate the offer," Tom responded, "but maybe we'd attract too
much attention if you started that in here."

"You're right," the cowboy said, staggering to his feet. "You're absolutely right. I'm goin' to go outside where I can sing to my heart's
content without havin' to git into a fight about it."

But before he left he did a surprising thing. He made a courtly bow

and said, "Pardon me for not introducing myself. My name is Drake, Ramble Drake." And with that he went happily outside.

Three days later Tom, riding the powerful bay which he'd started to call Morgan, owing to his bloodline, knew he had reached Joe Hill's ranch. A white-bearded neighbor in a sod house at least six miles back had warned him off, saying, "Them fellers are nothin' more than cut-throats and outlaws, and you'd be best advised to circle wide around 'em. They got a few houses and pens and such in the flatlands a few miles short of those hills northwest of here," the man had said, pointing to them. Then, as Tom rode in that direction, the dirty old man with a white beard stained from chewing tobacco juice had shrugged, as if saying to himself that he had done his best to give his fellow man good advice, and he acted as if he found nothing strange in the fact that this had been ignored.

With misgivings, Tom rode in, noting the large but poorly maintained main house, a ramshackle affair with shingles sliding off, leaving holes here and there. It had a roofed porch at the front and around both sides. A number of chairs sat randomly upon the porch along with a few tables. With his eyes fixed on this as his destination he only caught other quick impressions: some pens and a large corral with tall cedar posts as uprights and three rows of horizontal poles attached to them instead of rails. A long bunkhouse sat off about a hundred yards to the left, and a shack lay up a slight incline behind it. At the side of it, a bent-over figure tended a smoking barbecue pit.

Feeling a few butterflies in his stomach, the familiar fear of the un-known, Tom looked around, trying to get the lay of the land. He in-spected the pens more carefully and saw near them a dilapidated barn and a shed off of it which likely was where they kept their saddles and other gear. A number of bony small horses, the kind you see in Mexico, stood in the corral. Nothing unusual really. In fact the ranch looked so normal, so much like others he had seen all through his life, he began to feel relieved. The tension drained away as he pulled up beside the main house. A hitching rail stood off to one side and he tied Morgan to it. No grass, just dry hard dirt for a yard, without bushes or trees. The sun cast an unusual golden-yellow light that seemed to hang in the air in the late afternoon, leaving long shadows on the east side of the dwelling.

Two dogs off to his right barked incessantly, one of them running up and, when Tom faced him, backing off, teeth bared, but with his tail wagging, showing that he was only doing his duty. Faces appeared at

the windows of the bunkhouse and several men came out. But none
bore arms; Tom felt no threat.

On reaching the steps leading to the built-up porch, the front door of
the house opened and a tall man in his late forties with a three-day
stubble on his face appeared. He had prominent cheekbones, sunk-in
cheeks, and dull eyes shadowed by a skull-like brow. At his left side was
a sheath holding a broad-bladed knife slanted for a cross draw for the
man's right hand. An empty pistol scabbard hung on the right side of
his belt. The man didn't smile or say a word of greeting. He stood there
in the half-open door and waited.

"Mr. Hill?"

The tall man with the cadaverous face nodded ever so slightly in
acknowledgment, but still he didn't speak.

"My name's Tom Germany, I'm a long way from home, and I'm
looking for work. Been cowboyin' all my life, and I'd be a good hand."

Hill looked at him, his eyes studying Tom, seeing the dirt stains on
his clothes and face, eyes falling to the two guns worn low. He looked
over his visitor's shoulder at the muscular bay horse, which pulled back
on his reins at the hitching rail, neck curved, ears pointed, as the dogs
drew near, making growling noises. Then the bay lashed out with his
hind feet and the dogs scurried to safety, turning at fifty feet away and
showing much more bravery.

Hill stood at least six feet five and his gaunt, big-boned frame towered over Tom. After waiting for a good two minutes, he reached out
and shook hands with his visitor. Hill inclined his head toward two
sturdy homemade chairs on the porch and said, "Let's us set a spell and
talk."

Hill wore no hat and had a homespun-looking shirt with long sleeves
that didn't reach his knobby wrists. Soiled and wrinkled dust-colored
cotton pants that people had started to call khakis were tucked into
high-topped boots with worn-down heels.

When the two men had sat down, Hill said, "I guess you're on the
run from somewhere. That don't matter to me. Most who come out
here this far from any friendly town must do it for one reason or
another. What that may be is their business and none of mine. But I'd
like to ask, why'd you come to this place in particular? There are plenty
of other ranches needin' cowhands. You didn't see much livestock on
your way through my land, and you can tell I got a good many men
without enough to do. So why should I hire you?"

Tom didn't answer at first. At last he spoke up: "Guess I was just

hopin' you needed at least one more. The word is that you pay better wages than most, and to a man who's broke, that's of interest."

Speaking very quietly, Hill asked, "Why would you suppose I pay more than other men might?"

"I wouldn't know."

"Yes, you do." Fierceness flared in his flat dull eyes for an instant and he burst out, "Don't take me for a fool. Everyone in these parts knows about Joe Hill. And you rode in here askin' for me *by my name.*"

The tremor that Tom noted in the man's hands went away. The glow in his eyes gradually died down, and then Hill spoke matter-of-factly. "I think you rode here all the way from Texas looking for this particular range because you need a place to hide." He didn't show any emotion as he spoke.

Tom didn't see any reason to answer; Hill clearly had more to say.

"You're here because of trouble. The grips on those guns of yours look worn, like you work with them. Your regular cowboy don't really practice much, which you know as well as I do." Joe Hill looked searchingly at Tom as though he were trying to make a decision and it caused him difficulty. Then he seemed to relax.

The big man said, "I guess I came to this territory for much the same reason as you. I'm from Texas myself, from El Paso, and still have kinfolk there. Now, no sense pretending to me that you're just a workin' cowboy. You're well aware that I don't need men to look after stock; but I do work cattle—in a manner of speakin'—and men who can handle difficulties when they come their way can be of help."

Tom hadn't known what to expect. He sat there, pretending to be at ease in spite of the tension that gripped him, waiting for Hill to continue.

Joe Hill said, "I pay pretty well, but I expect more from my men than most would. We depend on one another, and when good fortune comes our way, we share it."

Another awkward pause seemed to hang in the air between them. Tom broke the silence. "Do you want to know anything in particular about me?"

"None of your past means much here. The others out in that bunkhouse all have things they've left behind. Maybe not as much as you. Hell," he snorted, "that don't matter, nothin' does. The only word of caution I'm goin' to give is this: you got to be careful with these boys of mine. They're not all that bad, but they get nervous now and then."

Tom's easy smile crossed his face. "Am I to understand that I'm hired?"

Hill nodded and rose to his feet. "Come on," he said to Tom, "I'll introduce you to the rest of the men." The two walked down the steps and across the hard, packed dirt with the two dogs following close behind them.

Off to their right Tom saw a long pit, like a shallow grave, with a low fire in it. Over reddened coals and charred short branches an iron grate held a heavy side of beef which dripped sizzling fat into the flickering red and yellow tongues of flame. A sudden whirl of wind gusted and blew smoke and cinders into the Mexican cook's face. He blinked and squeezed his eyes shut, moving around to one side, getting away from the blowing sparks and ashes.

The cook held a stick with a yellowish-brown wet cloth at one end of it. From time to time he stooped forward, dipped this in a pan which had an oily liquid in it, and smeared basting sauce on the searing, five-foot-long side of beef. Gritty smoke stirred from the smoldering pit, and the compelling aroma of cooking meat seeped through the air.

As they walked across the dusty ground, five cowboys filed out of the bunkhouse. They formed an uneven line and stood looking at the newcomer suspiciously.

"This here," Joe Hill announced to them, "is a new man who calls himself Tom. He looks all right to me. Make up your minds right here and now if you agree."

Not one of them uttered a single word.

"It's decided then. He'll join us." Hill turned to Tom and said, "Every outfit has to have one boss, and I'm him. There ain't no second guessin' allowed. What I say goes, and that is that."

One of the cowboys started to laugh but choked it off when Hill glared at him. "In our business we got enough trouble without things gettin' out of hand here at the Bent Snake ranch—that's my brand and the name of this place. So one of the rules that can't be broke is that there ain't no fightin' or anything of that sort to take place. Anyone who gits out of line just has to saddle up and ride out. And anyone who don't do what I say will regret that he ever got borned."

He turned to the cook and said, "Miguel, I'm ready for supper. When you plannin' to feed us?"

The men looked uneasily at one another. They introduced themselves to Tom without offering to shake hands, using only their first names, and then all of them went in a group toward the cook, who was

slashing at the smoldering carcass with a long butcher knife, spearing chunks and slices and sliding them onto dented pewter-colored metal plates. The cowboys stood in line, waiting their turn, speaking in low tones to one another. They got a splash of pinto beans, dark brown, hot with pepper, along with the beef. Grasping knives and forks and tin cups of coffee, they sat cross-legged on the ground before attacking their evening meal as though half starved.

Joe Hill sat among them, bony broad shoulders slumped forward as he ate, looking down at his plate. Beside him a skinny kid who'd said his name was Hugh finished quickly, eating half as much as the others. He had a blond mustache and oily unwashed hair that hung down almost over his prominent ears.

Tom looked at the others. One had features which could only be those of an Indian, but on closer examination could be seen to be a half-breed—with dark brown hair, not quite black, and hazel eyes. Next to him Tom saw a heavy-set older man with a big belly and hardly any rear end at all. He sat with his greasy hat pulled down so that his face could hardly be seen. Two others had moved off under a solitary tree. One of them must have said something funny, for the other chuckled dryly. Tom hadn't caught most of their names but decided it didn't really matter.

The boy named Hugh moved over beside Tom. "You might think," he volunteered, "that Miguel is cookin' an awful lot for no more than you see here, but Lucas and four others are comin' in tonight or maybe tomorrow."

"Lucas?" Tom asked, puzzled.

"Been off on one of our raids," the young mustached cowboy said with a touch of pride. Then he added, without explanation, "Without Lucas here, it sure is a lot more peaceful. When he's around, a man don't hardly dare to move without bein' careful about it."

The youngster took his plate and knife and fork and cup over to the cook and dropped them in a large enameled white pan which had some rusted spots on it.

After eating, Tom walked back to the house and then led Morgan to the corral where he unsaddled him, found a currycomb, and cleaned the dried lather and sweat-created mud off his back. Checking Morgan's feet, he used a knife to get out a rock that had lodged in one, then slipped off the bridle, giving Morgan a friendly word and a whap on the rump. He watched as the bay trotted off, head high, looking far superior to the smaller horses which gathered at the far end near a water trough.

Tom found some hay, broke it out, and left as he saw his horse approach it.

He put his saddle and blanket and bridle in the shed he'd seen earlier, finding a hairy mecate rope suspended from the ceiling with a loop which he hooked over his saddle horn. Then he carried his saddlebags and bedroll into the bunkhouse, surprised on entering to see its size. Much bigger than he'd thought, it held some twelve or fifteen cots. Plenty of room. He picked out an unused one and dumped his things on it.

Then, pulling from his bedroll a wrinkled but clean set of clothes, he walked outside in the late summer light that would last in all likelihood until past eight that night, and wandered to a small rocky creek he'd seen below the house. It had a few cedars growing near it.

A slight breeze cooled the heated air and made the cedars rustle. Tom unbuckled his wide, tooled leather gunbelt and carefully folded it upon the ground, placing its heavy holsters and their cargo clear of any contact with the dirt. After this he moved quickly, shucking off his spurred brown boots and then his pants, shirt, underwear, and socks. Then, with a sigh of pleasure, he waded into the two-foot-deep, clear running water and sank down in it, scrubbing off the dirt as best he could, washing his hair, and then crawling out to lie upon the dry grass which still held the sun's warmth from the July afternoon. His bones ached but he felt refreshed and, best of all, clean again.

He reflected a moment, arguing with himself, with logic winning over the tiredness and the aching in his bones and muscles. Then, making himself act, he rose abruptly, grasped the dirty clothes and socks, and washed them vigorously in the running water. Returning from the shallow creek to the bank, he spread the wet garments on the cedar to dry. He'd retrieve them the next day, he decided. Then he lay back down again, and for a moment almost fell asleep stark naked on the bank, in spite of the strangeness of the circumstances.

Gooseflesh rippled across his stomach as he heard footsteps approaching. He rose to a sitting position and then stood up, leaving his back to those who had approached.

A voice behind him inquired, "What on earth are you doin'?"

Another said, "Buck, ain't you never heard of a man takin' a bath?"

They came closer and Tom turned around, leaning forward to grasp his clothes. He slipped on his fresh underwear, his wrinkled but clean and dry pants and shirt, savoring the way they felt on his skin even under these awkward circumstances. Then he sat down in order to pull

on his socks and boots. Rising to his feet, he buckled on his gunbelt, automatically taking the time to fasten the tie-down thongs which held the twin scabbards securely to his thighs.

Feeling less vulnerable, with the layers of thin cloth giving him the sense he'd put on armor, Tom felt prepared to face whatever might come next. With a careless, graceful sweep he leaned forward, grasped his hat up from the ground, and put it on.

While he'd been dressing, the others had hunkered down upon the ground. One chewed on a stem of grass while the others watched Tom's every move.

"Stranger," the young man named Hugh, the boy with the blond mustache, said at last, "I've seen some tore-up men before, but it looks like some gang done wrapped you in barbwire and drug you a mile or two. Never seen so many scars on one body in all my life."

The older man with the big belly and almost no butt husked out gruffly, " 'Twarn't barbwire done it. You can see from the scars on his back that he's been bullwhipped."

The others showed the older man respect, Tom noted.

This person heaved to his feet, grunting from the effort due to having the burden of his great belly, and then he came closer. "I'm George Perkins. Been in this game too long to do anything respectable anymore, I reckon. I didn't catch your name before."

"I'm Tom Germany—from Texas."

"Ain't we all," Perkins responded. "I mean, all of us came from Texas oncet." The others rose to their feet and in a group they trailed back toward the bunkhouse.

Perkins's breath wheezed the way some men do who smoke all the time, as if they've got some paper stuck in their windpipe and it makes slight whistling sounds. He said, "There's no mistakin' the scars of bullet wounds. Them puckered blue and red scars where they go in, and the big ones where they go out, if you're lucky enough to have one pass clear through. I didn't take the time to count, but I wonder that you're alive."

"He likely would prefer to drop this conversation, George," a tall cowboy who hadn't spoken much before rasped out.

This man said, "My name's Buck Lewis. I've rode with Joe Hill for some time now. The three of us can be trusted. At least we get along all right with one another. But as a word of caution, look out for the others."

"Would you care to explain that?" Tom asked.

The tall man named Buck Lewis said, "You've already met 'em. I'm talkin' about the half-breed, calls himself Joe, and Digger is the one with the crooked nose, busted, I guess, the man who probably ain't said a word to you. Injun Joe prides himself on bein' a good shot, and he's what I'd call 'difficult,' I mean he's hard to get along with.

"But Digger is worse. He likes to test men out, loves to see 'em back down. The thing is, he's handy with a knife and you don't want to allow him to push you into that kind of fight."

"I go out of my way to avoid any kind of fight," Tom said.

George Perkins laughed shortly, and young Hugh said, "Hell, I do too."

Buck Lewis added finally, "The most important thing of all is this: don't get crossways with Joe Hill. Last year he had us hang John Farmer from the rafters in the barn."

"What did you say?" Tom couldn't believe what he'd heard.

"It's true," Perkins said, "but it ain't a thing I like to think back on. Poor John took a long time stranglin', and all because he tried to stand up to Joe Hill. *Jesus.*" George shook his head, grimacing in distaste.

Tom glanced about and saw Hugh's young face, which had turned gray as if he were sick at his stomach.

The four men walked silently toward the bunkhouse. Tom suppressed an involuntary shudder of horror. "What have I got myself into?" he asked himself.

# THIRTEEN

IN THE NEXT WEEK Tom spent time with young Hugh and the tall cowboy, Buck Lewis, moving scraggly rustled cattle which had been penned in a box canyon eight or ten miles away to a fenced "horse trap," as they called it, over a few low hills southeast of the Bent Snake headquarters. With little to do, they didn't hurry and stopped frequently to use up part of the day.

During those first mornings, Tom would go to the corral and, in an effort to break the boredom, he'd rope from the milling horses the most lively-looking of the scrawny Mexican ponies, vaguely hoping for some excitement, but after a few obligatory pitches they settled down—and plodded the rest of the day. He didn't enjoy riding them but decided he might as well give Morgan, his own horse, a chance to rest after the trip from Texas.

Big-bellied George Perkins always found some excuse not to work with cattle, saying he'd surely like to help but he had a misery in his back that required him to stay off a horse right now.

The half-breed named Joe never offered to lend a hand. He would wander off hunting, and the men on the ranch would occasionally hear the ring of a far-off rifle shot, followed by the echoes that came back from the stony steep-sided mountains just to the north.

Digger, the sullen big brute whom the others told Tom to avoid, spent much of his time alone behind the barn. He would pull his knife and square up some fifteen feet from the unpainted upright boards, slowly raise his arm, holding the blade's tip, and then he'd make a whipping motion, and the sheath knife would twirl, flashing in the sunlight, until it plunged with a whack into a splintered rough cedar plank, the handle quivering back and forth. Digger spent solitary hours in this way.

Late Saturday night, Lucas and the four men with him arrived late.

They woke the others when they thudded into the bunkhouse, swearing, kicking off their boots, then falling down on cots.

Old George Perkins sat up and asked in a sleep-blurred voice, "Well, you boys have any luck?"

"We burned a store over in Texas," a voice replied from the dark.

"Any reason to do that?" George asked.

"You answer him, Lucas," the same voice said.

Tom lay still, listening.

A hand lit a coal-oil lamp and it threw yellow shadows on the walls. A man with black hair and a thin black mustache on his sun-darkened face adjusted the lamp's wick. After this he pulled from his holster a six-gun with an unusually long barrel, about twelve inches in length, it appeared, and inspected it, turning the cylinder, then reholstering the weapon. In a hollow-sounding voice he drawled, "We got more than a hundred dollars in cash and a fair amount of free ammunition, not to mention some groceries."

"They just see fit to give all that to you, Lucas?"

"You know better than that, George. I took it."

"Anybody get hurt?"

"The owner tried to stop me. But I don't think he got hurt. Bastard never knew what hit him."

Another of the men who had just entered the bunkhouse commented, "I guess that's right. When it happened, it startled hell out of me—Lucas shot him right in the face, dropped him in his tracks."

"So that's why you burned the store. With him in it."

"Well, of course we did, George," Lucas said, as if reasoning with a child. "What else was there to do?"

One of the new arrivals had a coughing fit which ended with his hawking and snorting and spitting.

"There's a full moon," Lucas said. "And I saw a fine horse in the corral. Which one of you stole him?"

No one answered. Lucas cupped his hand above the lamp's glass chimney and blew out the light. "Well, we'll bargain for that horse tomorrow; right now I'm goin' to bed."

When Sunday dawned, Tom rose while the others slept. He dressed silently and checked his matched Colt .45s. After this, he went to the corral where he slipped up to Morgan, put the ends of his reins around his neck, spoke to him softly until the horse calmed down, then slipped on the bridle. After cinching the saddle, he pulled out the Winchester,

levered a cartridge into the firing chamber, then slipped it back into its slanted scabbard.

Tom rode in the purple grayness that preceded the sun's arrival, took a few deep breaths, then headed over the cactus-covered rocky rise which lay between the house and the horse trap. He spent some time there, riding around the cattle, wondering what the day would bring. Later, returning to the ranch, he found most of the men around the fire where the cook, Miguel, had slabs of bacon with the rind on it frying over a brisk fire.

Tom dismounted, tied his horse at the bunkhouse, and walked over to join them. The man named Lucas wore the same clothes he'd had on the night before, a sweaty faded blue shirt with white salt circles under the arms from dried sweat. Seeing him in daylight, Tom decided that he must be in his middle thirties. The two men stood a moment, staring at one another.

Joe Hill approached from the direction of the house. "Welcome, Lucas. Heard you had good fortune. This here," he said, gesturing toward Tom, "is a new hand who hired on to ride with us. Calls himself Tom Germany."

Lucas looked at Tom and then at the Morgan, which was drawing back his head and arching his neck. "What'll you take for that horse, cowboy?" he drawled.

Tom's cold, pale blue eyes looked steadily at his questioner. "He's not for sale," he said at last.

Perhaps it was the way he stood, relaxed, gun butts standing slightly away from his legs, or maybe it was because of the timbre of his voice, but there was something about him that carried authority. Every man there sensed it, and Lucas, not wanting the others to think he was backing off, said, "Well, we'll see about that after I've got rested up.

"God damn your lazy bones, Miguel!" Lucas stormed at the cook. "I brought that bacon all the way from Texas, and if you burn it up, I'll strap *you* on that griddle and fry your Meskin hide, you hear me?"

The men ate, drifted about aimlessly, a few of them restarted old quarrels but then dropped them as being more trouble than they were worth. Several gathered at a place which had two small holes dug in the ground, some twenty feet between them. Taking large metal washers, they began a game, trying to pitch the washers into the holes. Staking small wagers, the cowboys, one by one, would stand there, squinting, swinging an arm back and forth, and then swinging it smoothly, tossing round metal washers in high arches toward the farthest hole. When the

gamblers each had had their turn, they'd go up to find who got the closest. None put his missile in the target's sunken dirt for several rounds, but after each group effort they'd argue about who won, although this was for the honor of winning and not for money; then repeat the process, pitching the pierced metal spheres at the hole where they'd been before. Finally a cowboy rolled a washer into the hole, whooped and hollered, and collected from the discomfited men around him.

"It's too hot fer this," a loser complained querulously, and the other losers agreed, walking away from the crowing winner, who pocketed bits of change.

"It's the Sabbath day," George Perkins opined, sitting on the shaded veranda of Joe Hill's house, leaning back in his chair. "A day of rest, according to the Good Book." He picked up a bottle and drank from it and handed this to Lucas, who lazed beside him, boots up on the railing.

The two had been drinking since midmorning. Lucas pulled off his hat and let it fall to the porch's buckling floor. "God, it's hot," he said. Then, twisting in his chair a bit, he said, "Tell me about the new man."

"Can't say I know much. Seen him takin' a bath down at the creek one evenin', and he's been shot up bad. Not to mention cut with whips and God only knows what all. But it don't seem to have affected him none, or leastways not that a man would notice. He don't say much."

"Why'd he come here?"

"Hell," George answered, "why did any of us? How should I know?"

"I don't like him," Lucas said.

"Well, you got to wait your turn. Digger don't neither, and Injun Joe is buildin' up to a fever pitch about him. Tom Germany, to my mind, is just fine, but I know how you fellers are. You got to push new arrivals a little. That's why I've looked forward to this Sunday. I'll jest set up here on the porch whilst you all hooraw him, like you usually do, but as a word of caution, this here waddy has a way about him that gets your attention. At least, he gits mine. There's somethin' about a man with eyes that cold. Besides, he wears two guns, and that by itself is enough for me to advise you to tread soft."

"Never seen a real gunfighter who wore two guns, it's the kind of tomfool thing a pissant kid would do—it's just for show. In a little," Lucas drawled, pausing to take a drink from the bottle's mouth, "I'll let you see what I mean."

The day wore on. Miguel, the cook, with half a dozen cowboys ob-

serving expectantly, tried to stage a cockfight between two ragged-looking roosters, but they didn't want to fight, and in a fit of irritation the cook picked one up and wrung his neck. Then, angry at himself, he killed the other rooster the same way after chasing him for ten minutes and finally getting him in a corner. Heaving from exhaustion, Miguel began to grouse. He sat down and began picking feathers, his day of rest now ruined.

Around noon, Tom located Joe Hill sitting on the shaded veranda on the east side of the house. This place caught the south breeze and—with the sun now standing high in the south and moving west—would be, if not cooler, at least more bearable. Hill had a pocket knife in one hand and was whittling aimlessly on a dry stick. Tom had ignored the stares the men with Lucas had been directing at him and had walked up to the main house—noticed George Perkins talking to Lucas on the west porch—and then directed his steps toward the side Hill occupied alone.

Tom took a chair beside him. "I've been meaning to ask you a question."

Joe Hill didn't look up from his hands but kept shaving curls off the stick. These fell upon his lap and on the floor. A wind flurry swept dust from the ground and blew past the porch, carrying the shavings off against the wall in a cleansing gust.

"When I was in Texas I ran across a man who rode one of your horses, or at least it had the Bent Snake brand on it."

Hill looked around, fixing his eyes on Tom.

"What did the man look like?"

"I'd say he was around forty, give or take a little. Chewed tobacco, had a kind of dirty brown-colored mustache, a long one that hung down on both sides below his mouth. Let's see, what else?" Tom acted as if this weren't important. "The rider had a hooked nose, deep creases going down from it. Spoke to me only once, had a hoarse-soundin' voice as best I can recall."

"Shoot," Joe Hill said with a slight grin, "you're talkin' about that damn Wrangler Hull. Cain't be no other. You described him down to the minute."

"He work for you?"

"Might say that," Hill answered. "I been wonderin' what Wrangler might be up to. You see, an old compadre who rode with me long ago sent a wire askin' me to meet a friend of his at the Russell Hotel in Tascosa on the last day of May. Instead of goin' myself, I sent young

Hugh. And he brought back two hundred dollars along with a proposi-
tion. Seems that a mighty powerful man out near Fort Concho had
some rival that was causin' him a problem and he wanted to hire a gun.
That is to say, he wanted the man put down, if you follow the drift.
Anyhow, that's just the kind of thing that Wrangler prides himself on.
There was big money in it but it required a hell of a lot of ridin'.
Anyway, Wrangler took the job. He was to get in touch with some
judge, if you can believe it—Hugh could tell you more than me—as that
was the contact Hugh had been given. That judge would give Wrangler
his instructions. But Wrangler left some time ago, and we haven't heard
back from him."

Miguel served a thin, disappointing stew made from his two dead
roosters, ladling this into cups held by the cowboys. They dipped these,
when emptied, back into the pot of gray liquid with little yellowish
globules here and there on the surface, trying to satisfy their grumbling
bellies on the unsubstantial fare. Filling up on squares of corn bread and
frijoles, they complained with some bitterness before dropping the subject. After this they went back to the packed earth area where another
interminable game of pitching washers at the holes went on. Boredom
filled their blank faces.

Before the meal Tom had led Morgan back to the corral and unsaddled him. Now he sat on the ground away from the others, mending a
broken rein by splicing two ends together skillfully.

As if by some prearranged signal, although it was a coincidence,
Digger stalked around the corner of the barn and headed toward Tom
just as the half-breed known as Joe came riding in from the hills, three
bleeding rabbits tied behind his saddle's cantle.

Observing what was happening, Lucas took one last draw from his
nearly empty bottle, dropped it to the porch floor, and stood up,
stretching out his arms and yawning.

"Well," Tom said to himself, seeing the three men approaching him,
"here it comes." He stood up and walked over to a saddle lying on the
ground, its skirts and fenders crumpled under it. By the horn, tied by
saddle strings, hung a short running iron, a bent piece of steel which, in
most parts of the cow country, could get its owner shot or hanged. The
main use for running irons was to change brands, and certainly this
explained why most of the Bent Snake cowboys carried one. When
cattle they rustled had been "hair branded," which is to say branded
hurriedly on the surface without scarring the hide, the original brand

soon faded from view, so they could with impunity burn a new one on the animal. Or, at other times, the old brand could be blotched or changed into a new one. And on such stock these men would use their "runnin' irons" to make the jagged burn that looked like forked lightning —the "Bent Snake" brand.

Tom pulled the short, heavy L-shaped piece of iron free from the leather thongs which bound it. Cradling it between his hands, he sauntered toward the clot of men who lazily tossed washers through the air in their endless game. On arriving at the fringes of the group, he stood as though oblivious to the still mounted half-breed and to Digger.

The last named had been drinking, it appeared, for he staggered ever so slightly, his muscular, great shoulders dipping as he did. He had a turned-up pug nose with its hairy nostrils prominent in the center of his small-eyed face.

Digger stopped a few feet from Tom and said, "I don't like the way you give yourself airs."

"Don't know what you mean by that," Tom answered with an easy smile.

"You act like you're a boss or somethin' like that, when you're no more than a workin' cowboy like all the rest of us."

"Well, I *am* a cowboy. I don't know if that goes for all men here, and come to think of it, I don't recall seeing you on horseback tending to the herd. But if you say that you're a cowpoke, I'll take your word for it." His first words had been harsh, but then he'd eased them at the last, ending on a conciliatory note.

Digger patted the handle of his sheath knife. "Take off them guns and stop all that big talk, you sorry bastard. A real man fights with his fists or knives, and I'll give you the choice."

"Fight!" young Hugh called out at the top of his lungs, in sudden excitement. Men who had been in the bunkhouse or lazing around the grounds surged forward, anxious not to miss anything, intent upon the scene before them. Digger, small eyes glaring, head hunched forward, backed a few steps from Tom, his hand fondling the handle of his sheath knife.

Joe Hill suddenly showed up, saying, "Whoa now, you know my rules." But then he said, "I don't mind a little horseplay, boys, as long as it's fair. Just can't have no serious fights."

"Back off, Digger," the half-breed named Joe grunted. He looked down at the two of them as he reined his horse backward a few steps.

"That man has looked through me as if I wasn't even here. I'm the one that's goin' to take him."

Injun Joe held a rifle low in his hand. Raising his right leg from the stirrup, he smoothly lifted it over his saddle horn, pivoted, and slid down, landing lightly as a cat upon the ground. He leaned forward and a strange light came into the oddly hazel eyes in his Indian face.

Injun Joe's horse walked with his head held sideways so as not to step on the reins dragging on the ground, and approached the other horses behind the fence of the corral.

Lucas neared them then, drawling out the words, "I think the three of us should have some fun with this here stranger. What do you think we ought to do with him, Injun? Hold your rifle on him while we decide. First off, maybe we ought to make him get in a knife fight with old Digger here. But, Digger, just cut him up, like Joe Hill says, keep it like horseplay."

The brutish-looking man called Digger pulled out the wicked, curve-bladed knife he'd been throwing and waved it, point held low. A cruel grin spread across his face. The cowboys fell back, leaving a wide circle around this man and his victim.

Joe Hill stood with the others. "Well, what the hell," he said, acting as if he disapproved but with his voice wavering from excitement, "I said we'd have to be fair, and that means only one of you at a time gets to kick around with this here new man. Two on one won't do, you hear me?"

Tom said, "I'd just as soon not fight anyone at all."

Digger whispered loud enough for all to hear, "One of them sissy boys, are you? What's this, you don't carry a knife, is that your problem? Hand him one, somebody."

A man pitched a knife toward Tom's feet and it plopped on the ground beside his boots.

Digger began to circle. "Pick it up," he said, a fierceness on his features.

"Well," Tom said, turning his right side toward his assailant, "I've been took on often enough before now, but usually for some reason. I don't know what offense I've caused you, but if I've done something you think rude I'll be more than willing to say I'm mighty sorry it happened."

"You cowardly son of a bitch," the brute of a man snarled.

Tom's right hand, holding the branding iron, lashed out sideways into Digger's pug nose. Blood spurted, the man reflexively fell back and

sideways, and then Tom's hand, holding the bent steel bar, slammed it on the top of his skull. The awful sound of steel striking bone cracked through the air, and Digger fell like a poleaxed steer, dropping in his tracks in an unconscious heap upon the ground. Blood pulsed from what little remained of his flat nose, and his mouth hung wide open.

Injun Joe, rifle in his hands, had it going toward his shoulder. Lucas instinctively held his long-barreled six-gun, sliding it from his holster.

Ignoring them, Tom strode through the clot of men around him and proceeded toward Miguel's barbecue pit. He had his back toward the two who threatened him.

Heavy curses filled the air; several cowboys looked down in shock at the bloodied prostrate form of Digger; then all of them turned their heads, watching Tom stride toward the still smoky cook fire. All of the men followed, as though they couldn't help themselves. Joe had his rifle fixed on Tom's back, and Lucas had drawn his Colt.

"I'm not going to fight you men," Tom said, not looking at the people behind him. "There's no reason for it."

Lucas hissed, "You might-a been lucky droppin' Digger when he wasn't lookin', but this thing is serious now. I'm holsterin' my gun, yellow belly, so you got no excuse not to face my way. Don't make me shoot you in the back."

The cowboys standing near him hurriedly scrambled a safe distance away.

"What about Injun Joe?" Tom asked, still not looking behind him, standing with his back toward all the men.

"He ain't no part of this."

Hill said, "All right, the rest of you back off. Lucas is right, we can't have two on one. It's between him and Tom Germany. You Injun son of a bitch, git off the warpath and put that rifle down."

The half-breed didn't acknowledge the order.

Ominously, Hill said, "The last man who didn't do what I said ended up kickin' his feet in the air at the end of a rope."

Injun Joe immediately lowered his rifle barrel, then laid the weapon off to one side.

"Looks like the way is clear now," Hill said, satisfied that his authority had held.

"Turn around, waddy," Lucas barked, contempt in every word.

"I don't think you want to do this, friend," Tom said, slowly turning about to face the man.

Lucas took off his hat and tossed it to one side, revealing oily un-

kempt straight hair, black as darkest night. His narrow black mustache made a curving line under his nose. The man stood with his right shoulder down, hand out a few inches from his gun butt, giving the sense of a rattler about to strike.

Tom went a few steps off to one side and put a dirty tin cup on a chopping block. Then he walked back from it some thirty feet. Lucas watched him, frowning, puzzled.

"I'd really rather we didn't lock horns," Tom said pleasantly. "Now here's why I say this: it gives me grief to have to fight. I'm sorry, but that's how I feel."

Tom spoke again in a reasonable, conversational way. "Watch this for a minute, and take your hand away from your gun. I want to show you something. What's about to happen is no threat to you. But if, after this is over, you still think you want to throw down on me, we'll talk about it."

"What?" Lucas glared at Tom, who had his eye upon the cup sitting on the chopping block.

At that instant the metal cup seemed to explode, a crash came simultaneously, a gun was in Tom's left hand, appearing there as if by magic. The tin cup spun up—another blast sounded, the target ricocheted, screaming off even higher.

The right hand flashed, truly faster than the men could see, and now that gun bucked twice and the cup's trajectory jerked first one way and then the other as two more bullets tore it.

The hardly recognizable remains of the tin cup bounced upon the dirt with a tiny clang as Tom swiveled about, his two guns leveled on the eyes of the thunderstruck Lucas.

"No sense in fightin'," Tom said very softly.

"I guess not," Lucas muttered, sun- and wind-burned face turned to a sallow greenish cast.

"Judas H. Priest," said George Perkins.

Injun Joe, the half-breed, stood stoically, very still, and had his eyes fixed on the sun's late light on the cap rock of a mountain.

"I've heard tell of hands quicker than the eye," young Hugh said as if to himself, "but till now I never believed it."

Joe Hill, as astounded as the others, said, "Hell, the boys was just funnin'. Tom. I know you was too. No harm done—jest some reg'lar Sunday horseplay," he rambled on, perhaps trying to help his men save face.

Then he concluded lamely, "Let's forgit all this." With that he went thoughtfully back to his big dilapidated house.

When he got to the steps he hollered, "Tom, if I could see you for just a minute."

Followed by Tom, Hill went back to his chair on the east side of the house. The two men sat where they had earlier in the day, in chairs that sat a few yards apart on the weathered porch.

Hill said finally, "That was quite a show just now."

Tom didn't reply.

"Mind tellin' me what your real name is?"

"Does it matter?"

"You came lookin' for me, so I guess it does."

"No, I'm not looking for you. And you were right when you said at first that I came here because of trouble. But it hasn't got to do with you."

Hill sighed, obviously relieved. "Friend, you've got a way of makin' a quick impression. If all you want to do is hide out awhile, that's fine with me. But up till now the boys have only had one boss. They do what I tell 'em without question. Things might get a bit confused with you here."

He didn't know quite how to explain himself and he sat there scowling into the night. "You see," he went on, "I've got 'em buffaloed. Cain't do to have some of these men decide *you* could do a better job than me."

"I have no interest in stayin' long. Don't believe I'd be one to get into your line of work anyhow," Tom said, a smile breaking now across his face. "In fact, I'm waitin' for word that the coast is clear to leave for Texas. A friend said he'd send me word by the telegraph line in Lincoln when things got calmed down back home."

"I see," Hill remarked, looking more comfortable all of a sudden. "Then why don't you head over to Lincoln? I was plannin' to send Hugh with the wagon to get some supplies pretty soon anyway—so you could go with him."

"I'll ride my own horse alongside Hugh's wagon just in case I have to move on."

"That's just fine, Mr. Germany," Joe Hill said, a faint spark of humor showing on his massive skull-like face. "In fact, you might want to head out now, you and Hugh, because Digger was knocked out cold during

that display you put on. By tomorrow we can likely straighten him out, but when he comes to his senses tonight he might want to stick that knife of his in your belly while you sleep."

Tom grinned. "Looks like a nice evening for a trip."

# FOURTEEN

THE WAGON made creaking noises and the rim iron on the wheels cracked sharply when crossing rocky patches, but for the most part it rolled silently across a grassy prairie. Hugh held reins leading to the mouths of the two-horse team, occasionally slapping these long leather lines against their backs. He made clucking noises with his mouth, laboring under the time-honored assumption that the horses would understand that this was his way of urging them to hurry. "Git on," he'd say from time to time, "we're on our way to Lincoln."

The full moon caused the night to glow softly. Off to the left the craggy mountain looked as if it were carved out of shadowed ice, silver and white boulders littered on its sides. Tom rode slowly beside the wagon, listening to the young man who seemed so excited at the prospect of this unexpected trip—who kept talking to the team of horses.

"Here we go," Hugh chattered, "on a Sunday night. No work tomorrow, goin' to see them purty ladies without a crowd around us." He grinned at Tom. "Seems like a dream come true."

Then he said, as Tom sidled Morgan closer, "You surprised the very hell out of me and all the boys back yonder at the ranch." Shyly he asked, "Are you famous? Are you one of them real gunfighters I've read about?"

"Lord, no."

"I'll bet you are. There cain't be no man livin' quicker with a pistol."

"Hugh, I was shooting at a tin cup. It was just the surprise of the thing; you didn't expect it at the time. I've done some practicing on fool games like that, but it's like a card trick. If I could deal off the bottom of a deck, I'd have quick hands, but that hasn't got a lot to do with what it might be like if I had to face some gunslinger. Letting off shots at a cup is an entirely different thing from standing up against someone who plans to blow a hole right through you."

"I guess so," Hugh said, "but all the same . . ."

Tom interrupted, trying to change the topic of conversation. "How far is it to Lincoln?"

"We ought to get there around four or five in the mornin'. It ain't all that many miles from here, but we got to go around these mountains." He added with a trace of pride, "Don't worry—we won't get lost; I know the trail real well."

Hugh persisted; he couldn't stop talking about the demonstration he had seen. "I expect you've been in real gunfights before. In fact, I'd bet on it. If I was fast as you I'd go up against *anyone*. Hell's bells, I bet you could even whip the meanest man in West Texas—I'm talkin' about Tom English. Then you'd *really* be famous. Git your name in the newspapers. Maybe in some of them books."

"I swear this to you, Hugh," Tom said with great seriousness. "I'd rather shoot myself than try anything that crazy."

"Guess you're right," Hugh responded. "They say he's a huge hombre —half again your size. And I've heard tales told by men who've actually seen him shoot Meskins down with no more reason than that he likes to see 'em kick. Can you imagine? He's a terrible, terrible man."

"I've heard those stories," Tom replied, "but I doubt their truth."

"There's somethin'," Hugh confessed reluctantly as though embarrassed, "that I think I ought to tell you. I've never shot nobody."

He sounded as though he had just announced some mortifying truth about himself. "I've been on the edge of situations where I've heard gunfire, and once or twice I've been chased, had men shootin' over my head. Scared the livin' hell out of me."

"How did you happen to get mixed up with Joe Hill's bunch?" Tom asked, genuinely curious.

"I grew up in Lincoln—never knew who my daddy might-a been, and my ma went off with someone." He mumbled almost inaudibly, "Before that, I'm told, she hung around saloons." Then, in a stronger tone, he continued, "I hardly remember her either. But a lady I called Aunt Agatha raised me. When I hear preachers talk about saints, I wonder if they was half as good as her. Anyway, when I got left on my own—that was after Aunt Agatha died—I worked at the stables. Then all that trouble came about, and everybody got on one side or the other. The best thing was to git clear out of sight, so I went off with some cowboys and helped wrangle their horses."

"I used to do that as a kid," Tom said softly.

"Then I got to ridin' with them. Held the horses when they went off

on foot—this was when they was on what they called one of their 'raids.' Anyhow, it just seemed the only thing to do."

"Maybe you should think about moving on, finding a real job somewhere."

"Mister," Hugh replied, "I wouldn't know how to go about it. Besides, I don't really know how to do nothin'."

"What's your last name?" Tom asked.

"I don't have no idea," the boy replied, "but I call myself Simmons after that saintly lady who raised me."

It was almost noon when an outbreak of barking erupted, disturbing Tom's sleep. A pack of mangy curs scurried through the torn earth of the fenced lots and disappeared.

Tom came instantly awake, saw Hugh off in a corner, curled up on some burlap bags. And then he realized where he was. Hugh had gone straight for the stables where he'd worked throughout his youth. The awakened drowsy owner swore at Hugh but after this permitted him and his companion to release their horses in the small pen out back. Then Hugh had led Tom to the feed bin which lay under a shed roof near their horses.

Sitting up, he saw Morgan through a fence's rails and, on the other side of the small corral, he observed the two horses Hugh had driven: standing apart, eyes closed, sleeping on their feet.

A short time later, having given Hugh some money for breakfast, he set out on foot through the town to reconnoiter. He came across a restaurant and, after a full breakfast—in spite of the hour—of steak and eggs and hot biscuits dripping with butter, plus several mugs of coffee, he felt half human.

Tom went to a boardinghouse, paid four bits for the privilege of taking a bath, and dressed in fresh clothing. The lady who ran the place agreed to do his laundry for a modest fee, and he promised to return for his things later.

He wandered down a street and found a man sitting on a chair on the board sidewalk that ran in front of a line of frame buildings. He saw a general mercantile store, a place selling feed and saddles, and next to them a saloon with batwing swinging doors. In front of it, perched on a rickety chair, sat a man with a scruffy beard wearing a derby hat.

"Mornin'," Tom said, approaching the seated man.

"Howdy," the man responded. "The damn sparrows woke me up at dawn again. Their constant chatter is goin' to drive me clean out of my

mind. I've done all I could think to drive them off, but they nest under the eaves of the roof, right next to my window, and hot as it is I have to keep it up. I've tried shotguns, fire—nearly burned up my own house once—and have more than once flung coal oil out there on their nest, but they don't pay me no heed at all."

"Sorry to hear that," Tom said, stifling a smile.

"Birds are goin' to control the world if we don't take strong action. Mark my words."

"I've always liked birds," Tom remarked.

"That's part of their cunning," the man replied.

He took the stiff brim of his derby hat and with a flip of his wrist spun it on his head. It made several turns. "My head is completely round," he said proudly. "Never knew another man who could spin a hat like I can."

He took off his derby and tilted his head forward, revealing a totally bald pate. "Lookee there," he said, "round as a billiard ball."

Baffled, Tom said, "It sure is." Then he explained, "I was looking for the telegraph office."

"Across the street," the derby-hatted man stated, "next to the sheriff's office. If you want to send a message you'd best be quick about it. There's a line of birds sittin' on the wire right now; they'll be destroyin' it soon, would be my guess. That'll leave us out here at their mercy."

Tom nodded a farewell and walked across the street. "Lord, Lord," he said to himself, "I do get a kick out of listening to people."

Off to his left a wagon jolted along, its bed holding what appeared to be parts of a windmill, and these jangled against one another each time the wagon bucked over a dry rut. On reaching the telegraph office he went inside. A barefooted man wearing a pair of pants and the sweated top of a set of long underwear in spite of the heat sat up on a canvas cot. "The line's down agin'," he said. "No use tryin' to send a message."

"I was expecting to hear from someone," Tom said.

"Got a few here," the telegraph operator said with a sigh, his rest interrupted. "What's your name?"

"Tom Germany."

The man riffled through a few slips of paper on the unvarnished pine table beside his transmitter. A wire curled from it to the wall, leading to the line of poles and trees which linked this modern miracle to distant receivers and transmitters.

"Here you go," the operator said, sounding vaguely surprised that he was actually doing business. "Came in two days ago from, let's see, looks

like it's from someplace in Texas." With a professional nod of his head he handed the slip of paper to Tom and lay back on his cot. He held his arms out stiffly to each side and stretched before asking, "Is Crazy George still mad at them birds? Seen you talkin' to him."

"He sounds right concerned."

"Last week it was wasps and bugs that was goin' to take over the world," the telegraph operator said. "George is a worrier."

Tom walked out of the office and leaned against a hitching rail in front, reading the short message:

To Tom Germany, Lincoln, New Mexico. Your case remanded for retrial. Return home. JEDEDIAH JACKSON.

"Well," Tom said softly to himself, "things are looking better."

He allowed himself to think of Sally now and of Rebecca and Ben, the children. A wave of pleasure swept through his body as he began making plans for the trip back home.

Tom didn't even notice the three men who came up behind him as he leaned back upon the rail. The hot high sun left their shadows angling a short distance from their feet.

"Raise your hands slow, mister," a voice said sharply. Tom looked about to see three men holding pistols leveled on him.

"Don't try nothin'," the same man said.

Tom saw a star on his chest. "Am I under arrest, Sheriff?"

"You are. Don't move a muscle. Jed," he directed, "take his guns."

One of the men, after holstering his own weapon, walked cautiously forward and disarmed Tom, pulling the two Colts away from their scabbards.

"What's the charge against me?" Tom asked.

"We'll talk about that in there," the sheriff said, nodding toward his office, which lay only one door away. "Get inside and face the wall— lean on it with your hands."

When the four men reached the office, the two deputies patted around Tom's waist, pockets, and boots, searching for a hideout gun or for a knife. Then one of them nodded.

The sheriff said, "Set yourself down and give us an account of what you're doin' here."

"I came to get word from the telegraph office. Now I aim to head back home to Texas."

"You were seen in the company of young Hugh Simmons this mornin'. The boy's harmless enough, we've knowed him all our lives,

but he's took up with bad company. Rides with Joe Hill now. So we figure you're part of that outfit."

One of the deputies said, "We know the kind of things you outlaws been up to—robbin' banks and stagecoaches, hirin' out in range wars—killin' innocent men and such as that. Not to mention horse thievin' and rustlin'."

"I'll admit that I stayed a week there on my way in, but I'm no part of Joe Hill's bunch. My name is Tom English and I ranch along the North Concho River in West Texas."

The men looked thunderstruck. "Tom English?" one of them whispered in disbelief.

The sheriff tilted back his chair and examined Tom under his hat-brim for a long time. At last he exclaimed, "Well, I'll be a son of a bitch!"

He settled his chair back on all its legs and opened a drawer. "You got any proof of your identity?"

"Not on me."

The sheriff pulled out a sheet of creased paper and smoothed it with a callused hand. "This here is new," he said half to himself, "it just came on the last stagecoach."

He looked down at it and then at Tom's face, narrowing his eyes as he concentrated. His brow furrowed and he pushed the sheet across to one of his men. "Look at that, Bill."

The man addressed by the sheriff did so and said, "It's him all right. No doubt about it. Looks like we've earned ourselves a reward."

Tom experienced a spinning in the pit of his stomach.

The sheriff picked up the poster and handed it to him. Tom took the limp sheet of paper in his hands and looked at it numbly.

# WANTED—DEAD OR ALIVE
# TOM ENGLISH

Under these large bold-type letters he saw an engraving of a photograph of his face, one he'd seen before in newspaper stories, and with it the legend:

$1000 DOLLARS WILL BE PAID TO ANY MAN WHO CATCHES OR KILLS TOM EN-GLISH. He is wanted by the Law in Santa Rita, Texas, where he has been convicted for

the crime of murdering a man named Wrangler Hull. A court has sentenced this wanted man to death by hanging. The reward, put up by the Citizens for Law and Order of Tom Green County, is payable on delivery of Tom English or his body to Sheriff Reuben Baxter, Santa Rita, Texas.

"Looks to me to be your picture," the sheriff said.

"It is," Tom admitted. "But there's to be a new trial." He handed over the slip of paper he'd received from the telegraph operator.

"This telegram was sent to 'Tom Germany,' " the sheriff said, laying slight emphasis on the last name.

"I called myself that while on the run. My lawyer—he's the man named Jedediah Jackson who sent the wire—got the authorities in Austin to get me a fair trial. I took another name since it didn't seem real smart to use my own."

One of the deputies moved nervously to one side, keeping his six-gun pointed at Tom's belly.

Another of them pulled a sheet from the small stack of wanted posters which the sheriff had on his desk. It showed a drawing of a man with a mustache.

A drawn smile stretched the deputy's face; it looked unnatural, as though he rarely showed a sign of pleasure. He held it up for the others to see the unusually lifelike drawing.

Tom stared at it—looked at the face—and saw a man with a hooked nose, lines leading down from it, with dull eyes and a heavy, drooping mustache. He saw the likeness of the man who'd been sent to kill him.

"We got a curious situation, Sheriff," the deputy holding the poster said to his boss. "All of us know there's a hundred-dollar reward put up for Wrangler Hull, dead or alive. We got the strange situation of one murderer gunnin' another. Don't know that, given the circumstances, he ought to collect. What on earth do we do now?"

"My concern," the sheriff said deliberately, "is to keep the peace in these parts. Tom English ain't wanted here. We can talk to Hugh Simmons, and it's my guess he'll back up his story that English has never been part of Joe Hill's gang."

The lawman rolled a cigarette, streaming tobacco from a limp sack into a bent paper held by his fingers, then rolled and licked it, and scratched a long wooden match on the sole of his boot. Wisps of sharp

sulphur smoke made him squint his eyes as he took a long draw on the limp cigarette before continuing. "Wrangler Hull was about as sorry as they come. You shot a miserable snake of a man, Mr. English. And while I've heard all manner of stories about you, to my knowledge all your fights have been fair. So it don't seem to me that we should tie you up and haul you back to Texas and try for that thousand dollars. Particularly when it looks to me like you got yourself a new trial. That ought not to cause you much trouble, considerin' the nature of the man you killed."

"I didn't know his name at the time of all the trouble," Tom said. "They must have found out about it later. But I saw his horse had the Bent Snake brand, so I came out to try to learn who he was and why he'd come gunnin' for me."

"Well, now you know his name. You learn anything else?" a deputy asked.

"It don't matter now," the sheriff said, "since the bastard's dead— and good riddance." Once more he tilted his chair until it balanced on its two back legs, its spindled backrest propped against the wall. "Wrangler Hull murdered men for hire. That was his special pleasure, and now it's a relief to know he's done for. So, Mr. English, what I think I ought to do is take you down to our bank so they can pay out the hundred dollars you've earned by ridding the world of that varmint. And besides that, I'll give you a letter of commendation to take back to that new trial you spoke of. When you go in with it, they're bound to turn you loose."

Tom English shook his head. "I'm not anxious to face that judge again, but I reckon there's no other choice."

"Don't worry none," the sheriff said. And then he added, "Naturally, I've heard about you."

A slow smile spread across his face. "I'll be blessed if I ain't the first man to get the drop on Tom English. Maybe you boys will show me more respect in the future."

The deputy called Bill replied, "Baker, if I hadn't been here to help, you'd-a never been able to do it. Me and Jed got equal credit with you."

The sheriff rose to his feet and said, "My name's Baker Eckert, and I'd be proud to shake your hand, Mr. English. Before you leave town I want my kid to see you. His name is Bobbie. Smart as a whip, particularly when it comes to arithmetic. And he'd get a kick out of tellin' his friends he'd met you."

.  .  .  .

Tuck Bowlegs came from the direction of Clear Creek, carrying a wild turkey he had brought down with a silent arrow—along with a string of catfish.

Waiting for him, propped against a log, sat Calvin Laudermilk. "We've had us a fine day, Tuck. Killed a turkey, caught a big mess of fish."

"*I* had a fine day," Tuck said with more precision. "*You* been sittin' in the shade."

"We'll be ridin' back to Santa Rita soon," Calvin said, ignoring his Indian friend. "Of course, you and I are still wanted for murder, although all we meant was to help poor Tom get away from the hangman's noose. However, I have word sent by Jedediah Jackson that he's tryin' to get a pardon for us from the governor himself, owin' to the peculiarity of the circumstances we got caught up in. Jedediah allowed as how he couldn't come up with a legal way to argue our way out of this particular predicament."

"I think I'll stay out of sight until the white men decide not to string me up," Tuck said as he tossed the still squirming broad-bodied catfish upon the ground beside the feathered turkey carcass.

Calvin rose to his tree-trunk legs with an exaggerated show of effort, punctuating his laborious movements with grunts and snorted curses. He grasped his broad-brimmed hat, jammed it on his head, and then plunged down through a ravine that led to the creek, up the far slope, and energetically plowed his way through brush and shinnery until he reached the grounds surrounding the Bench home. A small boy named Mac and a little girl named Beth played in a sandpile.

Calvin spoke to them earnestly, watching them build houses and hills and trenches in the sand. "Playing is much more important than work. Remember that, children, all of your lives. Don't ever let grown-ups fool you into thinking that work has any value." The children, intent upon their efforts, paid no attention to him.

Edmund Bench stood on the porch waiting for him. "Where'd your Indian friend go?"

Calvin looked about, saw the turkey and fish beside a tree, but saw no sign of Tuck. "Beats me, Ed. He must mistrust you since you're one of them white men he's always grumblin' about."

"But what about you?"

"Tuck's accustomed to me. Besides, because of my size, I'm like him; which is to say he looks on me as an outcast too."

The two old friends went inside a comfortable sitting room. Like all

Germans Calvin had ever met, they had a sturdy well-kept house, and this room showed the warm personality of Ed's wife Sara. She looked up from the book she'd been reading and smiled her welcome.

"Calvin," her voice rang out in resonant contralto tones, "about time you came back. Ed's been cooking all afternoon and he'd be disappointed if you'd carried out your threat to leave us."

"Sara," Calvin said, sweeping off his hat, "when did you ever know me to miss a meal?"

Her marvelous laugh, like the pealing of fine bells, rang out and caused Ed to beam at her. He had a slightly round face and a somewhat full figure, for he appreciated good cooking. And he was an expert cook. His once bountiful head of hair had thinned after an illness he had suffered, and Sara teased him about it. But he took this good-naturedly, laughing with high notes, causing a contagion of smiles to break out if others were about.

"My," Calvin said to himself, "if I could only have a companion for life like Ed has. It's not my nature to suffer a lonely old age." But as he thought of Elvira he winced. "She'd make me go to Bible studies ever' damn Wednesday night, and more than likely would disapprove of the fellowship I seek at the Concho Street Saloon, not to mention my afternoons devoted to picking up the spirits of any downcast cowpokes who might be moping around the Lost Hope Saloon."

Edmund left Calvin with a large glass jar of homemade wine while he went off to the huge kitchen in the back of the house. Aromas swept throughout the stone dwelling, and Calvin's mouth watered. He rose to observe the preparations for the feast and watched while Ed skinned the catfish, using a knife and then a pair of pliers for the task. Then he cleaned them, cut them with a razor-edged knife into fillets, and dropped them in batter and then into a popping skillet with clear bubbling grease in it. The iron stove threw heat through the room and Calvin, who considered himself particularly susceptible to discomfort, had to excuse himself.

Later, Edmund served a goose he had roasted, filled with his special dressing; green beans from the garden made rich with salt pork; black-eyed peas; jalapeño corn bread; and fried catfish. Mugs of German beer accompanied the many courses. At last Edmund Bench remarked, after his third plate of catfish, "These are startin' to taste a little mossy."

Calvin roared with laughter. "Never was another one like you, Ed."

"I thought we'd save the turkey for tomorrow," Edmund remarked.

"Don't apologize, old friend, I think we had enough." Calvin had put

away a remarkable amount, even for him, and now he wondered if he could rise or if he'd be doomed to spend the next two days in the ample sturdy armchair that had been pulled to the table for him. While he worried about this, Tuck's face appeared at the window.

"Come on in and join us," Sara called.

Tuck shook his head. "I ate already." He directed himself to Calvin. "Some men are comin' on horseback. I'll be in those trees in front of the house."

With that he disappeared.

Calvin, his discomfort forgotten, moved surprisingly swiftly to the sitting room. He buckled on his gunbelt and walked out toward the porch.

Hand on his revolver, he passed through the front door just as three men rode up. "Howdy, Calvin," their leader said.

"Well, good afternoon, Sheriff Baxter. What are you doin' way out here?"

From the corners of his eyes he saw another ten or fifteen riders appear. Then to his surprise he saw Tuck emerge from the trees with his hands tied behind his back. Four men on foot walked behind him, holding pistols in their hands.

"Time to take you to jail, Calvin. You and that Seminole friend of yours can hang along with Tom English."

"Tuck resents bein' called a Seminole," Calvin protested. "He's proud of bein' half Comanche. He'd prefer you call him that."

"What in the hell is that fat man talkin' about?" a man holding a rifle asked the sheriff.

# FIFTEEN

"THIS IS INTOLERABLE," roared Calvin Laudermilk, heaving his monstrous body back and forth while holding to the bars. He hadn't done this before and rather enjoyed the sensation. The side of the old iron cell swayed and made cracking noises as the entire structure shuddered; it had not been designed to withstand such stresses.

"Damn your bones," a white-faced jailer screeched in alarm, slamming a rifle butt against the same bars, "git over there in the corner before you tear the building down. You want me to have to shoot you in the leg?"

Calvin retreated, apparently mollified. "No, young man. I merely wanted to get your attention. It's seven o'clock and I normally have my supper by this hour. So notify the cook that I'm ready to be served."

The bewildered deputy—who had been left in charge all by himself owing to all the things occurring outside—said, "You'll git fed when I feel like it."

"Petty bureaucrat," snarled Calvin. "Drunk with power like all your kind." He turned his back upon the man and addressed Tuck Bowlegs.

"Jedediah swears he's got a pardon on the way for us, but if it don't get here quick we'll have to take our satisfaction from the knowledge that these scoundrels are about to hang two innocent, or near innocent, men."

Outside on the courthouse grounds the sound of hammers rang as a scaffold neared completion. The long hot summer day hung on, the sun lingering in the bloodshot western sky.

Tuck Bowlegs had not spoken now for two full days, but this didn't deter Calvin from continuing their one-sided conversation.

"At least they let Tom English go—pretty well had to—seeing that he came with a letter of commendation from the authorities in Lincoln over in New Mexico Territory for gunnin' Wrangler Hull, who had a price on his head. None can be blamed for killing a hunted outlaw."

At last Tuck spoke up. "You and I were wanted by the law, had prices on our heads."

"And insultingly small rewards they were, too," Calvin growled. "But anyway, that's different," he emphasized. "We're about to get pardoned. And if we do I'm sure that Noah and Japheth Massie will be greatly relieved, for they carpenter the caskets for our fine community and keep a small stock out in their storeroom. However, as you'll recall, Noah came over yesterday and told me that I wouldn't fit in any that they've got. Made me feel right uncomfortable as he stood outside those bars, measuring me with his eyes, deciding just how big a box he'd have to build. Of course, even though Noah is a good friend, at the same time he's a professional woodworker, and I could see that he was plannin' to do a good job. It goes without sayin' that my choice would be to spare him that bother."

A crowd had gathered in the town even though the double hanging scheduled by the judge wouldn't take place until Wednesday, almost two days off, since it was only Monday night. As the sun disappeared, a breeze kicked up dust puffs on the grassless ground beside the raw boards of the strange construction, and observers stood in random clumps while several workers doggedly hammered away.

When darkness fell a few brought out flares, torches made of long sticks with oil-soaked rags tied to them. They held these up and allowed their smoky yellow light to throw irregular shadows on the few who toiled and on the silent men and women who stood by, watching them. A few children, bored by the absence of activity, began to play a game of chase, running around in circles.

"People in this town take weeks to build a simple fence. Never saw folks showin' more energy," Calvin complained. "I'd as soon they took their time." He didn't expect an answer and he got none. "Would you look at that, Tuck? I've never seen it to fail. There'll always be six loafers watchin' for every man doin' any actual work."

The old jail had two windows in its stone walls. Calvin stood at one of these and the deputy stood at the other, on the outside of the cell. Each stared at the scene before him in fascination.

A carnival sense of excitement buzzed upon the courthouse square when the great crossbeam was finally raised in place. A murmuring began as the man in charge, an outsider who wore an old black suit in spite of the heat, stood on a ladder and tied two special ropes to it. He descended the ladder to the platform's floor and stood beside the dangling hangman's nooses. He reached up and pulled hard, testing them—

first one and then the other. The trapdoors underneath his feet made a hollow noise and rattled when he'd swing up on the ropes and then drop down.

Miss Hattie and two of the girls who worked for her in the white frame house, denounced as being of "ill fame" from the Baptist and Methodist pulpits, stood woefully at the fringes of the crowd. The three women began sobbing into handkerchiefs, put their arms around one another, and departed. "Bless their hearts," Calvin said without bothering to explain to Tuck what he meant.

Men wearing hats appeared all around the scaffold in the flickering light as if they were an audience gathering to observe a performance on the stage. Others carried bottles as they scuffed unsteadily down the road and around the corner, walking from Concho Street where they would have spent all afternoon in various saloons—talking about the executions. They stopped when they got near and stood in clusters, watching the swarthy, sweating hangman who'd come all the way from Huntsville in East Texas. With the help of two bystanders, he put a great sack filled with sand on a heavy rope, pulled the lever which sprang a trapdoor, and watched the sack fall through, making the scaffold jolt as a surprisingly loud clanging noise rang out.

The deputy stared as if mesmerized, arms propped on the windowsill. "The hangman says he's never had a customer who weighed over three hundred pounds before, Calvin. Wants to do this right, but the thing that concerns him is this: if he drops someone your size the normal distance, then the amount you weigh might cause your head to pop right off—and that would be, in his view, a personal disgrace. The man takes pride in what he does."

Calvin winced. "You don't have a great deal of sensitivity, do you?"

The deputy laughed coldly. "I can't see why we couldn't of got a simple hangin' done with before now. However, only yesterday afternoon I was over at the Concho Street Saloon and heard Judge T. J. Hoskins say he wants this execution to be handled in a real formal way. He said it'll set an example so folks will *know* the law he lays down must, by God, be obeyed."

"Our trial wasn't all that formal," Calvin complained. "Took about ten minutes, and I wasn't given the chance to speak at all." He brooded over this a moment. "I had a spellbinding oration worked out in my mind, and now it's locked in there, festering away because it had no chance to be released. And in addition to that, lawyer Jackson got no

time to talk on my behalf, which makes me think that maybe I didn't get
my rights—even in an informal way."

Tuck Bowlegs sat cross-legged in a corner, staring straight in front of
him. Calvin sank carefully upon the single cot in the room and then lay
back, looking at the rough-sawn boards of the ceiling above the wooden
rafters and all the cobwebs, old and new, above him. A spider waited
motionlessly in the center of one web.

"There's a black widow, Tuck, the kind of spider that mates and then
eats her husband. I've long been convinced that mankind can learn a
great deal by studying nature and examining the lessons set out before
us. After careful thought I've decided that maybe this is the best thing
that ever happened to me. It certainly isn't the most dignified way to
make my exit, but at least it's no more final than a more peaceable end
would be. And maybe this is Dame Fortune's way of putting her arm
around my shoulders and helpin' me. It wouldn't-a done for me to live
out a normal life. Might even have hitched up with Elvira, and who
knows but what that could have turned into a reg'lar hell on earth. But
she's been most solicitous, coming out here every day, weeping like a
fountain. It does cause a warmth to rise up in my bosom when I see that
at least one person cares if I'm alive or dead."

He paused momentarily in his monologue before adding, "Excuse me,
Tuck, for mentioning that last word, it just slipped out. But while I'm
on the subject, allow me to make one more observation. There's an old
sayin' to the effect that we are to count no man happy until his death.
But I don't go along with that—I've had a happy time of it regardless of
the way I happen to die. No sheriff or judge or man from Huntsville
can change a thing about my past, and I'm well satisfied with it."

He raised his head and peered at Tuck but noted with disappoint-
ment that his Indian friend had not been listening. In fact he had risen
to his hands and knees, looking keenly at the jailer, then he crawled
alongside Calvin and began to whisper quietly.

"You broke the bars loose at the ceiling a minute ago. With a big push
at the top, they might go over on top of the guard."

Calvin, suddenly alert, rose nonchalantly from his cot, backing away
from the window all the way to the far side of the cell away from the
guard, who kept his chin propped on his arms, looking out the window.

Calvin turned his head, saw the hangman lengthen one of the ropes
and once again, with help from two men, strain to tie the heavy sack to
it. The black-suited executioner retreated to one side, put his hand on a
lever, and pulled it. At that instant Calvin rushed forward as though

shot from a cannon, all three hundred and thirty pounds launching into the air, and as the scaffold crashed this time the men standing near it heard a resounding boom from the direction of the jail.

Mystified, they looked at each other until one said in a tone that carried, "Must-a been an echo."

Not one of them noticed when Calvin and Tuck scurried out of the sheriff's shedlike office which adjoined the old stone jail. The two bent-over figures moved quickly around behind it and disappeared into the darkness.

When they reached the pens behind the Elkhorn wagon yard, Calvin found his gear and saddled Sully. By that time Tuck had bridled his mule and made his way bareback out on the street.

"Did you kill him?" he inquired as Calvin led his horse out of the wagon yard.

"Dead men rarely swear, and as we left I heard someone underneath those bars groanin' and sayin' some terrible cusswords. My guess is that he's got quite a few broken bones."

"We better go different directions," Tuck said when Calvin hauled himself up into his saddle and then leaned back, sitting comfortably astride the Percheron. Then Tuck's walnut-colored face cracked into a rare smile. "Nobody but you could have broke that jail wall down." And then he rode off into the night.

Calvin used his rein ends as a quirt, in spite of Sully's looking back at him with somewhat angry eyes. And then the workhorse lumbered into a heavy jolting gallop, pie-plate hooves banging on the dirt.

Tuck would be headed south into land whose every crease and fold he knew. They'd never find him. But Calvin decided that he and Sully might not be able to blend into the landscape. He turned north toward the Lazy E. If anyone could protect him, it would be Tom English.

A crystal chandelier shed soft candlelight upon a long oval mahogany table in Max Hall's dining room. Glinting lights reflected from the bottles and glasses on a sideboard and from a long breakfast cabinet filled with silver serving dishes and chinaware. All these things had been brought to Texas by Max's father when the banker's family moved there after the war. The five men sitting at the table ignored their surroundings.

Jedediah Jackson, a widower in his middle seventies, but erect and proud despite his years, said, "The pardon for Laudermilk and Tuck Bowlegs is on its way—I got a wire from Austin this afternoon. But it

was a near thing." The lawyer looked across the table at Tom English. "The fact that they busted loose saved a lot of bloodshed."

All the others knew what he meant by that. Tom had assembled a large group of cowboys from the many branches of the widespread Lazy E. They responded to his summons and arrived over a period of days at what they termed the Lower Ranch, the one only six miles from town that Jason Field had left to Tom in his will. Jedediah said, "If they had tried to hang Tuck and Calvin, I know the Concho would have run as red as Shiloh Creek."

Hall sat at the end of the table, acting as host, filling glasses before they emptied. His round and normally happy face showed concern. A big man, over six feet tall and weighing more than two hundred pounds, he usually showed great enthusiasm. But tonight he looked tired.

"We've been faced with one crisis after another for so long that we're losing sight of what is really going on," Max said. "First a man rode onto the Lazy E to bushwhack Tom, and then the law tried to execute him for the 'crime' of self-defense. Then he had no sooner got out of that jam by the grace of God—since the man he shot was an outlaw—when Calvin Laudermilk and Tuck got into their fix. We need to look behind all these things and get to the cause of the trouble, not their symptoms."

"You're talking like a doctor," Jedediah said.

This caused Max to grin. He took a drink and said, "I guess I am. What we need is for Santa Rita to get healthy again. I know my bank is strained to the limit, and every store in town is in serious shape. Retail sales have almost died—and the little they can still sell has to be on credit since none of the ranchers can pay their bills. The blame for this falls squarely on the bank set up by Julian Haynes and their 'easy credit' notes. What I predicted has come about: those notes have been called in for payment. The Haynes bank has seized ranches and herds they held as collateral all over this part of the state. The damnable part is that Haynes installed his own man, T. J. Hoskins, as the judge to enforce his liens—to do his bidding. It's a ruinous thing."

"Business goes in cycles—couldn't that be what's happening?" the lawyer asked.

"I don't think so—this isn't something that's happening elsewhere," Max answered. "West Texas seems to be suffering all by itself this time."

Three men hadn't spoken. One of them, a young man, sat at the side of Tom English at the far end of the table. Another, John Robert Hale,

the famous Texas Ranger captain, sat by himself across from Tom. He cleared his throat and the others turned toward him.

John Robert Hale had a low voice and, when he spoke, men listened. A man of average height and build, he leaned back in his chair and said, "I can't address such problems. I don't know much about business. But I do think that we've got to clean house. There are men who've come to Santa Rita who can cause harm. As you know, I've been out in the Davis Mountains for quite a time. While I was gone, a man named Reuben Baxter from El Paso got named sheriff for Tom Green County. I can tell you a little about him."

The others gave John Robert their full attention.

"Baxter has the reputation of being a hard man. You wouldn't expect Julian Haynes to bring any other kind if his plan was to take over the town. Anyway, I've heard that Baxter made a name for himself in a range war in New Mexico. After that he got mixed up with some outlaws around El Paso. That's where Haynes comes from as well as T. J. Hoskins, the judge you mentioned. I've been unable to learn anything about Hoskins except that he's never been a judge before."

"I could have told you that," Jedediah Jackson said curtly. "And he's no lawyer either."

John Robert concluded, "I've found out nothing about Julian Haynes —the man is a total mystery to me. Max probably knows more about him than I do."

Max said, "I've tried to learn what I could from other bankers. Friends at the Fort Worth National and the City Bank of Dallas ran a check for me. Haynes has powerful friends at the state capital and maybe in Washington due to the fact that he makes a lot of political contributions. He has over five hundred thousand dollars in cash, not to mention those ranches around here he foreclosed on—or bought at fire-sale prices."

"Don't forget the cattle," Tom broke in. The others turned toward him.

Tom said, "He foreclosed on herds as well as land—and the word is that he has sold some ten thousand head to the XIT in the panhandle. He stands to make a big profit there—since the cattle didn't cost him ten cents on the dollar."

Max said, "We know he'd been trying to get access to the North Concho through your property. I thought that cattle sale you mentioned was to take place next year."

Tom shook his head. "He apparently made a new deal, and the cattle

are on a drive to the XIT right now. Thanks to Asa Coltrane and the cowboys on Hester Trace's ranch, it looks like Haynes's men gave up on their chances of cutting our fences.

"I introduced all of you earlier to Hugh Simmons, the young man sitting by me, when we came in. There's a reason I asked for this meeting, and that's to listen to his story. Before he starts, I need to let you know a little about how we met."

Then Tom told them briefly about his escape and about the ride with Calvin and Tuck to the fishing shack on the South Concho. He recounted his conversation with Calvin and Tuck about the man who'd tried to kill him, and how he had described to them the man and his horse with the jagged slash across its hip. And then the way he'd learned from Tuck about the Bent Snake brand, and where the ranch lay in New Mexico Territory.

"So I went there as much in desperation as anything," Tom concluded, after telling them about the way he met the young man with him. "It's time for you to pick up the story, Hugh."

The boy shifted nervously in his chair. He obviously felt ill at ease in Max Hall's house. He'd never seen anything like it in his life. "Well," he began so quietly that the others couldn't hear him.

"Speak up, son," Jedediah Jackson said. "My hearing's not what it used to be."

"Yes, sir," Hugh replied. "I talked to Mr. English about all this. He can tell it better than me, but he said I should go into what happened." His face flushed with embarrassment. Seeing the amused patience on the faces of the four men around him, he began to speak—first with confusion but then directly and simply.

"Joe Hill called me in when he got a wire from somewhere in Texas. He told me an old friend he'd known since his days in El Paso had sent him a wire that there was what he called 'a big-money job,' or something like that, to be done. Hill said I was to go, according to the telegram he got in Lincoln, to the Russell Hotel in a town called Tascosa. Had to get there by the last day of May."

"Tascosa lies in the middle of the XIT," Tom said. The others nodded. All of them knew about the place.

"Anyway," Hugh Simmons said, "I finally got there, about a day late because I got lost, but anyway, I went to the Russell Hotel. I did what Mr. Hill told me: I asked around for the friend of Baxter's."

John Robert Hale looked up sharply. "What's that?"

"Mr. Hill said his friend who used to ride with him was named

Baxter, he's the one who sent him the wire about the job to be done. Anyway, a man wearing a coat came down the stairs and met me in the bar. He asked who I might be, and I said I'd been sent by Joe Hill. This made him mad because he thought Hill himself would come. So then he said he wasn't going to say more except that there was important work to be done.

"He sat awhile, seemed to be thinking, and then he must have decided I could be trusted since Joe Hill had sent me out alone. Then, without saying a word, he got up and left; I guess he went back to his room, but anyway he came back in just a few minutes carrying a small satchel. He handed this over to me and said I was to take it to Joe Hill. I picked the thing up and was right surprised at its weight. I looked up at him and saw him studyin' me. He had slit eyes, don't know how a man can see who keeps his eyes closed that way, but anyway he said, and I remember these words exactly—they made a strong impression—'Boy, there's two hundred silver dollars in that case. You're to take it to Joe Hill—and if one dollar ends up short, I'll get some Mescalero friends of mine to burn you over a slow fire.' "

Hugh winced at the memory. "You don't forget things like that. Anyway, I told him I was just a messenger, and that I would sure as hell deliver all the money to Mr. Hill.

"The slit-eyed man said, 'All right, you do that. But tell Hill from me that the next time he's not to send a boy on a man's errand.' And then I asked, 'Is that all?' and he said, 'No, it's not. When Hill, or the man he might choose for the job, goes out—he's to ride to Santa Rita, a little town across the river from Fort Concho in West Texas. When he gets there he's to see the judge—who will tell him what he has to do to earn the two hundred dollars.' "

Hugh fell silent. Then he said, "And that's all there was. I took that satchel back to the Bent Snake ranch and gave it to Joe Hill along with the message."

"Did the man at the Russell Hotel ever give you his name?" Hale asked.

"No, sir," Hugh answered.

"It had to be Julian Haynes," Max Hall said. "He would have been up there makin' his cattle deal with the XIT people. And the description the boy gave sure fits him." He mused a moment. "Wonder what Wrangler Hull did with the money? Probably left it hid somewhere under some rocks."

Tom burst out laughing. "Trust a banker to worry about money."

The others joined him.

"Thank you, Hugh. You've sure cleared things up as far as I'm concerned," said Hale.

Tom glanced around the table at his friends. "I advised Hugh he was still young enough to get a fresh start somewhere; he's never been directly involved in trouble, as I may have told you before. He said he didn't know how to do anything, but I explained that in that case he'd fit in just fine at my place. As you know, we're short some men on the Lazy E."

A tension fell upon the men at these last words. They knew the closeness that had existed between Tom and the five Mexican cowhands who had died trying to rescue him.

"Let the law take care of this matter," John Robert warned.

Tom English didn't answer.

# SIXTEEN

JUDGE T. J. HOSKINS sank into a soft upholstered chair in the waiting room near the tall plant with drooping green leaves in its dull red pot. He always felt uneasy in Julian Haynes's bank for some reason; the formality of the furnishings seemed out of place. Looking down, he saw a design of small unicorns and leopards in a border around the edges of the oriental carpet. "I wonder where on earth Haynes got this rug," he said to himself.

A lamp glowed steadily upon the table, throwing wavering light upon the wall, which held an oil portrait of an austere lady who stared everlastingly off to one side, as though she had made a pact with herself to overlook the things that might take place within her sight.

The door of the private office at the corner of the waiting room opened, and a very young Mexican girl came out. She looked disheveled, her hair matted and her eyes fierce as she wiped tears from them. Julian Haynes appeared at the door, buttoning his white shirt. Behind him, lying on the long sofa, Hoskins saw Haynes's frock coat and, on the floor, his tie.

"What do you want?"

"Christ a'mighty, Julian, all hell's about to break loose. What do you mean, what do I want? Tom English has gathered thirty or forty men out at his ranch. He's come to town with the Texas Ranger, and at this minute they're over at Max Hall's house—gettin' ready to make their move."

The two men entered the private office, closed the door behind them, and sat down. Haynes took his place in the black leather chair behind his broad uncluttered desk. Hoskins sat nervously on the edge of an armchair's seat in front of him.

"Calm down, T.J., we've known this might happen ever since we saw English come into town with that boy. And we worked out exactly how to handle the situation."

Haynes held a brandy snifter cupped in both hands, warming the contents as though in prelude to savoring the fiery liquid, but instead he gulped it as though throwing down a shot of raw tequila. He clenched his teeth against the effect and then asked, "How long have we known each other, T.J.?"

"Since I was just a tad, after I showed up at your daddy's ranch."

Haynes nodded. "You grew up there with all us 'Meskins,' alongside Jaime and Chato and all the others—including me. And worked for my drunken old daddy. He quirted the two of us almost every night. In that way, I guess, he treated you as if you were a brother." Bitterness etched his face.

"We've been together quite a spell," Hoskins admitted cautiously. He knew not to cross his companion when he'd been drinking and he saw the half-empty bottle of brandy on the desk.

"Old Dad was a cutter," Julian Haynes said, leaning back. He poured more brandy and sipped it slowly as he spoke. "He had a good education but left for the West to gain his fortune. Well, he did that in a manner of speaking. He lost what money he had in a poker game when, for some damned reason, he'd wandered into Socorro County in the New Mexico Territory. So he hired on as a cowpuncher at the Estevez ranch not far away from Frisco. And in six months he'd married the only daughter of old Joaquin Estevez. At the time my dad had just passed his twenty-eighth birthday, and my poor mother was only fifteen. I don't remember her at all, of course. I'm told she looked a little like her mother, the one in that picture outside in the waiting room— that's Joaquin's wife. A padre painted it in Mexico City, the story goes; he did it from memory after seeing her in church—and later sent it to her. Can you beat that? Anyway, my maternal grandmother didn't last long after she moved to New Mexico."

"Why are you tellin' me all of this?" Hoskins asked.

"Well, T.J., my opinion is that we're going to have some company soon, so I'm just passing the time. You don't object to that, do you?" An unspoken threat lay behind the question. Haynes had always, since childhood, been able to bully Hoskins even though his friend was older.

"As you know, my mother died while giving birth to me in the big house that Joaquin Estevez built when he thought he'd have a large family. My mother's father, old Joaquin—he always had me call him 'Abuelo'—had always wanted eight or ten kids but ended up with just himself and one pitiful little girl with no one to carry on his name. Then, after Joaquin died, Dad owned it all. He held title to that ram-

bling thick-walled adobe house with heavy Spanish red tiles on its roof, along with the dried-out range. He owned forty sections, give or take a little—over twenty-five thousand acres—and ran some scrawny spotted Mexican cattle. He had more help than he needed: vaqueros wandered in from Old Mexico, and then their families followed. Built shacks, planted little plots of frijoles, raised some goats, and somehow managed to hold body and soul together.

"That's where I grew up, and you did too, with my bastard half brothers and half sisters in the shacks around the ranch—while Dad drank whatever kind of whiskey or tequila he could get his hands on. Until he finally got hold of that bad batch and went blind."

Hoskins didn't break the silence that fell at this moment.

"Which brings us to the time when my luck turned," Haynes said. "I had him sign a power of attorney, giving me the right to do whatever I wanted with the property. I built the ranch up and put it in my name. Then I took off for two years, that time I went to Santa Fe and got an education of sorts—while you stayed behind and ran things for me. And then I sold most of the ranch to J. B. Slaughter."

Julian Haynes started to reach forward, his eyes on the bottle, but, thinking better of it, sank heavily back into his chair. His dark face flushed and he looked up with the two fringed slits that were his eyes, and a cruel smile without humor bent his mouth.

"My God, you'd have thought I'd killed him from the way Dad squalled when he heard what I'd done. He'd gotten so weak he could scarcely get up from his bed, but in spite of that I found him outside in the shed next to the corral, clawing at that old saddle of his for a rifle. Said he planned to kill me for selling his land—that a family like his *had* to own their land. He whirled around, waving his rifle when he heard me laugh. That worn-out drunk who used to whip the blood out of me —there he stood, waving his egg-white eyes around as if he thought he might actually see me if he tried hard enough. Then those blind eyes began to cry and tears actually streamed down over his wrinkles. This ruined old son of a bitch stood there saying, 'No man can take my land from me.' And I said, 'Well, Dad, it belongs to Mr. Slaughter now.' Then he dropped the rifle to the ground and stumbled back toward the house. Fell down on the steps, and I went over to help him get back inside. He never spoke to me after that."

"I hadn't heard about his trying to shoot you."

"Well, that's what happened. But the old man has stayed alive, dried out as a gourd, but still living on chicken soup, I guess. I didn't sell the

house, and kept a little land, about three or four sections. The shacks are still there. Goats and chickens and frijoles—enough for the people to live on. My bastard half brothers and half sisters look after him, I guess. They probably keep him supplied with tequila, too."

Haynes said, "If worse came to worst, T.J., you and I could go rest awhile out there. After all, it still belongs to me. And, come to think of it, the only child I've got is there. A boy who's both my son and nephew."

"Macha? Am I to understand that you and Macha . . ." Hoskins couldn't conceal his astonishment. Huskily he added, "I knew that Macha was pregnant when we left—and didn't have a husband—but God, Julian, she *hated* you."

"Hell, I know that, T.J.—I hated her too. It had reached the point where I had to hold a knife to her throat whenever Chato Verdugo brought her to me."

They heard sounds in the waiting room and then a knock on the office door. A moment later Reuben Baxter entered.

"You're late," Haynes said.

Sounding surprised at the rebuke, Baxter answered, "The girl just gave me your message. I was with the men. We've got lookouts in place, the way we talked about, but English and the rest of 'em won't come till mornin'."

"What's goin' on here?" Hoskins asked.

"Now, Judge, just calm yourself. We've got a situation that we've talked about time and again," Haynes replied. "The only difference is that it's no longer something off in the future. It's about to take place."

Haynes opened a desk drawer and took from it a small blue steel derringer. After placing it beside his empty brandy snifter he said coldly, "The only one who can cause us trouble is that boy. His name is Hugh Simmons, I hear. As you may know, Jedediah Jackson has sent for the circuit judge, one Amos Host, and plans to cause us difficulty. Simmons can testify that a man named Baxter sent a telegraph message to Joe Hill, and Simmons can say he met me in Tascosa. And he can give witness that I told him to have Joe Hill's man come see the judge in Santa Rita—that would be you, T.J."

"There's still no crime in any of that."

"Well, maybe not, but it can cause a scandal, for the man who came was Wrangler Hull, who trailed Tom English. We don't need scandals, Judge. I'd prefer to stop this before it goes further."

Haynes looked at Baxter. "We could have saved ourselves a lot of

trouble if you'd taken Tom English out yourself instead of sending word
to your old friend in New Mexico to do your work for you."

"At the time we all agreed that would be best," Baxter said harshly.

"Well, I guess you're right. But when it comes to facing English, do
you think it can be done?"

Baxter said deliberately, "I'm sure of it. You see, I've figured out his
weakness."

"And what might that be?" the judge asked.

"He has an overpowering sense of honor. It gets the best of him,"
replied the sheriff.

"I don't know what you mean."

"You will, Judge. You will."


A rooster crowed, straining with all his might, forcing the stretched-
out sound up toward the violet sky of early morning. Shadowed men at
the sagging old corral of the Lower Ranch roped and saddled horses.
Outside the house John Robert Hale stood with Tom English and Asa
Coltrane.

"You instructed your men?" the Ranger asked Tom.

"Yes. There's to be no gunplay unless I give the word."

"We're not goin' into town to start a war," John Robert said. "The
governor himself has sent instructions for me to get things straightened
out, and I intend to do just that. First, I'm takin' over from Baxter as the
only 'law' there is in Santa Rita. He'll give his badge to me. Amos Holt,
the circuit judge, will be here by Friday, and he'll sit at any trials that
may take place. T. J. Hoskins and Julian Haynes and their kind don't
run things anymore. Law and order has come to Texas; we can't allow
men to take over towns with a pack of outlaws."

He spoke in a matter-of-fact way, as though discussing a routine
chore. John Robert Hale had a clear understanding of the concept of
duty and never wavered from it.

"The three of us will ride ahead of the men. Reuben Baxter and all
those gunslingers he and Julian Haynes brought in will be waitin' for us,
naturally, and so I want to make it clear that we're coming in to parley.
If things get out of hand, we ought to be able to handle it," John Robert
said with a slight smile. "Most of 'em will have their eyes on you, Tom.
Havin' 'the most dangerous man alive' alongside us ought to unsettle
'em," he said with a grim chuckle. "In addition, I've seen more than my
share of trouble and so has our friend Asa." He turned to their compan-

ion, the cowboy from the Hester Trace ranch north of the Lazy E who
had become acting foreman for Tom's neighboring spread.

"As for the rest of Tom's cowboys, we'll have them along for support.
They'll look fierce enough but, like most cowboys, they're not much
when it comes to real gunplay. In point of fact, the most danger they'll
be in if things get out of hand will be from themselves: likely to shoot
their feet when they draw, or maybe each other—their horses' ears—or
God knows what. But it shouldn't come to that."

John Robert continued, "You haven't said much, Tom. You're broodin'
about the death of old Santiago and the other four—I know how much
they meant to you. But this isn't the time for revenge. There's been too
much blood in these parts. If we're ever goin' to show that we've got the
law to take care of wrongs, this is the time for it. Can I depend on you?"

Tom listened through a muffling haze, a redness that may have been
a reflection of the sun cresting on the horizon, but which seemed to
creep inside his head. "I won't start anything, John Robert. You know
that."

The Ranger captain nodded. "Let's go," he said.

Tom watched the cowboys step into their saddles, some horses spinning, one fat black mare bowing up her back with ears flattened threat-
eningly but then relaxing, accepting the inevitable. Most of the cow
ponies bore the sudden weight placidly, and the familiar sight reminded
him of happier days. He realized that Hugh Simmons hadn't joined
them. "Well, it's not Hugh's fight," he rationalized. But still he wondered where the boy might be.

The long procession jolted along, accompanied by a drumming noise
of hoofbeats. At times a horse would squeal when another, in the grip
of early morning meanness, would give way to temptation, seeing hindquarters within reach, stretching out bared blunt teeth in order to take
a savage nip. The injured plunging mount would kick in retaliation
while its rider cursed hoarsely and hauled on his reins to get control.

Jouncing noises, like squeaking leather bags flopping up and down,
came from the long procession while here and there horse tails raised
and nature called without a pause in their progress. The sun loomed
higher and long shadows floated on the silvery dew upon the short grass
of the prairie.

Lagging somewhat behind the others, Severn Laycon rode beside his
old friend Ira Turnbull. "What are we doin' gettin' mixed up in this?"
Severn asked petulantly. "I hired on to work for the widow woman, and
then we looked after English stock on his ranch after all his men got

theirselves shot, and now damned if it don't look like I'm taggin' along so the same thing can happen to me. And all I ever planned to do was work cattle and get my pay oncet a month so I could git into the bar at Villa Plata now and again."

"If trouble breaks out, Severn," his friend Ira replied, "we'll find ourselves a ditch and hunker down in it."

Appearing mollified, the old cowboy said, "It ain't that I'm scared, you understand."

"Hell, no, me neither. It's just that we might as well be cautious."

They spurred their horses so as to catch up, relieved that they'd formulated a battle plan.

The cowboys slowed their horses from a jolting trot to a walk when they reached the scattered houses on the north side of the town, mostly Mexican huts, a few jackals, and one adobe store. Off to one side was the bare ground where the year before the people of Santa Rita had held their first stock show. There had been a horse race; the whole town—men, women, and children—had been present. Now the site, a stretch of treeless hard dirt with the remnant of an unpainted wooden grandstand already falling into disrepair, stood silently, ignored by the intent riders.

They reached the rutted road called Chadbourne Street and slowed even more. Dismounting, they took their rifles from saddle scabbards, loosened pistols in their holsters, and fell into an uneven line. The nervous skirmishers eyed their comrades as they moved forward. Overhead, unnoticed by the cowboys, dark clouds moved in from the west and a sudden wave of wind from a squall line bent the limbs of an old mulberry tree off to their left.

Ahead of them John Robert Hale, Tom English, and Asa Coltrane stayed on horseback, approaching the courthouse and, across the road from it, a crowd of men clustered about the one-story stone building that housed the old jail and the sheriff's office in its attached frame shed. On both sides of the jail, a barricade had been constructed, made of kegs and casks dragged from the hardware store, several water troughs, a few overturned wagons, and scraps of lumber. Weapons bristled from these defenses, rifle barrels pointing at the three riders.

John Robert Hale, the Ranger captain, moved ahead of Tom and Asa, holding up his right hand as he called out, "We've come to talk."

Reuben Baxter emerged from his office holding a double-barreled shotgun, both triggers cocked. Six men came with him, three on either side, holding pistols at hip level aimed at the three approaching riders.

"I'm here in the name of the governor of Texas, Baxter. Don't reckon you plan to take on the whole state."

"Don't make any quick moves," the sheriff said, "or I'll blow you to kingdom come. I don't care whose name you come in, this looks quite a bit to me like the Lincoln County range war, and you've just took up sides with Tom English instead of with Julian Haynes. Maybe English hired you just like he did the rest of them men out there." He glared past the Ranger at the cowboys standing on the courthouse grounds, more than a hundred yards away.

Hale said shortly, "You know better than that."

At a sign from Baxter, his six armed followers—pistols leveled on the three men on horseback—moved forward.

"Git down and hold your hands up," Baxter rumbled.

The three men dismounted but stood together, not raising their hands.

"Take their guns," the sheriff said.

A strange light came into the unblinking pale blue eyes of Tom English. "I wouldn't try that," he said. Although he spoke softly, his words carried and the six men stopped in their tracks, looking back at Baxter for guidance.

The more than thirty cowboys from the Lazy E and Trace ranches had their pistols and rifles up by now, and they moved forward. Dust and sand slapped into their faces as the storm approached, and over the whining that the wind made in the brass weather stripping in the windows of the sheriff's office could be heard the sounds of levers cocking rifles and the metallic snaps of pistol hammers clicking back in place.

The sheriff's men waiting behind the barricades sank down and leveled rifle barrels. On both sides, hearts pounded, mouths went dry, tension heightened.

"This thing is between you and me, Baxter," Tom English said.

"You might be right," the sheriff said, surprisingly cool. "But I hear you've practiced with those .45s of yours quite a bit, which leaves me at a disadvantage."

Tom didn't answer.

"Well, no use causin' all these men to git involved," the sheriff said. "It's true that the real trouble is between us. But I've heard of all your tricks, the way you can fall down and shoot at the same time with either hand. How you can hit a coffee cup from thirty feet or so. But face to face, that wouldn't make much difference. You may not have heard a lot about me, English, but I've had my share of gunfights. Mostly close up

in bars, not out in the street for show like you," he said with a sneer, "with newspapermen there to watch."

"I'll meet you under any rules you want to lay down," Tom replied coldly. "I stood at the window of that jail cell"—he turned his head toward it—"and watched while you and your men killed five of the best friends I'll ever have. It took place right here—where I'm standing."

"We'll go over yonder," Baxter said. He uncocked the shotgun and leaned it against the wall of his office. Then he walked across the dirt road to the broad grounds of the courthouse and waited beside the raw boards of the scaffold that had been constructed for the double hanging of Calvin Laudermilk and Tuck Bowlegs.

Tom followed, pausing as he reached the eight-foot-high walls of the scaffold. He watched Baxter proceed up the wooden steps to the platform and retreat to one side, putting a hand on one of the two heavy uprights that held the crossbeam with two hangman's nooses still dangling from it.

The midmorning sky turned dark as twilight, a bruised blue shadow tinged with yellow filled the windswept air; and from the west, tall tumbled thunderheads glowed with pent-up lightning. Tom climbed the steps to the pine floor and stopped there, about ten feet from Reuben Baxter.

The sheriff's mouth crimped nervously before he spoke. "This close, I've got as good a chance as you—and there's no room to throw yourself off to one side or pull any of those tricks I've heard about."

A feeling of unreality surrounded Tom as he walked across the creaking platform to the far side, turning to face his adversary. A flickering of gooseflesh rippled up until it reached the nape of his neck.

Both hands hanging easily, fighting tenseness, Tom kept his eyes on those of Baxter. He could always see the signal there first, the sign that flashed the barest instant before the other would make his draw.

Around them a hush fell on the armed audience on both sides at the bizarre sight of two men standing on a scaffold, prepared to kill each other.

A seeming theater had been created with a central stage. A flash of jagged lightning snaked down in the west, followed almost instantly by thunder. Men behind the barricades rose, not thinking, from the protection of boards and barrels and overturned wagons. The cowboys across the way from them stood in a rough half circle, mesmerized by the drama.

"Jesus Christ," Severn Laycon breathed out, unable to believe his

eyes. He and the other men with him unconsciously lowered their weapons as they stood, riveted by their fascination—transfixed by horror.

The gunmen brought in from El Paso moved past the overturned wagons and kegs and overturned water troughs, also allowing their rifle barrels to droop earthward, as they moved closer so as not to miss seeing what would happen.

A wind whipped across the courthouse grounds and the rope lanyards on the flagpole slapped against dried-out splintered pine. The somewhat ragged flag was not in place except on special holidays.

Reuben Baxter's face flushed red, and in spite of the whipping wind, beads of sweat traced lines down his unshaven cheeks.

"I can't handle this because . . ." His voice broke off. "I thought I could—but you know, and I do too, that I don't have a chance. You'll kill me sure as hell." He raised both hands away from his sides and said, a note of terror in his voice, "Don't draw on me—for God's sake."

He turned away from Tom, speaking just loud enough for him to hear. "I can't back down in front of my men."

Tom didn't answer.

Still not looking behind him, Baxter pleaded, "Ain't there some other way than this? What is it that you want?"

"Turn in your badge to the Ranger. You and the judge and Haynes give yourselves up to stand trial. It'll be a fair one."

"All right. Hell, that's fine."

Baxter seemed weak with relief. He put his left hand on a long metal bar as though to steady himself. He said, "Come over a little closer, I don't want any of them men of mine to hear what I've got to say."

He listened to the creaking of the platform, the hollow thuds made by Tom's boot heels, the chinking sound of spurs. Then with a plunging movement his hand threw the lever and the trapdoors under the hangman's nooses fell open. Baxter whirled as he threw the lever, right hand grasping his revolver.

As the world fell out from under Tom's feet, his two .45s exploded simultaneously.

The transfixed multitude saw Tom English drop like a shot, disappearing as if into thin air, and Reuben Baxter, feet out in front of him, hurled as though by a catapult backward off the scaffold—and they heard the thunderclap crash of two heavy-gauge cartridges exploding as one.

Men shrieked, blood-crazed, astounded, mouths and eyes stretched wide. And then they stared at the form of Reuben Baxter, spreadeagled on his back with a gout of scarlet as thick as a man's wrist erupting from the center of his chest.

# SEVENTEEN

JOHN ROBERT HALE and Asa Coltrane held Colts leveled on the six men before them, but there was no need for this. The followers of Reuben Baxter, shaken by the spectacle that had taken place an instant earlier, seemed paralyzed.

The other mercenaries brought into Santa Rita by the sheriff looked at their fallen leader with disbelief, standing in front of their tumbled barricades. Not that they really gave a damn about him. The pay was what counted—they'd ridden hundreds of miles on getting messages that he offered good money.

The lifeblood of the paymaster formed an astonishing pool about him —how could that much liquid be inside a single body? At the front of the sheriff's office the six men, averting their eyes from the grisly sight, moved closer to one another, holstered their weapons, and after a moment's indecision scuffed away toward the horde of gunslingers who had retreated behind the tipped-over wagons.

A sudden, roaring, invisible wall blew through the town, the storm's blunt leading edge. A tidal wave of wind struck gray and purple shadows of cloud-darkened stores and buildings, while a sound like that of locomotives roared through the day turned night. Stinging dust and dirt flew horizontally, and over the heads of crouching men shingles torn from roofs and bits of paper whirled through the air. Cowboys and their momentarily forgotten foes braced themselves, turning their faces away from the onslaught, instinctively bending their heads down. At that instant a lightning bolt split through the boiling darkness of the sky and a cannon roar of thunder shook the windows of the town. And then a sandstorm swirled, drawing a reddish-brown curtain some fifteen yards away from John Robert and Asa, while the sheriff's men disappeared behind its gritty folds.

The rain came down: slanting through the sand and dust, turning the hardened crust of earth into a slick and glistening and unsure surface.

Puddles formed and tiny spouts of water seemed to leap upward in them as hurtling raindrops pounded across their surface.

John Robert and Asa moved back onto the small porch of the sheriff's office and stood behind a solid waterfall that streamed from the shed's roof. Soaked to the skin by wind-driven slashes, they backed farther, entering the office's shelter.

The two stood at the open door, feeling the driven mist in their faces, not speaking, as though stunned by double body blows: first man's violence and then nature's. Through angled transparent rods, the long thin reeds of rain, they could barely make out a figure limping toward them.

Tom English entered the office, looked about him, then took off his sodden hat and dropped it on the floor. He sat down in a rickety ladder-back chair in front of the scarred desk and methodically reloaded his weapons, putting a single cartridge in each six-gun.

"Are you all right?" John Robert Hale asked at last.

"Turned my ankle," Tom replied.

"How on earth did you manage to fire those shots?" Asa Coltrane asked in an awed tone.

"I have no idea, Asa. I really don't," Tom English said. "It all took place too fast for me to have time to think. I'm as puzzled about it as you are."

The following day a haze hung in low places, an early morning fog. A warmth of sunlight burned this away, and a clear blue arc of morning sky spread from one horizon to the other. It seemed as if God had once again forgiven all the sinfulness. Shafts of brightness struck upon the torn limbs of uprooted trees, a roofless barn, and the littered, branch-strewn streets of a drenched and forlorn small town crouching by the swollen Concho.

Once firm land had turned into a sea of mud. Moist south wind blew a musty smell, like wet woolen blankets or rotting wood, as it drifted past. Men on foot walked with teeth clenched tight, lifting their knees while ankle-deep muck made sucking noises as their unrecognizable boots pulled free.

The normally slender, twisting stream now spread across a flat at the bend below Beauregard Street and made a brown, wave-swept lake. Trees floated down the flood along with doors and other parts of Mexican shacks. In spite of its almost placid appearance, the rolling far-spread river's current carried underneath its frothy surface a power that defied description.

A small house went by with a cat perched in amazement on its roof. Cowboys and townspeople stood on high ground and watched, spellbound. Across the water they saw the distant small figures of a scattering of cavalrymen, even officers, doing the same thing.

"You don't often see dry country like this, what some call semidesert, when it's under water," Calvin Laudermilk said to no one in particular. "They say it rained close to fifteen inches in one day upriver around Water Valley yesterday." Since receiving his pardon, Calvin had been earnestly celebrating—much to John Hope's disgust because he had almost cleaned out the Lost Hope Saloon's inventory.

"Where's your friend Tom English?" The question came from the best bootmaker for many miles around who happened to be standing nearby.

"Left yesterday afternoon with his men for the Lazy E main headquarters some thirty miles north. Took his wife Sally with him, Rector."

"He was in luck, gettin' west of the river before the flood struck last night," the bootmaker said. Then he asked, "Did you see it? I was workin' at my shop and missed everything." Rector didn't have to be more particular. Everyone in town was talking about the confrontation between Reuben Baxter and Tom English.

"No, I didn't," Calvin responded. "I've talked to a hundred men since, however, and all of them claimed to have been eyewitnesses. And I heard a hundred different stories. Soon a thousand men will claim that they were there, and God knows what tales we'll hear. After that, the best talkers around will pick and choose, taking the best parts from all those yarns, and before long we'll hear a fable that will sound something like the ones about those brave old boys in England who would take after fire-breathing dragons with nothing more than their swords."

Rector laughed.

Calvin, delighted to have an audience, said as they struggled back on foot toward the swamplike center of town, "Out of all those witnesses, there's one whose word I'm prepared to accept. Considering that he has no imagination whatsoever and has never once in all his life told me a lie —and since he may be the best friend I've got on earth—I tend to believe his account. I'm talking about Tuck Bowlegs, my fishing companion and spiritual counselor." Calvin ignored the perplexed expression on Rector's face.

"Tuck has always been a cautious soul, and after the dignity of the law decided to hang him by the neck until he was dead, he has turned even more cautious. He don't read, so a piece of paper from the gover-

nor saying that the white man had decided *not* to hang him holds no weight with Tuck. No one but me has seen hide nor hair of him since we got our pardon. That is to say, except for Jimmie, his woman who cooks at the Lost Hope Saloon when she's in a mood to do that. Well, he happened to be out of tequila, or maybe he wanted his woman's company two days ago, so he slipped into town. And, forgetting himself, spent the night. When he got up, he told me, he found all them gunslingers who backed Reuben Baxter millin' around the place, so he laid low.

"Then, the first thing he knew, here came Tom English, John Robert Hale, and Asa Coltrane on horseback with a passel of armed men on foot backing them up. Tuck slipped out of Jimmie's shack, which lies off behind Hope's saloon—and slipped through the tall Johnson grass in a draw up to where those chinaberry trees are that got planted and then forgotten."

He added parenthetically, "You know where they are, Rector, off toward the west side of the courthouse grounds. Weeds and shinnery have grown up around them, and Tuck can slither through such undergrowth like a garter snake. He can turn invisible when he's a mind to. And so he had a clear view of what occurred and he told me the true story."

"Well," Rector asked, fascinated, "what really happened? I'm like you —I've heard all sorts of things."

"Tuck said that a hawk flew over in front of the storm, a feather fell from the sky, and he knew on the instant that this was what he calls a 'sign.' For at the very moment that it struck the ground—not two feet away from where he lay on his belly in the weeds—both men on the scaffold suddenly vanished from sight with a terrible explosion. Made his ears ring. Tuck has thought about all this carefully and is sure he knows exactly what occurred."

"And what was it?"

" 'Hawk-feather magic.' That's what Tuck said to me, and I'll take his word for it."

Calvin bade Rector a gruff farewell as they neared the Elkhorn wagon yard, mumbling inaudibly about something he needed to get behind him. Laboring through the mud, he walked north and then west, soon looking as though he had been caught in the previous day's downpour, although the moisture that soaked him came from inside instead of outside his clothing. Secondhand fumes of alcohol hung about him like an invisible cloud as he forged ahead. The day's heat built, and

steaming humidity rose from the morass that normally was a rutted road.

"I can scarcely breathe," the complaint echoed in Calvin's mind. But he had a fixed purpose; it could not be postponed a single day. The spinster Elvira East had been much on his mind. Each day she became more possessive.

"No," Calvin barked, "never in a million years," intent upon his mission, not noticing how his rumblings startled two young boys who played nearby. They jerked up their heads as the sweat-soaked monster squashed ankle deep down a road that looked like a well-used hog wallow.

"My freedom," Calvin said to himself, "means everything to me. I must simply break off with Elvira. There's no reason, of course, that we can't remain friends. But this is bound to break her heart." More perspiration traced down his face.

Arriving at his destination, Calvin plodded up the flagstoned front walk, pausing at the steps to try to scrape the clinging balls of mud from his boots. Giving up, he sat down on a porch swing on the veranda and pulled them off. Cleaning his hands by scrubbing them repeatedly on his pants legs, he approached the front door in sock feet. It opened before he knocked, and he saw Elvira standing to one side, waiting for him to enter.

"Alvin isn't in," she said, referring to her brother. Her tone left the clear impression that Calvin was once more staining her good name by intruding on an unchaperoned single lady.

"Good," Calvin said shortly.

"Could I serve you some hot tea?" Elvira asked uncertainly.

"Don't need warmin' up right now," Calvin responded, panting from his exertions. Sweat streamed down his face and he mopped his forehead with a forearm. "I could do with a drop of whiskey if you have any handy."

He observed her shocked expression. "No, I guess I don't want any of that. Wouldn't take it if you offered it to me. Of course, if you insisted, I'm not a man to cause offense."

Elvira ignored his ramblings. "I've spent many sleepless nights thinking of you—and about our future," Elvira said.

"That's why I'm here. I've got the same thing in mind, and I couldn't let another day go by without coming here to discuss it." His words trailed off lamely. "How on earth," he thought, "can I tell her this without absolutely breaking her heart?"

"Calvin, I cannot marry you. It simply won't do."

"What?" The question began deep in his bulging stomach, worked upward to his great chest, and issued from his throat in the form of a roar. "What is that you say?"

"We have nothing at all in common. You would never be a part of my world, you don't want to live a God-fearing life, we'd never live like normal people: go to church, socialize in town, and all the things that are important to me."

Calvin's face turned scarlet. "Woman," he finally stammered, "are you *rejecting me?*"

"I fear I am. And yet I truly do love you."

Calvin approached her tenderly, folded her within his arms, pressing her head against his great sweaty bosom. "Don't act in haste, Elvira," he said, "we aren't in any rush. We can keep company like the best of friends, go for buggy rides and such."

He thought in horror, "What are you sayin', you damn fool?"

And then, as if his will had totally lost control of his words, he continued, "Why, darlin', you mean the world to me. Although it's true I can't stand bein' in town for any stretch of time—and can't abide most Baptists." He sought to hold her but she struggled from his grasp.

"What are you doin'?" he asked, aghast, as Elvira picked up her best china teapot, a delicate white one with a curved spout. And hurled it in a fury into the fireplace where it shattered into a million pieces. Tea splashed all over the floor.

In the hush that followed, Calvin finally managed to speak. "Is that the action of a God-fearing woman?"

"Oh, Calvin, I don't want you for a friend."

He led her to the couch and sat with her in his arms. "Let's discuss this calmly," said Calvin, feeling for some obscure reason inordinately proud of himself.

But Elvira did not deign to talk. She planted a kiss squarely upon his mouth.

"I'll buy you another teapot at the Wedgwood and Spode Shop that Miss Cornick just opened at her house," Calvin said.

"Hush up," Elvira said, kissing him once again.

In the month that followed the great flood of '86, Manuelito, a young horse wrangler from the Lazy E, returned from Durango in Old Mexico with three dark-eyed former neighbors of old Santiago Acosta and his son Benito. They'd grown up with Pepe Moya and Luis Batalla and Juan

Suarez. And they came to Texas after hearing that these five men had died violently—in an effort to save Tom English from hanging. They knew and respected English, they'd been with him in the brief range war that began at Three Points years before. And they had a great sense of duty. Besides that, they welcomed the challenge.

So Perez, Montealegre, and Jimenez arrived with Manuelito, who had grown four inches in height in the last year. The four would be the new "Mexican Cavalry" protecting Tom English.

Since their arrival, the five men had gone to the hills toward the west and practiced with their rifles and pistols under Tom's careful supervision. Spending almost all their time together, they struggled with a blending of their two languages until a Tex-Mex polyglot jargon emerged which served as a means of communication. Perez, fortunately, spoke fairly good English, so he acted as translator whenever Tom's "ranch Spanish" proved inadequate.

Montealegre rode a curved-neck blue roan horse with dappled spots and a long mane and tail. He had a massive saddle with a flat round horn and drooping tapaderos over the stirrups. Perez, with a laughing face, always in a good humor, had a head for figures, and in a short time Tom found himself depending on his new recruit, seeking his advice, getting a second point of view on plans he made for the ranch. While Jimenez, a lofty person with a great sense of personal dignity, didn't say much. He oiled his weapons, checked his gear each night, and a sparrow landing on the bunkhouse roof would wake him.

Tom told Jedediah Jackson about these men when the old lawyer came from town to see him. He arrived along with Jim Boy Irons, reestablished now as sheriff.

"We have bad news," Irons said to Tom after they reached the house. "You'll recall that you lost track of that boy from New Mexico, the one who came to Santa Rita with you."

"Hugh Simmons."

"He was to be our primary witness in the proceedings against Julian Haynes and T. J. Hoskins," Jedediah commented shortly.

"You never found him, is that what you're saying?" Tom asked.

"We found what was left of him," Jim Boy Irons replied with distaste.

The three sat in homemade rocking chairs, built of mesquite limbs with the bark still on the parts which had not been whittled down into rough tenons that were wedged into crudely chiseled mortises. The seats and backs were made of cowhide. The front porch of the once painted ranch house, now sandblasted by wind until the weathered pine

showed through, faced east, looking down over the sloping pasture that led to the tree-lined North Concho River. Beyond it, at the horizon, they saw the land rise back from the river valley to the rolling slopes of blue hills.

"Found his body back of the bunkhouse at the Lower Ranch. One of your boys remembers hearing someone outside calling his name—the night before you and Asa and John Robert Hale rode into town. Hugh went to see who wanted him and didn't come back. There were so many cowboys around at the time that no one paid any mind. He was new—hadn't had time to make any friends."

"What happened?" Tom asked tersely.

"Some men gagged him with a bandana. Tied his hands behind his back with a piggin' string, then cut his throat. Left him that way, covered up with brush. A few days after that, the cook went out to chop some wood, saw a cloud of flies, and discovered him."

"No one told me," Tom said distantly.

"Not much doubt that Julian Haynes had it done, but we can't prove a thing," Jim Boy Irons said. "In the old days that wouldn't have mattered, but times have changed. The whole town rose up behind John Robert Hale and you and Asa. And we're going to live by the law from here on out." He touched his badge with pride.

"So where does that leave us as far as Julian Haynes and T. J. Hoskins are concerned?"

"Tom, there's no case to be made against them," Jedediah stated. "But they've lost face in town. Most people know what they were up to —and that the things that Reuben Baxter and his gun hands did would have been under their direction."

"I did hear that those two left town," Tom said so quietly that the others almost didn't hear him.

"That's true, they've headed for El Paso. It's over, Tom, we've won."

Tom rose and excused himself. Moments later the others saw him riding toward the south.

"Where's he headed?" Jim Boy Irons asked.

"Going off to be alone so he can think, I'd guess," Jedediah Jackson replied.

Sally English appeared with a wooden tray and put it down on a low table. She spoke courteously to both men, smiled her affection at the old lawyer, then served a glass of straight bourbon to Jim Boy Irons. After this she poured a steaming dark stream from a blue willow pot

into a matching cup, then handed this to Jedediah Jackson. Hot coffee, she knew, would be his preference.

Wordlessly she took her own coffee, tasted it, then looked at Jedediah. He held his cup in both hands, staring over the valley at the ancient hills which blended with the darkening sky.

He had a classic face, still handsome although ruined: a parchment skin as wrinkled as crepe paper, shot through with tiny lines and creases, fissures leading into crevices; a patrician profile, with sunken intelligent eyes under a broad brow.

A gentleman, Sally English thought, studying him. A true gentleman.

"I'm approaching my seventy-fifth birthday," Jedediah remarked, "but, except for the aches and pains, I feel much as I did fifty years ago. Of course," he added, "I tire more easily."

Addressing Jim Boy Irons, he said, "You know, we're almost all of us alike in so many ways: we flinch at unexpected loud noises, blink to keep sand out of our eyes. All these things are reflexes, we don't think about them. If we slip down—and this holds true for a little child or a grown man—we throw out our hands to break the fall. It's instinctive."

Jim Boy Irons looked at Sally, raising his eyebrows humorously, as if to ask if she could make heads or tails out of these nonsensical comments.

"I keep thinking about what took place on the scaffold in town a while back." The lawyer glanced at Sally, knowing that he shouldn't speak of such matters in front of her, but he seemed unable to stop. After a certain age people develop the habit of saying what is on their minds.

"An *ordinary* man," Jedediah continued deliberately, "would have grabbed at the edge of that trapdoor when it fell out from under his feet. It's only human nature to protect yourself, and I suppose that Baxter bet his life on that. He must have figured that Tom would have caught hold and clung there, helpless before Baxter's gun.

"But Tom English is not an ordinary man," Jedediah concluded, staring once more across the river valley.

"What happens now?" Sally asked. "He's been unlike himself the last few days. Hardly says a word."

"Max Hall told me," the lawyer replied, "that Tom has sold his part of that ranch in Montana to his partner up there, Hap Cunningham's boy. He's raising all the cash he can and is in touch with J. B. Slaughter in New Mexico about selling much of his herd to him."

Sally nodded. "He asked me about these things, wanted to know if I'd

mind, but of course that's his decision. Tom told me that Max's bank needs capital, that he'll end up putting all he can into it, although he doesn't want to own more than a third of the bank—and he definitely will have no part of running it.

"The very thought of having to sit at a desk all day would drive him crazy. But he's been a director along with you and Max for some time now, and says he enjoys the excuse your meetings give him to go to town and see friends and sit around and talk, while claiming that he's 'doing business.' "

"It's more than just talk," Jedediah said. "Some of the ranchers who lost their land may be able to buy it back with the help of Max's bank. Time will tell."

Jim Boy Irons, who hadn't much to add to this conversation, left the two old friends and wandered off toward the bunkhouse. He saw Asa Coltrane out there with some of the new cowboys, as well as the men from Durango. Asa had come to this part of the Lazy E to serve as foreman now that Santiago was gone. His former employer, the widow Hester Trace, had given him her permission. Asa, nonplussed by Tom's offer at first, had finally accepted the job and took his new responsibilities with great seriousness. At least, that's what Jim Boy had heard. He walked eagerly out toward Asa now, determined to "hooraw" him about becoming a boss.

The old man and the young woman sat together on the shaded ranch house porch, bonded by affection and respect.

Sally said to Jedediah, speaking of her daughter, "Rebecca has stayed with Hester Trace at her ranch. She won't come home until her dad puts up his guns. He knows this—and it breaks his heart."

A slight frown crossed her unlined forehead for a fleeting moment. "She comes by that stubbornness from *his* side of the family."

Taking a deep shuddering breath, she said softly, "I wake sometimes in the night to find him sitting bolt upright beside me. He touches me, says, 'Go back to sleep,' and then gets up and leaves. When morning comes he rides off with the new men from Mexico and I hear gunfire from the hills."

She turned abruptly toward Jedediah. "This cattle drive he's planning to New Mexico worries me sick. I heard him talk to Asa just the other day about going to El Paso after they see Mr. Slaughter."

"I'll speak to him, Sally. It's not like Tom to seek revenge. He's had to spend too much of his life avoiding trouble from all those enemies he's got."

"I know."

"He's always been reluctant to face a man—even when a fight's forced on him."

"I thought that too, Jedediah. But he doesn't seem himself somehow."

"He misses Santiago," Jedediah said, "and the others. But more bloodshed isn't the answer."

Exhausted by the trip, he closed his eyes. Sally reached a hand out, suddenly concerned, but then he looked at her and smiled.

The two sat side by side, lost in thought, feeling helpless. Their heads raised simultaneously and they looked up into the twilight sky. A hawk flew overhead, gliding silently, fixed upon the evening's errand, the routine ending of another day, waiting for its next kill.

"They say time heals all things," Jedediah stated, "and in my experience, that is most certainly true. Tom has more sense than to go out after Julian Haynes. That's simply not going to happen. The trouble is over—and peace has come to the Concho Valley again."

"Has it?"

The old man, drained of energy, said, "I hope it has." He tasted his coffee but it was cold. Focusing on the face of the worried woman who leaned toward him, he took her hand in his and said, "Peace will come back—it always seems to, even after the most savage, the most violent times. It's so welcome—and people cling to it. But then it goes away. Peace never lasts for very long."

A thought struck him and he grinned, looking twenty years younger. "I guess that peace isn't a natural state. That hawk we saw a second ago would starve to death if he had a peaceful nature."

"Men are different," Sally said.

"Most of them are," Jedediah agreed.

A baby wobbled out upon the porch, pulling a soft wool blanket behind him. Ben Westbrook English stared at them solemnly, then held up his arms, knowing without question that his mother would pick him up.

P9-DNV-626

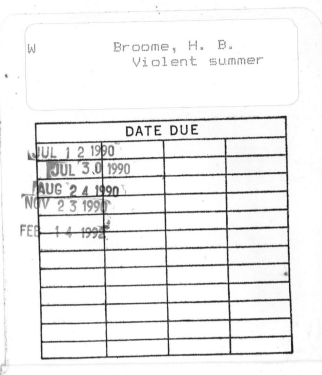